Counting Daisies

by Nicola Haken

Counting Daisies

Copyright © 2016 Nicola Wall

Cover Design by Reese Dante

http://www.reesedante.com

Edited by E. Adams

ISBN-13: 978-1533494757
ISBN-10: 1533494754

Please note: This book contains graphic descriptions of intravenous drug use which may be distressing or uncomfortable to read, or pose as a trigger for some readers.

Help, information, and advice regarding the issues discussed in this book can be found on the following websites. Please don't struggle alone.

http://www.talktofrank.com

http://www.samhsa.gov

Dedicated to Oor Janie. Thank you for being my friend. I love you.

For all the Dylan's and Cameron's out there. You are strong. You are brave. Keep going.

Contents

Prologue

~Dylan~

CAMERON O'NEIL HAD been my best friend since primary school. We'd been inseparable since the day Mrs Nugent sat him next to me in reception year. Only when we reached the age of fourteen did our friendship develop into what we thought was love. I say *thought* because kids are stupid.

School was over and we were chilling out in my room while my Granny Roberts cooked our dinner. I'd spent all day wishing the end-of-day bell would ring so I could be alone with him. I couldn't touch him at school, not like I wanted to. I couldn't even hold his hand. Sometimes I'd wrestle with him on the grass just so I could hold him, and that was acceptable because all the lads wrestled and play-fought with each other.

"Play me something," Cameron said, scooching closer to me on my bed, nodding

"Play me something," Cameron said, scooching closer to me on my bed, nodding towards my dad's guitar. It was a stunning instrument; a 1929 Martin that my dad always said was worth thousands, but I didn't know how true that was. I knew it was possible because it was really old. My granddad passed it down to him before he passed away when I was four.

"Nah." I shrugged, staring mournfully towards the guitar. Playing it was something I only did alone, when I could close my eyes and remember my dad without feeling embarrassed when it inevitably forced tears to my eyes.

"You miss him today?"

My gaze didn't leave the guitar, which was propped up against the chair that my dad's leather jacket was draped over. I used to wear it at weekends. It was too big for me, the sleeves fell over my hands, but I thought it made me look cool. "I miss him every day." I had since the day he died the year before. I'd missed him since the very moment the police turned up at my grandma's door to tell her he'd been killed in a car accident on the M25, and that the house I was spending one night in would be my new home. I missed him, and I always would.

Counting Daisies

My mum died, too. There were complications when she gave birth to me, something to do with her placenta, though I'd never been told the specifics. All I knew was that she bled out on the operating table and never got a chance to see me. The saying 'you don't miss what you've never had' is bullshit. I missed my mum. Whether it was *her*, or the idea of a mother, I didn't know. But I *did* miss her.

I missed both of them.

"You're gonna have to play in front of someone eventually if you want to be a musician, Dyl."

"I don't want to be a musician anymore," I said, the words quiet and sorrowful on my lips.

Growing up, I watched my dad try to make it, playing in pubs and clubs whenever he could, in between his shifts at the supermarket. He was a great dad, but always sad. Even when he smiled I could tell he was sad. He missed my mum, and because of that he never really smiled...until he picked up his guitar. Playing made him happy, which in turn made *me* happy, and so I decided that's what I wanted to do when I grew up, too.

I wanted to play. I wanted to sing. I wanted it to bring me the same joy as it did my dad. But then he died and, ever since, music just made me really fucking miserable.

"Maybe I'll be a chef like you." I couldn't prevent the teasing grin that accompanied my words. Cooking sounded so boring to me.

"You'll be laughing on the other side of your face when I'm presenting MasterChef," Cameron said, jabbing me in the shoulder.

I jabbed him back, making him laugh, and it quickly escalated into a full-blown pillow fight.

"S-stop! Stop!" Breathless and crying with laughter, Cameron could barely get his words past his throat as I straddled his hips, hovering a pillow above his head. "I surrender!"

My lips twisted into a winner's grin and I tossed the pillow on the floor before collapsing onto the mattress beside him. He rolled onto his side, and I stared at his face which, being fourteen and permanently horny, gave me an instant hard-on. We hadn't done anything except kiss a few times yet, but I wanted to. I had no doubt I was gay, and that Cameron would be the person I'd eventually lose my virginity to. That's why I was planning on coming out to my grandma soon. I imagined she'd take it pretty well. She was a huge fan of Elton John.

"You're smart, Dyl. You could be anything you want to be."

Draping my arm over his waist, I brushed small circles on his back through his T-shirt with my thumb. "You think?"

"I *know*. You're clever enough to be a doctor, or a shit-hot lawyer. You'll be something really great, I know you will."

"Yeah," I agreed with a smile. I worked hard at school. I adored my dad, but I wanted more from life than what he had. I wanted to get away from the council estates I'd grown up on. I wanted a nice house, a flashy car. I didn't want to live with my curtains drawn in case the bailiffs showed up. I didn't want to have to decide between buying food for dinner or paying the gas bill. "Maybe I will."

In that moment, as I pressed my clumsy lips to Cameron's, I envisioned our future. In my head I wore an expensive suit as I greeted him in his Michelin star restaurant after a hard day at the office. We were successful. In love. Out and proud.

Happy.

But then three days later my grandma died and I was packed off into the care system. I didn't even get to say goodbye to Cameron before my entire life turned to shit.

Everybody dies.

Chapter
One

~Cameron~

Sixteen years later…

"I WOULDN'T FEED that shit to my dog," I snapped, lowering the spoon from my lips. "Start again."

"Yes, chef."

Wiping the sweat from my brow on a towel as I weaved through the kitchen, *my* kitchen, I headed over to the pass to find someone else to yell at. "Do they look the same to you?" I nodded toward the two plates about to be picked up by a server before glaring at Kai, one of my commis. There was a good half-inch difference in size between the two pieces of salmon. Completely unacceptable.

"No, chef," Kai muttered, the struggle on his face as he fought the urge to roll his eyes glaringly obvious.

"Sort it!" I yelled. "What the fuck is wrong with you people tonight?"

Huffing in frustration, I stomped over to the pantry and hid inside for a couple of minutes, taking deep breaths.

"You're being an arsehole."

Turning my head, I saw Paul hovering by the open door. Paul was my sous chef, and best friend of ten years. He was my age, well, six months younger. We met in college and ended up working our way up the culinary ladder side-by-side ever since.

"Fuck off," I spat, glowering at him.

Pulling off his white hat, exposing his damp dark-blond hair, the fucker laughed at me. "As amusing as I find your Gordon Ramsay impersonation, that's not you. What's wrong?"

"Kevin," I muttered under my breath. Kevin was my ex, and the guy I believed I'd marry one day…until I caught him with his dick in my ex-pastry chef's arse, in my ex-house, on my ex-mattress. "He's back in town. Wants to give us another shot."

"And do *you*?"

"Fuck no."

"Then what's the problem?"

"The problem is I considered it. I considered it because I haven't been laid in six months and…well… I'm lonely. And he's fucking relentless. I'm worried I'll give in just to shut him up."

Kevin and I were together for three years. It was the only notable relationship I'd really had. Staying with him felt like the *adult* thing to do. He didn't make my stomach flutter, my heart didn't skip a beat when he kissed me, but that wasn't real life, right? Not once you'd grown up. Mostly, he was dependable. He treated me good, well, until he cheated on me, and we had a lot in common. Some people would never find those things in another person, so I clung to it…until he threw it away.

"Want me to beat him up for you?"

"No!" I said, even though I knew he was joking. "I need you to make sure I don't do anything stupid. You can't do that from prison."

"You need a drink. Several drinks." Cocking his head towards the kitchen, Paul patted my back. "Come on. Let's get service out the way and then I'll pay for you to get so smashed you won't even remember his name."

Blowing out a puff of air, I nodded.

"Great. Now, can we have Cam O'Neil back? Gordon pisses me off."

Stepping past Paul, I fixed my game face in place, lifted my head high, and did what I was good at; serving plate after plate of glorious food.

* * *

"Oh dear, God…" Clamping one hand to my forehead, I rolled over on the couch, only to land with a thud on the laminate floor. "I want to die."

"Mornin', sunshine."

Through a painful squint, I followed the sarcastic voice with my eyes and saw Paul sitting on the edge of the coffee table with a smug grin on his stupid, irresponsible face. What the hell was he thinking, allowing me to get plastered on a work night?

"I hate you." I intended to yell, but managed little more than a croaky whisper. "I've gotta get to the restaurant," I mumbled, crawling onto my knees. "Fuck." Seemingly, the art of moving was too strenuous on my hungover body. My elbows gave way and it was easier to let them than to fight, so I lay in a sprawled heap on my stomach instead.

"You need to get to *bed*. I'll cover the restaurant until evening service."

The cool floor felt soothing against my flushed cheek so I didn't move as I watched Paul stand and stroll over to the coat-hook by the door.

Grabbing his jacket, he hooked it onto his finger and slung it over his shoulder. "Quit the dramatics and go take a shower. You stink."

"Love you, too."

Shaking his head and grinning, Paul left my apartment, slamming the door behind him. The sound made me want to crawl into the foetal position and die and I was sure he did it on purpose.

Fuck...

* * *

I still felt like reheated shit when I walked into my restaurant, simply named *O'Neil's*, later that day. Blaming Paul made my head hurt less which is why I scowled at him the second our eyes met.

Taking a brief pause from dicing carrots, which wasn't his job but I didn't have the energy to ask why he was doing it, Paul smirked before carrying on with his prep. "You look like shit." He sounded amused. *Tosser.* "Your parents are in tonight. Your mum rang about an hour ago."

"Oh for fuck's sake," I grumbled, leaning back against the counter Paul was working on, arms folded across my chest. I loved my parents, but it pissed me off that they thought I could magically make a free-table appear from my arse, prepare them free food, serve them free wine, all to impress their friends and with only a couple of hours notice.

"They're just proud of you," Paul argued. "They like showing off their award-winning son and his fancy food."

"Hmm. Sometimes I think I should add them to the wait-list like everyone else."

"And that would make you an arsehole."

He was right, and I'd never actually considered it. It was my bad mood and hangover from hell talking.

Counting Daisies

"Right. I'm gonna get changed and check over this afternoon's delivery." So that's what I did. Then I popped a couple of aspirin and chilled out in my office with the lights off until service began. *I'm never drinking again.*

Several hours later, while service was in full-swing, I accompanied my parents' meals to their table because I knew my mum would serve me my balls for breakfast if I didn't. They sat with two friends, a man and a woman, who I didn't recognise, and when I approached and saw my mum stand, clapping her hands, I had to fight the urge to grit my teeth.

"Here he is!" my mum practically sang, loud enough to make other diners turn their heads. She threw one arm around my back, hugging me close while wearing a smile so wide it brought out the wrinkles around her eyes. "This is my boy! He owns this place."

Smiling awkwardly at the strangers staring at me, I offered my hand for them to shake. "Nice to meet you. I hope you enjoy your meals." *Your* free *meals.*

The woman looked down at her plate, raising an eyebrow in approval. "I'm sure we will. This smells delicious."

I stayed a minute or so, exchanging pleasantries, before kissing my mum and dad on the cheek and excusing myself. No doubt I'd see them again in a little while when they asked for the bill they knew I'd waive.

The rest of service continued like any other Friday night. The kitchen was tense as my staff and I strived for perfection. The atmosphere was hot, sweaty, and filled with expletives. But also as usual, the moment the last plate left the pass a round of satisfied smiles and congratulatory shoulder claps erupted.

"Great job tonight, guys," I said, tossing my dirty apron into the laundry bin.

Most nights I stayed behind until the restaurant had been cleaned to my standards, but today I wanted to feel sorry for myself in a dark bedroom so I handed the keys over to Derek, my head pastry chef and second best-friend next to Paul, and asked him to lock up for me.

"Wanna grab a drink?" Paul asked, handing me my coat before reaching for his own.

I'm sure the piercing death-glare I offered conveyed my answer well enough.

"You're gettin' old, mate," he said, laughing.

We walked out of the restaurant side by side and then I turned for the car park behind the building. "See you tomorrow!" I called over my shoulder as Paul carried on walking towards his flat above the barbershop a couple of streets away.

Rummaging through my coat pocket for my car keys, I stepped past what I assumed was a homeless guy sitting against the brick wall, staring up at the sky. It was a common sight on the streets of London, and as always I felt a pang of sorrow, maybe even guilt, as I carried on walking to my flashy car, ready to drive to my expensive apartment to eat my luxury food.

"C-Cameron?" The timid voice that carried my name darted into my ears, paralysing me, welding my feet to the pavement.

It can't be.

"Cam, is that you?"

I seemed to turn in slow motion, my eyes squinting as I studied the face a few feet away, illuminated by the streetlamp above.

"*Dylan?*"

Standing, he strode towards me, each step hesitant and wobbly, and as he neared I had no doubt in my mind. "Oh my God. *Dylan!*" Automatically, I lunged forward, my arms folding around his body, around his leather jacket, his *dad's* jacket, and held him tight to my chest. Pulling back, I stared at his face, pressing my hand to his cheek to move back the side of his grey hoody. Christ, the feel of his skin on mine…it still sent tingles through my spine even after all these years. He still felt familiar. He still felt like home.

His nose was bloody, his cheek swollen, and his gaze was fixed on the ground. "Jesus, Dyl. What happened to you?"

"I, um, I was mugged. No big deal."

"Your nose is still bleeding. Let me take you to A&E."

"No, no," he protested, shaking his head and backing away from my touch.

Looking at him made my chest ache with sadness, regret, confusion. I barely recognised him, and not just because adulthood had added a couple of inches to his height, given him some facial hair and strengthened his features. His shoulders were hunched, his voice nervous, his clothes tatty and worn. Yet he was still Dylan, *my* Dylan. He still had the same fair hair – although longer and scruffier, the same green eyes, full lips and narrow chin. Seeing him made every emotion I ever felt for him flood back to the surface.

My heart hammered in my chest, making my pulse thud in my ears. He stood two feet away yet I could still *feel* him, just like I always could. "Come with me," I said, cocking my head. "I have a first-aid kit at home."

"That's, uh, no...I should probably get going."

"Bullshit!" I snapped, composing myself immediately afterwards. "I thought I'd never see you again. I'm not settling for a few minutes in an alley. Please?"

Sighing, Dylan nodded and followed me to my car without another word. For months, possibly *years* after Dylan was taken away I thought of things I wished I could say to him. I missed him terribly, and I often dreamt about seeing him again and telling him as much. But now he was here, riding in my car, and I couldn't think of a single word.

Dylan trailed behind with his hands stuffed into his pockets as I let us into my apartment. My home was small, open plan with only a bathroom and one bedroom off the hall, but the location was highly sought after and ridiculously expensive.

"Take a seat," I said, unable to stop staring at Dylan while I motioned towards the brown-leather couch with my hand.

While he got comfortable I grabbed the first-aid kit from the cupboard under the sink in the kitchen and made my way right back to him. I couldn't quite believe he was here after all these years, all the time I'd spent wishing I could see him again…and yet he seemed like a total stranger.

Setting the green first-aid box down on the lamp table, I joined Dylan on the couch, surprised when he scooted away from me a little. "Let me take a look," I said, reaching for his face.

"It's nothing," he argued, turning his face away. "It'll be fine."

Cupping his cheek, I encouraged him to look at me. "I said let me look."

Our gazes met for a few long seconds before what looked like deep, emotional pain forced Dylan's eyes closed. Sighing through my nose, I reached out to the green box and plucked out a sterile wipe.

"What happened to you, Dyl?" I asked, my voice unsteady as I began wiping away the blood that had dried around his nose.

He flinched, from the question or the sting of the wipe I wasn't sure. "I told you. I was mugged."

I didn't mean tonight. The hurt in his eyes came from something much deeper. Whatever haunted the beautiful boy I fell in love with all those years ago had been building for a long time.

"I looked for you," I told him, grabbing a fresh wipe. "After you left. My mum rang social services but they wouldn't tell her anything."

"I didn't leave," he spat, venom coating his words. "I was taken."

"Where'd they take you?"

"Up north, eventually. Town called Littleborough. My foster parents lived here in London when they took me in, but moved up there shortly after. I was allowed to stay with them when they did."

"Were they good to you? Your foster parents."

Dylan shrugged. "Sure. Until they got fed up with me and put me back in the system."

My chest felt heavy as my heart broke for the boy I used to love. I wanted to fold my arms around his shoulders, hug him and never let him go. But we didn't know each other anymore, so instead I finished cleaning his bloodied face. "I don't think it's broken, but I imagine it will swell some more before it heals."

Dylan smiled, though it appeared forced, like he felt uncomfortable being here with me. "So, uh, what about you? How'd your life turn out?"

"Grea-okay," I stuttered, feeling a peculiar stab of guilt. Despite his reluctance to talk, I had no doubt whichever path Dylan's life had followed, it wasn't a great one. "I became a chef," I added, a small smile pulling on the corner of my lips.

"Yeah?"

"That was my restaurant. Where we met tonight."

"O'Neil's. Of course. I didn't put the pieces together."

"It's a common name." But one I would've expected to make him wonder, at least.

"I knew you'd do it," he said, bumping my shoulder with his. The contact almost made me choke on my own breath as the most delicious of tingles swept through my spine. "I'm real proud of you, Cam."

For a few seconds, I stayed quiet, absorbing his words. If I closed my eyes, it felt like the last sixteen years had never happened. "So what did you end up being?"

Without warning, Dylan stood, raking his fingers through his messy light-brown hair. It was much longer now, falling past his ears. "I need to get going. Thanks for, uh-"

"Wait," I said, coiling my fingers around the top of his arm. For a moment he just stared at my hand, not moving, not talking. "You don't want to talk. That's okay. We'll just…sit. Don't leave yet."

The internal battle was visible in his expression and all I could do was hope. Hope he'd stay. Hope he'd…hell, I didn't even know. I just wasn't ready to say goodbye yet.

"Please, Dylan."

Nodding briefly, he sat back down, leaving too big a space between us. For a while we sat in silence - an awkward, nervous quiet, both too afraid to look each other in the eye. Eventually I plucked up enough courage to break the hush, taking his mind back to our childhood. At first it made for easy conversation. Over a few beers, we reminisced. We laughed. We each jogged memories the other had forgotten.

We laughed about the time we got caught wagging school when we were twelve and how mortified we were when the head-teacher dragged our parents into her office. We remembered when we filled Kieran Nicholls' lunchbox with dog shit for no other reason than we were little bastards. He reminded me of the time I decided I was going to talk in an American accent for the rest of my life when I was ten, and I took him back to the day he broke his wrist after trying to climb our primary school's fence during the summer holidays.

Then, we talked about the time Dylan 'ran away' from home when he was nine after his dad said he couldn't get a dog. He showed up at my house and my mum said he could stay forever, though now I was an adult I imagined she called his dad as soon as he arrived and told her she'd take him home the next day. It was the best evening I'd had in years, but discussing Dylan's dad made his mood slip instantly, making my heart sink into my stomach.

"It's late," Dylan said, and I knew what was about to follow. "I'm gonna go."

"Sleep here." The words fell from my mouth without prior thought, but that doesn't mean I didn't mean it. "The busses have stopped, and I can't drive because of the beers. It makes sense."

A flash of panic paled his face. "I, um…"

He never used to stutter or mumble and I wondered if it was a nervous habit he'd picked up. *But...why would I make him nervous?* "I meant out here. The couch folds out into a bed. I'll be in the bedroom," I reassured him. "I'll grab you a blanket and a pillow."

"Okay. Thanks."

Before he had chance to change his mind, I headed to my bedroom and took the spare quilt from my wardrobe and a pillow from my bed. "The bathroom is the door on the right," I said when I stepped back into the living room, throwing the duvet on the couch before pulling the leaver that released the cushions so I could unfold it. "In case you want a shower or anything before you sleep."

"Thanks."

Nodding, I tucked my hands in my pockets. "Okay. Um, goodnight then."

"Night, Cam. And thanks again."

"No problem. See you in the morning."

"Right."

"Right."

It took me a full minute to turn away, and another to resist the urge to turn back and hold him. After crawling into bed I thought about Dylan, how he'd changed, wondering what he'd been through, whether he'd been happy...

But most of all I thought about how much I still loved him.

How ridiculous.

* * *

19

Stumbling out of bed the next morning, I wandered straight to the bathroom to freshen up before checking on Dylan. When I'd finished, a lump formed in my throat the second I saw my empty couch. There was nowhere else he could be, given that my kitchen and living room were part of one open-plan space.

Dylan was gone, and worse than that, I didn't know how to find him.

It almost felt worse than the first time he left. Back then, it wasn't his decision. Back then, I believed he was heading for a new, happy life with a family who would care for him. Back then, he was my whole world.

Now? He was a stranger, and the only way I can describe how that made me feel is incredibly sad.

I flopped onto the couch, next to the folded quilt stacked in a neat pile with the pillow on top. I stared at the quilt for a moment, running my finger along the cotton as if somehow the contact made me closer to Dylan. Then, through the corner of my eye I noticed a crumpled card on the coffee table with several silver coins scattered on top of it. Pushing the money to one side, I picked up what appeared to be a worn and stained business card for *Rochelle's* – a nightclub in Soho.

Turning it over, I wondered if he worked there, if that's where I could find him, before reading his scribbled note.

Counting Daisies

Money's for the cheese rolls I took from your fridge. Great to see you again. ~~Love~~ *Dyl.*

Shaking my head, I tossed the note aside in temper, not caring where it landed. *Great to see you again.* So great I didn't even deserve a goodbye? I couldn't decide if that hurt the most, or the fact he'd crossed out the word 'love'. Not that I expected him to *love* me, not after all this time. We were different people; adults leading separate lives. But he must've felt it, if only briefly, for him to write it in the first place.

A knock on my door startled me from my depressive musings, shortly followed by Paul walking straight through, dangling the key I gave him in the air. "Jesus, you look almost as bad as yesterday. You been drinking without me?"

Standing, I exhaled a long breath, hoping my uneasy mood would leave along with it.

"What's wrong with you?"

"Nothing," I spat. Clearly, breathing out didn't fucking work.

"Liar. Spill it."

"I'm going for a shower. Put some toast on while I'm in there."

"Hey, you're not the boss here, mate."

You'll do it anyway, I thought, heading for the bathroom. Dylan was all I could think about while I showered, and then again while I ate breakfast. Memories flashed like grenades through my mind, one after the other. Memories of his smile, the husky laugh he used to have, the way he used to feel in my arms... I missed him all over again.

He was still in my head when Paul and I reached the restaurant and I had a peculiar, and somewhat inexplicable, feeling that he would never leave. *I've lost him.* Again.

"You know we've got a critic in from The Guardian tonight, right?" Paul asked, changing into his uniform in the staffroom.

"I know."

"Then you need to tell me what's going on in that head of yours before your foul mood seeps into the food. It's Kevin isn't it? You've slept with him."

"What? *No!*" I protested before dragging my hands over my face. "Did I ever tell you about Dylan Roberts?"

"Dylan," he repeated, as if scanning his memory. "Wait, your best mate from high school Dylan?"

"He wasn't just my best friend. I was in love with him."

Paul raised a sceptical, almost mocking eyebrow. "You were a kid."

"Doesn't matter. I loved him. Anyway, I saw him again last night."

"Yeah? Where?"

"Just before the car park. Right after you left."

"Wow. What are the chances? Must've been great seeing each other again."

I didn't realise I hadn't answered until Paul spoke up. "Or not."

"He was, I don't know…different."

"Of course he was. It's been, what, fifteen years?"

Sixteen. "I know, I know. But…"

"But what?"

"It's like he wasn't Dylan anymore. It was more than just being older. He looked so…so…*lost.* Hurt."

"You said he was put in care, right?"

"Yeah."

"Well there you go. You hear all kinds of horror stories about those places. That kinda shit is bound to change a person."

"Hmm. Maybe."

"Jeez, Cam. This has really affected you hasn't it?"

"I know I rarely mention him, don't even think of him that often anymore, but he's always been in here," I said, tapping the side of my head. "When I was with him last night it almost felt like, well like I still love him."

"Um…"

"I know it sounds ridiculous."

"I can't say. When I look back on my first high school love I end up laughing. He was a proper wanker."

Paul didn't understand and it made me sigh. "I know every teenager probably says this at the time, but for Dyl and I it was more than puppy love. It was *real.* I know it was."

Paul clicked his tongue while he pondered what to say. "Maybe after everything with Kevin you're just clinging to happier memories."

"Maybe." I shrugged. "I don't know. I just can't stop thinking about him."

"So see him again. Maybe you'll pick up where you left off."

My heart sank all over again. "He left. While I was sleeping, he just…left. I don't know how to find him."

"Wait…he stayed over?" Paul questioned, raising his eyebrows as he anticipated further detail.

"Yeah, but nothing happened. We just talked, then he crashed on my couch."

"You tried Facebook? Although…if he left in the night, maybe he doesn't want to be found."

"Why wouldn't he?" My tone was acidic, as if the angst I felt was all Paul's fault. "We were best friends. Why wouldn't he want to see me again?"

"Hell, I dunno," Paul said, surrendering his hands. "I don't know the guy. I'm just saying, when you want to see an old friend again you usually swap numbers or something. Maybe he's married. Got three kids and a dog."

Married? That seemed almost as ridiculous as me thinking I still loved him. "He left a business card behind. Rochelle's – the club. Do you think I should hang out there? Maybe ask around?"

"Sure. If your goal is to become a creepy-arsed stalker."

"He *wants* to see me again, Paul. We were best friends."

"*Were.*"

Huffing, I folded my arms across my chest. "Why are you being such a dick about it?"

"I'm being realistic, Cam. Not so long ago you were planning to marry Kevin, and now you're obsessing over a guy you haven't seen since you were a kid. I don't get it."

"Kevin…" *Ah, fuck.* Maybe Paul was right, but I didn't want him to be. "Kevin was different. I loved him, of course I did, but I wasn't *in* love with him. We became a relationship of convenience."

"That's called being an adult. It's not all rainbows, butterflies, and boners like when you're a teenager."

He didn't understand, and as much as I wanted him to, he was beginning to make me feel stupid so I changed the subject. "Fetch me the venison from the fridge. I'm going to make a start on prep."

"You're worrying me a little."

"*Venison*, Paul."

Sighing, Paul shook his head. "Yes, chef."

* * *

Later that night, I was the last one left behind in the restaurant. Service was over, the kitchen was clean and prepped for the next day, and I simply sat in the quiet, going over invoices that I paid little attention to. All day I considered Paul's comment about finding Dylan on Facebook, but I also thought about everything else he had to say, like how absurd my reaction to seeing him again was. *That's* why every time I reached for my phone I would dismiss the idea of searching for Dylan and put it away again.

Until I couldn't do it any longer.

Fuck it, I thought. *And fuck Paul, too.*

Opening the laptop on my desk in the office, I brought up Facebook and typed in Dylan Roberts. Hundreds, possibly even thousands, of hits filled the page with none of the tiny profile pictures bearing any resemblance to *my* Dylan. I tried to narrow my search parameters by adding *London*, then *Littleborough*, into the search bar after his name. When that proved unsuccessful I started going through the friends lists of old school friends to see if he appeared on any of those. When he didn't, I took a fuel break, making a sandwich and pouring myself a strong cup of coffee, before clicking open every single Dylan Roberts profile one-by-one.

Bingo!

It took me almost an hour, but I found him. For a while I just stared at his profile photo, which once again looked nothing like how I remembered him. It also didn't resemble the man I met last night. *This* Dylan looked older, but happier. Healthier. He looked like the man I would've expected Dylan to grow into.

Finding the strength to close the photo, I scrolled through the rest of his profile, only to find he was last active six years ago. There were a handful of old statuses, posted from somewhere in Newcastle. He had seven friends, half of which had private profiles and the other half had inactive accounts just like his.

Dammit!

Paul was right, and it hurt to realise it. Dylan didn't want to be found, and my reaction *was* irrational. I refused to start stalking a club which he may, or may not, have worked at. I refused to do *anything* else to actively hunt him down. I refused to be *that* guy. I was just going to have to accept the fact that, despite our chance meeting last night, Dylan was nothing more than a memory. Just like he'd been for the last sixteen years.

Chapter

Two

~Dylan~

WHEN I WAS little, if I was afraid or hurt, my grandma would tell me to count daisies. I remembered the first time she said it like it was just yesterday. We were in the waiting room at the dentist, and I was about to go in for my first filling. I'd been told I'd need an injection in my gum which could sting for a few seconds and, being eight years old, I was terrified.

"When you lie down in the chair," she began, *"Close your eyes and imagine you're picking daisies."*

It was easy to imagine, because in the summer it was something Cameron and I used to do all the time in my grandma's back garden. We always said we only did it to make pretty things for my grandma, because making daisy-chains was for girls. Truthfully, we did it because it was fun.

"Count the daisies, Dylan. Turn those bad thoughts into something beautiful. By the time you have a pretty little bunch in your hands, it will all be over."

I didn't really believe her when she said it would take my mind off the injection, but I did it anyway, and it worked. It worked when I heard strange noises coming from the radiator in my bedroom at night. It worked when Fat Alan kicked me in the playground because I wouldn't share my crisps. It worked when my dad died and I couldn't stop crying.

And it worked, even as an adult, in moments like this.

"Money first," I said, holding out my palm to the balding man with greasy skin.

The queasiness descended on my stomach as soon as I took the two twenty-pound notes from him, stuffing them into the hidden pocket inside my jacket. I always felt a little sick at this point, but since I had to stop hanging out on the richer side of town in case I saw Cameron again, it'd only gotten worse. The punters around here were sleazy. They expected more services for less money. The area around Cameron's restaurant could've earned me a hundred quid, easy, for what I was about to do.

Why the fuck did I go to him? If I'd stayed away, even if I'd just stayed quiet when he finally appeared, he would've kept on walking, and right now I could've been about to drop my pants in a swanky hotel room for a rich guy in a business suit. Going to find him was a mistake. It forced memories I'd fought so long to supress back into my mind and allowing myself to remember the life I used to have was a very dangerous thing. Now, I was paying for it by standing in a dirty public bathroom, passing a condom to an old guy with putrid breath and a beer-belly.

"I'll give you an extra twenty to go in bare," the man who made my stomach roll offered.

Lowering my hoody from my head so he could see my face clearly, I forced myself to smile for him. "No deal."

Shrugging, he opened the condom and, as always, I watched him roll it on before turning to face the toilet and pushing my worn jeans down to my ankles.

Leaning forward, I grabbed onto the cistern and waited for it to be over. Some guys came prepared, brought their own lube, but most didn't. When I heard the vile sound of Bald Guy spitting onto his cock I knew he was one of the latter and bit my bottom lip, preparing myself for the discomfort. Most of the time I had sachets in my pocket that I'd picked up for free in clubs, but I ran out a few days ago and…I was desperate. I needed money and I needed it *now*.

Time to count daisies.

One, two, three, four… Most guys never got to fifty, and I could count on one hand how many

30

reached one hundred. I yelled the numbers inside my head, drowning out his pathetic grunts. *Thirty-eight, thirty-nine…*

"Ah, fuck!"

Forty. Thank Christ.

Pulling away, I dragged my trousers back up my legs the very moment I heard him finish. Immediately, I reached out to unlock the cubicle door but he pulled me back, grabbing my forearm. A wave of panic coursed through my veins, tensing my muscles as the memory of the night I saw Cameron resurfaced. I was foolish that night. The man whose cock I sucked seemed respectable; smartly dressed, wealthy enough to pay me two-hundred pounds for the hour I spent with him. As a result, I let my guard down. Once he'd finished, taken what he needed, he ripped the money he gave me from my jacket pocket and punched me until I fell to the ground before kicking the shit out of my face with his boot.

Stupid. Stupid. Stupid.

That's why I went to find Cameron. For the first time in a *long* time, I felt so alone. Scared. Hurt. I needed someone to hold me. Help me. Tell me I would be okay. But as soon as I called his name I knew it was a mistake. Seeing his rich-brown eyes, hearing his voice again, made me realise just how much I'd let him down. I'd let *everybody* who ever mattered to me down. I was a mess, a total fuck-up, and I didn't want him to know me that way.

I should've kept my distance, as I had done for the last few months. Sometimes, I'd stand across the street from O'Neil's and wait for him to leave work for the night. It was winter, freezing cold, often with rain or snow seeping through my clothes and into my bones, and I'd just…watch him. The cold, the pain of the memories he brought to the surface, was worth it just for the two minutes I got to spend seeing him living his life. Watching him laugh with his friends as he locked up, seeing him smile. I missed that smile. Even from across the street and in the dark of night it was bright enough to light up his whole face.

Yes, I was a weirdo fucking stalker…and I should've kept it that way.

"Let go of me," I growled, my pulse throbbing in my ears.

He dropped contact immediately. "Sorry. Just wanted to say thank you."

"Whatever," I spat, opening the door. "Give my regards to your wife."

Walking out of the bathroom, I blocked the left side of my vision with my hand so I wouldn't catch a glimpse of myself in the mirror. I was a disgusting human being, a failure, and my reflection never failed to make me feel violently sick to my stomach.

My next stop was, of course, Dean – my dealer. He based himself out of a small, dingy pub called The Old Dog and, being a cold February night, walking inside felt welcoming on my skin. Dean sat in the corner, surrounded by a group of 'his' guys; the kind of guys that would break my nose in four different places if I ever got behind on my payments. Striding past his table, I gave a silent nod and carried on to the bathroom, knowing he'd follow. Our exchange was over in seconds, the two small baggies concealed in my pocket already calming the anxiety running through my veins as I made my way to what I called home.

Climbing the fire escape was the only way into my flat above the derelict video-rental shop below. I was grateful for the streetlamp outside my cracked window because it meant I didn't have to stumble around in the dark after dusk. Luckily, some furnishings had been left behind when I discovered the empty building; a brown sofa with the inner foam exposed on both arms, a chest of drawers – broken but usable, and several lamps which were rendered useless without electricity.

I tried not to think about what I did next, winding the belt around the top of my arm automatically. If I allowed myself to think about the steps it would only serve as a reminder of what a worthless piece of lowlife scum I was. So, I thought about how peaceful the moon looked tonight as I sparked the lighter under my spoon. I wondered what put the laughter in the voices I heard outside my window as I drew the heroin into the needle through a tiny ball of cotton wool. Then, as I pushed it into my vein, I allowed myself to remember all the people I'd lost in my life, let myself feel the intense pain those faces brought with them, safe in the knowledge in just a few seconds it would all disappear.

And it did.

I felt the warmth from the needle travel through every inch of my body. It was magical. As my breathing slowed, so did my mind. Every ounce of pain, every conscious thought, disintegrated until all that remained was a hollow, blissful shell. These were the moments I lived for, the only times my heart didn't hurt and my body didn't ache. I was an addict; a fucked-up, selfish and pointless excuse of a man. But in that moment it was worth it. The world wasn't a scary place anymore. I wasn't alone. Right this second life, and heroin, was beautiful.

That's why we do it, us addicts. If taking a hit wasn't the most exquisite, incredible sensation to ever exist, we wouldn't do it. The very moment the drug dances into your system makes all the other shit - the constipation, the fatigue, the impotence, the prostitution, the damage to your body and mind, the living as a social reprobate, an outcast, a useless piece of despicable shit - worthwhile. Take the best day of your life, the most intense orgasm you've ever had, the most wonderful food you've ever tasted, and multiply all those things by three million. *That's* what heroin is. *That's* why we do it. *That's* what we live for.

It didn't last of course. Never did. A couple of hours later I woke up in a sprawled heap on the cold living room floor, the empty syringe lying next to me where I dropped it, and the loosened belt still wrapped around my arm. The beginnings of an abscess was starting to form in the crook of my elbow and I stared at it for a few seconds, frustrated that I'd have to find a new vein next time. It wasn't a new thing for me. Abscesses were common, part of the parcel.

That's the moment the beauty turned to disgust, the moment I vowed to beat this crap once and for all, the moment I *detested* being a heroin addict.

Until the next hit, of course.

Scrambling to my knees, my muscles heavy and my bones aching, I cleared away the latest set of evidence that depicted how screwed up I was. For now, I felt relatively okay. I had enough gear to see me through the next two days, but my whole life revolved around preparing for the time my stash would run out. And so, after washing myself down in the grimy bathroom with cold, bottled water, I donned my sunglasses to disguise my sunken eyes and headed outside.

I may have been reckless and selfish, but I wasn't completely irresponsible. That's what I told myself anyway. In the beginning, I swore to myself every single time I sold my body that it would be the last. Once that naivety wore off, however, I decided if I couldn't stop it, I could at least control it. So, condoms were a deal breaker. I had, and would, never go near a guy without one. I had to believe I would never become desperate enough to forgo the only real rule I had.

Trouble is condoms were expensive. They weren't always available for free at clubs and I didn't approach clinics in case they required a consultation first. Therefore I usually ended up pocketing a couple of boxes before paying for the third. Small, independent shops had poor security which worked in my favour, but I was still careful, conscious of prying eyes and hidden security tags.

I detested what I'd become, which is why I lived my life on autopilot, refusing to dwell on the days' events, and rarely letting myself remember the boy I once was. That's why I couldn't afford to see Cameron again. Going to his restaurant and calling his name a moment of weakness, and one that had cost me dearly, leaving the image of him etched into my mind. I needed it out, needed him gone, and the only way to do that was to keep myself on a level of high that meant I could barely remember my own name.

It hadn't worked yet, but I'd keep trying. Which is why I planned to buy one of the reduced-price sandwiches nearing their sell-by date along with the condoms, before going home to shoot up again.

* * *

I was relieved to wake up later that evening. I slept a *lot*, heroin does that to you, but I didn't often remember my dreams. Not that I'd just had a dream. It was a nightmare. Torture. A loud bang outside ripped me from the painful torment after my unconscious mind sent me back in time, back to a day where Cam and I sat around the kitchen table, chatting with my dad.

They'd be so disappointed in me.

Counting Daisies

Coming back to this city was a mistake. After my first set of foster parents took me up north, I ended up staying there even after they'd had enough of me. I'd had four sets of foster carers by the time I turned eighteen, and then I was pretty much left to fend for myself. I pushed the lot of them away. Everyone has their limits, and I tested them until they broke. That's why it was for the best that I'd backed away from Cameron, before I broke *him* too. I'd find his limit, and I'd crush it. I was destined to be alone. No point in deluding myself, delaying the inevitable.

Social Services offered help and guidance, but I didn't fucking want it so I set off on my own.

I did pretty okay at first. I hung around Manchester for a year, got a few labouring jobs on building yards while I saved enough money to get out of the overrun hostel I was living in, and I met Sam.

Sam Maloney had been a labourer since he was fresh out of school and had enough skills, although not recognised officially, to rival any professional builder. After another year, we decided to team up; offering off-the-book jobs, fixing up roofs, repairing or installing garden walls and the like, all cash-in-hand. Within two months we had a steady enough income to rent our first flat together. It was tiny, but it was ours.

Life was good then, maybe even great. Sam became the first friend I'd had since my grandma died and life as I knew it was torn to shreds. We worked together, lived together, had fun and smoked weed together. I loved him like a brother. But like everyone else, I lost him too. He didn't die, but he might as well have. Sam met a woman, the daughter of one the clients who'd hired us to repair the roof of the summerhouse situated at the bottom of his gigantic garden. Within a matter of weeks, weed was for losers, nightclubs for teenagers, and Netflix for people who were too dumb to read. Sam's life became all fancy restaurants and the National Geographic Channel and I was slowly but surely phased out.

Everybody leaves. They left or they died. Either way, I was alone.

Without Sam I couldn't complete the jobs we'd accepted. Without a job I couldn't afford the rent on our flat, and without rent it didn't come as a surprise to find myself squatting in a boarded-up repo house two doors down from the guy who supplied my weed. It was the same guy who offered me something 'a little stronger' to help me forget the fact my life had turned to shit. Started with a little coke. Tried meth a couple of times. Then he offered me heroin and from that day on I became, and would always be, an addict.

It's not true, what people say about you becoming addicted after the first hit. The first time it feels incredible, like nothing you've ever experienced, but you don't *need* to do it again; you just *want* to. So you take it a couple more times. You start by chipping, limiting yourself to one hit a week, slowing down when you feel the first twinges of *reliance*, the first signs of being junk-sick, before resuming normal pattern once you've got a hold of yourself. You think you've 'got this', that you're one of the lucky ones who won't let it take over. But by the time you realise you're entering dangerous territory it's too late. Heroin *owns* you, and you'd do anything, *anything*, to have it just *one* more time.

Quite quickly after that, you need *more*. You build up a tolerance. You need extra to keep the withdrawal symptoms at bay. A little more to get you to sleep, to help you wake up, to keep you alert, to calm your racing thoughts, to quash fears you didn't even know you had before you started using. Suddenly, you need it to carry out almost every basic function every other human being takes for granted.

That guy was also the same man who, months later, had three men break my nose and snap three of my ribs when I couldn't afford to settle the debt I'd racked up with him. It was also that same guy who suggested I might have something worth selling while cupping my dick through my jeans with his nicotine-stained fingers.

I laughed in his face, right before I punched him square in the jaw. I might've been an addict, a thief, a waste of a life…but I had a shred of self respect left and I refused to let it go. I held onto it with everything I had. I clung to that self respect through another beating, through moving from hostel to hostel before ending up on the street.

I clung to it for two whole months before I gave it to a middle-aged man who wore a smarmy smile, in exchange for a twenty-pound note and a packet of fags. I didn't even smoke anymore, but I'd sell them on for a couple of quid.

I threw up the second he left the cheap hotel room he'd booked for the night. Then, when my dad's face entered my mind, I threw up some more until I felt steady enough on my feet to go and score a bag with the twenty-pound note that contained my self respect.

That night became routine over the next few weeks. Fuck, throw up, score. Fuck, throw up, score. Then one day, while stroking the polished wood of my dad's guitar, a used syringe at my feet, I realised where I was going wrong, what was making me feel so shit, so disgusted with myself. It was my dad. My *family*. It was like I could still feel them with me, watching me, being disappointed.

But they *weren't* with me. They were dead; gone like everyone else. I needed to let them go, so back to London I went. I walked, hitchhiked, took a train with the fifty quid I got for blowing a guy in a pub toilet, and headed straight to my dad's grave. He was buried with my mother, and my Granny Roberts was next to them. I sat there for hours, picking at the damp moss that had gathered over my parents' headstone. I couldn't bring myself to talk to him, to *any* of them, not that they'd have been able to hear me anyway. What would I have said?

Oh, hey family. So, I've been turning tricks to buy drugs the last few months. You proud of me?

Nevertheless, I said goodbye to them in my head, silently apologising for the fact I planned to never think of them again. That worked pretty well for a while. I lived my life in a heroin-induced daze, only ever thinking of where the next bag would come from. Life wasn't good, but it was bearable…until the night I ended up in a fight with my dealer and he plunged a knife into my side.

I ended up in hospital where I had surgery to repair the perforation in my bowel. I could've died, almost *did*, and yet…I wasn't particularly bothered. From there I was enrolled into a community rehab scheme and started on a methadone programme. My key worker helped me find accommodation for after my discharge, another hostel in a long line of many, and then I had to go to the local chemist every day to have my medication administered. Each time they would take me into a little side room, away from the *respectable* members of the public, and I'd have to swallow the bitter green liquid under the supervision of the pharmacist.

A lot of people think methadone is a 'safe' substitute for heroin, and those people are wrong. It's safer, sure, but it's *nothing* like heroin. You don't get the magical hit your body lives for. It takes a few hours to kick in, and so there's no rush. No warmth. No beauty. But it kept the shakes, the nausea, the sweating, and the debilitating ache in my bones away, so I persevered. The drugs nurse in the hospital gave me some hope. She made me believe I was taking the first step towards getting my life back and I believed her. She made me think if I got clean I could get a job, a *real* home. Maybe make some friends and not have to be alone anymore.

She was full of shit.

Ten months I stayed on methadone. Ten months of hard fucking work. Ten months of willpower. Ten months of believing good things were coming. But they didn't. The hostel I was living in was closed down due to underfunding, but it was okay because I was offered a room in another one. What I didn't know when I accepted was that my new room was a shared room...

With a junkie.

His very first words to me were, "Are you holding?" but they weren't enough to make me throw my ten months of hard work away. It took him shooting up in front of me to do that. The look on his face when the needle dropped made my heart pound and my mouth dry up. He looked like he was in heaven; so peaceful, so free of burden...and I wanted that.

So I had it.

Just this once. That's what I told myself. I said the same thing the next time, too. When it happened a third time, I told myself a different lie. I told myself I enjoyed being an addict. I told myself it was time to stop trying for something better because it didn't exist. For the first time in ten months I had something tangible to look forward to instead of just a dream that would never materialise. Scoring heroin was achievable. I was good at it. Ten months I'd waited for the good things that stupid nurse made me believe I could have, whereas it took me ten *minutes* to score a bag of the only 'good' stuff I knew deep down I would ever deserve.

So back I went to the only way of living that didn't cause me pain. I didn't give up the methadone right away even though I was back to using skag daily, because…free drugs. I'd have been stupid to turn that down. But then the pharmacy started asking me questions I didn't like. They weren't stupid. They knew what I was doing, probably because I wasn't the only one who was doing it, and also because part of the programme involved regular blood tests. So, I just stopped going back and cranked up my heroin use instead.

After a few years, I even made a new friend. Bubbles. She was an addict too. She *got* me. She *got* addiction. For a while we did everything together. We'd steal together, score together, couch surf, share our gear. We'd eat expensive microwave meals, drink posh wine, it's amazing what you can afford when you're nicking it, and she'd even cut my hair. We'd talk for hours some nights. She'd rip the piss out of me because I quit smoking on the basis it was bad for my health, usually with a needle sticking out of my arm. She was funny, bold, smart too. She'd had a shit life as well; sexually abused for years by her stepdad before running away from home when she was fifteen. We were both as fucked up as each other and that made for a great friendship.

But, of course, she left as well. She reunited with an auntie who paid for her to get into a shit-hot rehab facility; the kind that fucking celebrities go to. That was six months ago and I hadn't seen her since. I tried not to be angry with her for leaving. She wasn't abandoning me, simply grabbing a great opportunity. Still, I was hurt, maybe even a little jealous, and I combatted those feelings with drugs.

Life was easier when I was using. Heroin made it easier not to care, not to worry, not to wish for things I couldn't have. It never let me down. It never gave me false hope. Its effects were reliable, and I needed that. The worst that could happen was it would kill me, and some days that idea didn't seem so terrible. I was mostly numb, and life was manageable…

Until I saw Cameron again.

He'd barely changed. Sure, he was taller, had some stubble on his face, but I recognised him instantly. I thought talking to him would comfort me, but instead it took me back to my past, the past I'd lost and would never get back, and all I'd done since leaving his apartment in the middle of the night was curse myself for going there.

"What the hell?" I whispered to no one, scrambling to my feet when I heard what sounded like a door slamming. Moments later, footsteps pounded the stairs that led to the abandoned shop below and my muscles tensed instinctively, my body switching to fight-mode.

A man appeared in my doorway; twice my age, at a guess, dressed smartly in a suit and long overcoat. He rolled his eyes the second he saw me, shaking his head. "Thought as much," he said under his breath. "You can't stay here."

"Oh yeah? Says who?" I forced confidence into my voice, despite the fact my hands were shaking. I'd lived here for over four months without a problem. I wasn't hurting anyone. I wasn't getting in anybody's way.

"Says *me*. I just bought the place."

"I have rights." As the words left my lips I prayed there was truth in them. I'd heard of the term 'squatters rights' but I didn't really know what it meant. I was almost sure the owner of the building couldn't claim the property back while I was inside, so as long as I stayed put I'd be fine. Granted, I'd need to leave eventually if I ever wanted to eat again, but at least I'd have a few days to consider my options.

By options, I mean the streets or a homeless shelter. I'd survive either way. I'd lived pretty much everywhere over the years – hostels, people's floors, alleyways, inside tunnels covered in piss and graffiti. I'd be okay, it was just a pain in the arse.

"Sorry to disappoint you, mate, but the rules changed back in 2012. You're breaking the law right now."

Shit. For a moment the idea of a police cell sounded appealing. I'd be warm, clean, and fed three meals a day. But…I wouldn't have been able to score in there.

"Look," the man continued. "I'm not a monster. I'll give you twenty-four hours. But if you're still here when I come back tomorrow night I'll have you arrested for trespassing."

"I-I-" *Fuck.*

"Twenty-four hours, mate," he called over his shoulder with a dismissive wave, already returning to the stairwell.

"*Dammit!*" I yelled, kicking the wall so forcefully I dented the plaster. Frustrated, angry, and maybe even a little scared, I kept kicking, throwing in the odd punch too. "Dammit! Dammit! Dammit!"

Knuckles bleeding, I sank to the floor, throwing my head in my hands. I was back to square one. I had nothing and no one. *Again.* I wasn't stupid enough to believe the flat I'd been living in belonged to me, but the longer I stayed without being found the easier it became to pretend I had a right to be here. Not just the flat, but *here*. Alive. I had somewhere to call home. A place to go. A purpose.

I didn't need another hit yet, but I didn't need the thoughts running riot in my mind even more. So, crawling over to the sofa on my hands and knees, I picked up my spoon and the rest of my gear and set about forgetting the world for a while.

* * *

Taking a final glance around the flat, I made sure I had everything that mattered to me.

My leather jacket.
My guitar.
Heroin.

Holdall in one hand, my dad's guitar in the other, I carried my whole life with my fingers as I turned my back on the place I called home, climbing through the window and onto the fire escape.

For hours I just walked, using the fresh air to clear my head while I tried, in vain, to work out what the fuck I was going to do. Two hostels and one homeless shelter turned me away because they were full, and the council offered to put me on an accommodation waiting list which I knew was their way of fobbing me off, too. As evening drew in I tried a few doors on empty buildings but couldn't get them to budge. It was a cold night, the light drizzle in the air seeping through the worn patches of my jacket and stinging my skin as I settled onto a bench, using the guitar case as a pillow.

For the briefest of seconds, I considered going to Cameron for help. Then I wanted to punch myself in the face for allowing his name into my head. I didn't need Cam. I didn't need anybody. The cold was making me weak and afraid, but spring was approaching so it wouldn't be for long.

I'd survive on my own. Just like I always did.

Chapter

Three

~Cameron~

One week later...

"A SCARF? SERIOUSLY?"

"It's freezing," I protested, tightening the thick wool around my neck.

Raising an eyebrow, Paul exhaled a mocking laugh. "Pussy. It's almost spring."

"In *London*. Not Hawaii."

Paul didn't even zip up his coat as we stepped onto the street outside his flat, purely to prove a point no doubt. I stayed over at Paul's last night so, with him living so close to the restaurant, we were walking to work today.

"Hey, thanks for coming over last night," Paul muttered before forcing a nervous cough. "And, uh, sorry for whining. I had too much to drink."

Closing the gap between us as we walked, I bumped his shoulder with mine. "That's what friends are for. To be there in your hour of need, mop up your vomit, dry your tears."

"Fuck you. There were no tears."

But there *was* vomit. A *lot* of vomit. Mostly a vile concoction of vodka and, Paul's only addiction, Jaffa Cakes. "Do you think she'll take you back?"

Paul pondered for a moment, his eyes fixed straight ahead as the restaurant came into view. "You know what? I don't think I want her to. If she can't accept me for who I am then…" he trailed off, shrugging.

"Maybe she'll accept it in time." I gave Paul all the advice I had to offer last night, but given the amount of alcohol he'd consumed before I even got to his place, I imagined I'd be repeating a lot of it today.

Paul had been with his girlfriend, Heather, for only a month but he really liked her. Talking about her gave him that loved-up glint in his eye that you get in a new relationship, that coy smile which makes you look stupid to anyone who isn't getting any action. From what he'd told me they seemed to be a perfect match…until Paul told her he was bisexual yesterday and she flipped her shit.

"Doubt it. She's got some really backwards opinions about it. You know, the usual. Bisexuals are unfaithful. How can she be enough for me when she doesn't have a dick, yadda yadda."

"She's got fingers," I said with a sly smirk, earning me a swat across the side of my head. "*Ow!*"

"You asked for that."

Turning my head so he couldn't see the grin on my face, I pulled the restaurant keys from my coat pocket and bent down, twisting the lock to open the door. "I'm sorry, Paul. I know you liked her."

He replied with another shrug as we stepped inside, clearly trying for the nonchalance that he failed spectacularly at last night.

"You wanna talk about it some more or get straight to work?"

"Work. It's taking all my strength not to throw up right now. Talking is making it harder."

"That's what you get for drinking on a work night."

"I'm starting to wish I hadn't been so sympathetic when *you* were hungover. Arsehole."

Hanging up my coat and scarf on the rack in my office, I couldn't help laughing at the pout on Paul's face. "What can I say? You're a better man than I am." I wasn't a *total* bastard. I planned to get him some coffee and paracetamol while he started prep for lunchtime service.

Counting Daisies

"Give Derek a ring will you? Ask him to come in early to help with the fish. I can't handle anything with an odour right now."

Derek was a pastry chef, but I knew he'd still help. "A sous chef who can't handle the smell of fish? Now who's the pussy?"

"Just call Der…oh shit." With a face that'd turned a pale shade of green, Paul threw his hand over his mouth and darted towards the bathroom.

For fuck's sake. Rolling my eyes, I plucked my phone from my pocket and called Derek. Then, after deciding I'd need to send Paul's hungover arse home for a few hours, I phoned one of my commis who wasn't due in until this evening to come in early too.

* * *

Half way through evening service and I was sure anyone looking in would think I was stressed to fuck. A professional kitchen in the throes of service is a sea of bodies dancing around one another, glowing with sweat, barking orders and commands, while striving to make each plate as perfect as the last. It *is* stressful, but the adrenaline surging through your veins as the pace picks up creates such a delicious buzz, one that I'd never found doing anything else, and makes it all worthwhile.

I'd wanted to be a chef since I was just a kid and I was living my dream every single day. It was so much more than simply cooking food. I created works of art. Each component of every gourmet dish had to be as pleasurable on the eye as it was on the tongue and having that ability was something I prided myself on. There was no place for modesty in this business. I was a perfectionist. I excelled in my craft and I wasn't too shy to admit it. That being said, the tradition of sending the head chef out at the end of service to receive an applause, as had been the case in some of the restaurants I started my career in, is something I hadn't carried through to my own establishment. I was good and I knew it, but the only praise I needed was customers coming back for more.

"Hey," Derek said while tossing a tea-towel over his shoulder. "I think Twinkle's usin' your office as a brothel." He finished his statement by laughing, before plucking a handful of vanilla pods from the shelf behind me in the pantry.

By Twinkle, he meant Paul. Paul had a star, complete with rays darting from it, tattooed on his back two years ago while on holiday in Malaga. 'I was drunk,' was his excuse. When Derek caught a glimpse of it one day, referring to it as a tramp stamp, he came up with the nickname Twinkle. It pissed Paul off to the extent he threatened to break Derek's favourite palette knife, which of course made Derek more determined to never call him by his actual name again. So Twinkle stuck, and Derek started taking his knives home with him every night.

In return, Paul referred to Derek as 'Old Man', because in Paul's words, Derek is a granddad's name. They were both as childish as each other.

"Heather's here?" I asked, scrunching my nose in confusion.

"I dunno 'er name." Derek shrugged. "Tall, brunette, birthmark on 'er chin."

Exiting the pantry, I strode with purpose to my office, planning to eavesdrop; partly because I was nosey, and partly because if I found him fucking someone in my office, especially during service, I'd rip off his dick and pickle it in vinegar. I'd have been surprised if that *was* what he was doing. He felt well enough to come in for the evening shift but still only looked marginally less shit than he did this morning.

Holding my ear to the door, I heard voices. They were muffled and unintelligible at first, but grew louder as tensions in the room seemed to rise.

"I'm willing to try and forget it if you are."

"Forget it? You want me to *forget* I'm bisexual?"

"No, no. You're twisting it! I mean we can keep seeing each other. See how it goes."

"Sooo…today you've decided you don't have anything against bisexuality?"

"Oh, Paul. That's not fair. I'm not homophobic or whatever it is you're implying. Sure, I think wanting both sexes is a little unnecessary, and maybe a tad greedy, but I'm not-"

Oh, he won't like that. I knew I should step away but…well, I just didn't.

"Wow. I'm so sorry, Heather. That must've been such a tough decision for you."

"What?"

"Well, it sounds like you're saying you *chose* to be straight because you didn't want to be greedy, and not because you're simply not attracted to other women. I admire your strength. Here's me *choosing* to be bi because I don't have your kind of willpower to only stick to one kinda person."

"What the hell, Paul?"

"No, I get it. I've always been a greedy bastard. I used to tell my mum I didn't have time for lunch at school so she'd give me a double helping at dinner time."

"I shouldn't have come here."

"No. You shouldn't."

"So that's it? We're over?"

"Oh *shit!*" I yelled as the floor met my face. I hadn't heard footsteps approach the door before Paul opened it. *That's me busted.* "Sorry," I mumbled, clambering to my feet. "I didn't know anyone was in here."

The small rise of Paul's eyebrow told me he could smell my bullshit.

I was about to make my excuses and leave, but Heather started talking. "Paul?"

"Goodbye, Heather."

She opened her mouth to speak, but all that emerged was a stutter followed by an annoyed huff before she stormed out of the office, slamming the door behind her.

"I can't believe you were eavesdropping," Paul said, shaking his head.

"I didn't want to…but then it got all soap opera and I couldn't help myself."

"Hmm," was his reply, and as he ran his hand through his hair and looked at the ceiling, I couldn't tell if he was genuinely pissed off or not.

"You okay?"

"Not really. Think I left my favourite shirt at her place."

Stepping closer to him, I clapped his shoulder. "Well you know my thoughts on that shirt."

"Your dad likes it."

"Exactly."

Paul laughed, but it wasn't altogether convincing. He was clearly experiencing the post break-up blues, something which I kind of understood. I'd felt like shit ever since Dylan disappeared on me for the second time. I knew the comparison was ridiculous. I hadn't broken up with Dylan, given that we weren't together, but it felt like I had.

As Paul's best friend, it was my duty to cheer him up. As Paul's boss, however, it was my job to get his arse back out into the kitchen. "I'll help you drown your sorrows later. But right now I need you out there."

"Sure," he agreed, literally shaking himself off before straightening his back. "Oh, before I forget!" he called as I walked away. "I've been working on some new recipes for the summer menu. There're a couple I want to test out on you next time you're free."

"Sounds great. Tuesday? Derek's holding the fort so you can use my kitchen."

"Tuesday it is."

Nodding, I headed back to the kitchen, the sweltering heat punching me in the face the second I pushed through the swinging doors. I took a moment, as I often did, to admire my team working in perfect sync with each other. This kitchen was *mine*, the creations being placed on the pass were *my* ideas, *my* artistry brought to life, it was difficult to stand here and not feel pride swell in my chest.

As service drew to a close, I started cleaning down while everyone else worked to get the last few plates out. Of course, cleaning and dishwashing weren't part of my role, but my success hadn't made me too arrogant to get my hands dirty. This was *my* restaurant, *my* people, my family, and I didn't just think of myself as the head of the team...I was *part* of it.

A couple of hours later, once everything was done for the day, I sent everyone home, leaving just me and Paul. I was locking the day's takings in the safe in my office when I heard voices, shortly followed by Paul appearing in the doorway.

"There's someone here to see you. I tried to get him to leave, but he says he knows you."

"Why'd you ask him to leave?" I didn't really care. I was stalling, needing a few seconds to remember how to breathe. I knew who was here. I don't know how, I just...*knew*.

I hadn't been able to stop looking for him, searching social media, stopping by *Rochelle's*, despite Paul repeatedly telling me it was stupid. Seeing him again changed me somehow. Only after that night did the twinge of longing disappear whenever I heard from Kevin, which was often, and mostly by text. He hurt me, but a part of me still missed him…until I saw Dylan.

People say young love, first love, whatever you want to label it, isn't real. It's a dress rehearsal. Teenagers aren't capable or mature enough to understand what love entails. That's what people think. But *we* did. Dylan and I had a bond, an awareness of each other, even before we hit puberty and our friendship developed into attraction. Maybe that awareness, a sixth sense almost, is how I knew he was here right now.

"Because he looks dodgy," Paul answered, pulling me out of my thoughts. "He's wearing fucking shades at night for a start. Looks like some kinda homeless rockstar fuckin' wannabe. I still don't know if I should've told you or called the police."

"That won't be necessary. I know who it is." Blowing out a steadying breath through pursed lips, I stepped past Paul and made my way through to the dining room.

Even though I knew who it was, it didn't stop my pulse racing or my breath catching in my throat the second I saw Dylan.

"I, uh," Dylan stammered, removing his sunglasses as I walked over, stopping just inches away from him. "I'm sorry to bother you here. I didn't know where else to go. Maybe it was a bad idea. I should go. I'll go."

Reaching out, I grasped his arm, inwardly despising the material of his jacket that kept me from his skin. I couldn't believe he still had it. I recognised it the first time I saw it. The black leather was worn now, scuffed and scratched, and it definitely fit him better than when we were teenagers, although still a little too big…but it was his father's, I had no doubt. "No. I'm glad you came. What do you need?"

"I, um, I need…" Staring at my hand on his arm, his eyes filled with sadness, Dylan sighed. "I need help, Cam."

They were innocent enough words, yet they terrified me. A part of my mind thought I'd never be able to give him whatever he was asking for, but a bigger part of me knew I'd have to try.

"Everything okay here?" Paul interrupted, coming up behind me. He still sounded dubious, and he deserved an explanation, so I told Dylan to take a seat while I talked to Paul in the office.

Dylan disappeared from view as I left the dining room with Paul trailing behind me. A heaviness descended on my stomach as I silently hoped he'd still be there when I got back.

"That's him isn't it?" Paul said, closing the office door behind us. "That's Dylan."

"Yes."

"Jesus, Cam. Do you know what you're getting into here?"

"I'm not getting into anything. I don't even know what he wants yet." My tone was clipped and defensive.

"He asked you for help."

"And?"

"He wants money, Cam. You can't be that stupid."

Whoa. I flexed my fingers in an effort to relieve some of the tension building in my gut. I didn't expect Paul to understand my feelings for Dylan but he owed it to me, as my friend, to try.

"He was my best friend."

"*Was.* A *long* time ago. Who knows what kind of man he's turned into? Look at the state of him. He's filthy. He looks destitute for Christ's sake."

"Why are you being like this? You don't even know him!" My voice was low, so Dylan wouldn't hear, but harsh. I was angry with Paul, and I wanted him to know it.

"Neither do you! Hell, I can barely remember my friends from high school and you've been moping around since you saw him like you're still in love with the guy!"

Frustrated, I waved my hand in the air, dismissing him. "I can't do this right now. Go home. I'll call you tomorrow."

"You'll call me *tonight*," he countered, grabbing his jacket from the rack behind the office door. "I need to know you're okay."

"So, what? You think he's come to hurt me now, too?"

"Honestly? Yes, I do. I think you're gonna get hurt, Cam. Maybe not physically but-"

"Stop it, Paul."

"I think he's a junkie."

A humourless laugh burst from my throat. "And you know that after seeing him for under a minute? What the hell is your problem? Are you *jealous?* Do you feel threatened or something?"

"Now you're just talking bollocks. You know about my cousin John. I know the signs."

"Go home, Paul," I said, my tone void of emotion as I opened the office door for him. I'd had enough. I was angry, confused, and tired of his bullshit. I didn't understand how we'd got here. There was no reason for Paul's hostility. He didn't know Dylan.

But *I* did. I'd known him since we were four years old. I wasn't naïve enough to believe I knew what he'd been through, the life he'd lived as an adult, but I knew *him*. Inside. Deep in his soul, I knew him.

"Call me, Cam. I mean it."

I didn't reply as Paul walked away. I *would* call him because he was my best friend. I loved him and I didn't want him to worry, but that didn't mean I couldn't be pissed off as hell with him.

I took a few deep breaths after he left, trying but failing to compose myself. As I pushed through the doors to the dining room, I held my breath, only releasing it when I saw Dylan had indeed waited for me. Since hearing what Paul had to say, I found myself studying him, searching for the 'signs'

Paul apparently saw. Dylan hadn't seen me yet, so for a minute or so I just stared at him. He was thin, evident even through his clothes. His eyes were dark and sunken. His skin was pale, yet his nose was pink as if he had a cold. That didn't mean he was a fucking junkie though, and in that moment I hated Paul for putting that doubt in my mind.

Any number of things could've caused Dylan to look like he did. Maybe he wasn't sleeping. He could've been depressed, or had an eating disorder. To jump to the conclusion that he was a drug addict, here to hurt or steal from me, was a low, and frankly ridiculous assumption on Paul's part.

When I reached Dylan's table he looked up, greeting me with a smile saturated with so much sadness it tore through my heart.

Without thought, I grabbed a leather-backed menu from the rack by the servers' station on my way, and handed it to Dylan as I sat down. He looked like he needed a decent meal, but I didn't risk offending him by saying it out loud. "Choose something. Anything."

"You don't have to do that," he muttered, his voice timid, unrecognisable from the boy I used to know.

"Just do it, Dyl."

Smiling nervously, he opened the menu. I watched his dark-green eyes scan the list of dishes, and every so often he would squint a little, drawing his eyebrows together like he was confused. "What's a con...con-summer?"

"Consommé?"

"S-sorry," he stuttered. "I'm not up on all this fancy shit. Not that it's shit. I'm sure it's not shit. I meant-"

"It's okay, Dylan. I know what you meant," I assured him with a warm smile. I couldn't stop staring at him. His busted nose had healed, still a little yellow around the edges. I wanted to mention it, find out what really happened because I didn't believe he was mugged, but I didn't. "A consommé is like a clear soup made from meat juices. The confit rabbit leg in the dish you're looking at sits in the middle with some seasonal vegetables."

"Oh." He looked unsure. "What about…" Something caught his attention, interrupting his question. "Holy *fuck*. You charge one hundred and twenty-five pounds for this?"

Shrugging slightly, but unable to keep the grin off my face, I tried to justify the price list. "That's for three courses."

Dylan's eyes widened and he opened his mouth as if he were about to reply, but then closed it again. He carried on reading the menu, occasionally sounding out unfamiliar words on his tongue, before looking at me with a defeated expression. "Don't you do anything, you know, normal?"

"I can make you anything you want."

"Um…a burger? Do you do those?"

Smiling, I stood up and held out my hand. "Come with me." If Dylan wanted a burger, I would make him the best damn burger he'd ever tasted, and I wanted him to watch while I did.

Partly because I wanted him to see me doing all the things I'd talked about when we were kids, and partly because I wanted to keep him close so he didn't disappear on me again.

Dylan stood, but he didn't take my hand. For a few seconds he stared at it with a look of almost fear on his face, and then he stuffed his own hands into his pockets. Nevertheless, he started to follow, and I led him into the kitchen carrying a heavy knot of an emotion I didn't recognise in my stomach.

I wanted to talk to him, *needed* to find out his story, but I was so afraid of scaring him away that I stayed silent as I made his meal. He watched me prepare the minced steak, adding herbs and seasoning before shaping it into two round patties and placing them in a pan of sizzling oil. Putting a separate pan on to heat, I went to the fridge to grab some strips of bacon, keeping Dylan in my line of vision the whole time. I did the same when I grabbed some buns from the pantry, and while I fetched some garnishes from the chiller cabinet. It was as if I thought if I took my eyes off him for even a second, when I looked again he would be gone.

"Go sit down," I said, arranging the garnishes on top of the stack of meat, cheese and deep fried onion rings. "I'll bring it out."

Nodding, Dylan walked away without a word. The silence was painful, only because I knew there was so much we needed to say. And we would. At least, *I* would, but I wanted to enjoy his presence for a little longer first.

"Voila," I said, placing his plate on the table before sitting down to join him.

"Thanks." He smiled, but again it seemed sad. Everything about him seemed sad. He looked so fragile, so lost. It made my chest ache. "You're not having one?"

I shook my head. "I need to calm down from the buzz of service first. Plus I've been tasting all night. I'm not hungry yet."

Chewing on my bottom lip, I fixed my gaze on Dylan's face as he took his first bite, hoping he'd like what I made for him. I'd been judged by thousands of customers over the years, not to mention professional critics and, even scarier, my family. But in that moment Dylan's approval seemed to matter more than anyone else's.

"Wow," he breathed, wiping the corner of his mouth on his thumb. "This tastes incredible. What kind of bread is this? It tastes, I don't know, different."

"Brioche. Sorry, we only stock the fancy shit here," I said, winking as I repeated his earlier remark.

"It's delicious." He took another bite, while my eyes wandered over to the entrance doors.

Placed just next to the door was a holdall and a guitar case, the sight of which sparked a twinge of excitement in my stomach. "Oh my God. Is that your dad's guitar?" Now I knew where Paul's stupid 'rockstar' comment came from.

Still chewing, Dylan simply nodded.

"I can't believe you've still got it. Have you played for anyone yet?" I begged him repeatedly to play for me when we were younger, but he never would. Somehow, though, I knew he would play beautifully, just like his dad.

Taking another bite, Dylan shook his head. It was enough to make me think the guitar was something he didn't want to talk about, so I dropped the subject and carried on watching him eat. He looked like he should be starving, yet he ate in tiny bites, finally pushing the plate aside after eating just over half.

"This place is stunning, Cam. And fucking *huge*. That kitchen is like something I've only ever seen on TV." His words made me feel proud, but he was stalling, avoiding the conversation we *needed* to have.

"What happened to you, Dyl?"

His breath caught, a flash of panic invading his expression. "I-I'm just full. I might finish in a minute."

Reaching across the table, I curled my fingers around his forearm. "You know I didn't mean the food. You said you needed help. I'm here. What can I do?"

"I, um, I need a place to stay. I know I shouldn't ask, that we don't know each other anymore, but...I don't have anywhere and...and it's cold."

My God. My fingers smoothed down his arm, over his wrist, until they reached his hand. He flinched, tightening the knot in my stomach, but he didn't pull away. Taking his hand in mine, I brushed my thumb over the back of his scuffed skin, like I used to do when we were younger. "We *do* know each other, Dylan. And you can stay with me as long as you need."

"It wasn't an accident," he blurted. "When we ran into each other, it wasn't an accident. I knew the restaurant was yours. I saw an article about it in the newspaper a few months ago. I…I was waiting for you."

Knitting my eyebrows together in confusion, I straightened my back in the chair. "But…you left. Why? If you wanted to see me…"

"Because I knew it was wrong. It still is," he said, shaking his head and refusing eye-contact with me. "I'm no good, Cam. I'm not the same person you knew all those years ago."

"Everybody changes," I said.

"*You* haven't. Look at you, doing all the things you said you would. I knew you would, too. I believed in you, and I was right."

"I believed in you, too."

Dylan laughed, blowing out a sardonic chuckle while briefly glancing my way before looking down again. "You shouldn't have."

I wanted to know why. Why shouldn't I have believed in him? Why didn't he have a home? Why was he so damn broken? But I was already losing him; I could see it in his eyes. He'd pulled away from my touch. He couldn't look at me. He was afraid of something, and I knew if I pushed him any harder he would bolt.

"Come on," I said, standing from my chair. "Let's go."

I really should've cleaned the kitchen, but I just wanted to get Dylan home. Take him somewhere he could feel safe, have a shower and a good night's sleep. So rather than clear the mess I'd created, I locked up the building and called a cab, keeping Dylan close the whole time.

Chapter

Four

~Dylan~

I WOKE UP on Cameron's sofa, I hadn't folded it out into a bed last night because I was exhausted, my eyes flickering as they adjusted to the bright sunlight seeping through the crack in the curtains. As soon as I sat up the nausea descended. I was expecting it, but I'd hoped it would take a little longer. I hadn't had a hit in sixteen hours which is probably how I managed to convince myself I wasn't a delusional bastard by going to Cameron for help. Sixteen hours and I felt reasonably okay. My bones ached, my stomach cramped, and my head hurt...but it was all pretty manageable…for now. Did I think I could beat this on my own? Get my life back on track if I had the help of a friend and somewhere warm to rest my head? No, but I told myself I could, which is why I ended up at Cameron's restaurant last night.

His friend had me sussed. He saw what a selfish, destructive piece of shit I was. But Cam didn't. He saw the boy he grew up with, the boy he fell in love with. I tried to tell him otherwise, but he refused to acknowledge it. That boy died a long time ago, and unless I found the strength to do the right thing and walk away, he'd see that soon enough for himself.

"Good morning."

I hadn't noticed Cameron in the kitchen area that was adjoined to the smallish living room until I heard his voice. He stood behind the granite counter, bringing a mug to his lips. He was a beautiful man. Everything about him just…perfect. From his tidy brown hair, to his dark-chocolate eyes and athletic body, to his huge, caring heart. He was everything I always knew he'd be. Everything I wasn't.

"Can I make you some breakfast?"

The thought made my stomach roll. I needed to score, and I needed to do it soon. "No thanks. I'm good."

"You must be hungry. You didn't eat much last night. It's no trouble."

"Honestly, I'm good. I need to wake up properly first." Even if the beginnings of withdrawal weren't setting in I doubted I'd be hungry. That's the thing with heroin. It numbs. It stops you feeling anything, not just emotionally, but *everything*. Including hunger.

"Well there's plenty in the fridge and cupboards. Help yourself to whatever you want."

I wondered why he was doing this, helping me, but then I realised that it was because he thought there was something inside me worth saving. When he saw the guitar last night he must've known selling it would've helped me find a place instead of going to him for help. It was worth a few grand, easily, and I'd considered selling or pawning it several times in the past but I just... couldn't.

Cameron clearly thought the fact I still had it meant I was a decent guy. I could see it in his expression. When we got back to his apartment he started talking about my dad and how great I was for honouring his memory by keeping his guitar close to my heart. Sure, it was special to me, but I knew if I had to choose between my dad's prized instrument and heroin I'd choose the option that would quickly change Cameron's unfounded, and frankly ridiculous opinion of me. If he knew the only reason I hadn't needed to sell it so far was because I discovered I could earn enough cash to survive by sucking off strangers in toilets, he'd realise I wasn't the man he thought I was.

"Are you feeling okay? You look like you're coming down with something."

Shit. Swiping at my runny nose with the material of the long-sleeved shirt I'd slept in, another gift from my friend Mr Heroin, I nodded. "Getting a cold. Nothing serious."

Cameron looked a little dubious, but he didn't push. "I need to go to work soon," he said. "Will you be okay here on your own?"

I'd been on my own since the day my grandma died. It wasn't a big deal to me. "I'll be fine."

There was a pleading, almost desperate look on his face as he walked around the counter, heading over to me before perching on the edge of the coffee table in front of the sofa where I sat. "Will you still be here when I get back?"

There was a rawness in his voice that pierced my heart, stirring up an emotion I didn't like. Guilt. *I shouldn't have come here.* "Sure," I said, forcing a small smile that I hoped looked believable.

"Maybe we can talk later. You know, like we used to."

Nothing about us could ever be like it used to be. I wasn't that person anymore. I was too damaged. "Sure."

Cameron sighed, looking to the floor. "Dylan…" Raising his gaze to stare into my eyes, he reached out and took my hand. The simple touch felt so alien to me, so intimate, and all I could do was glare at his fingers. "I don't know what you've been through," he added. "What you're *going* through, but I'm here. Try and remember what we had. Try and remember a time when I was your best friend. I can be that again if you let me."

I pulled my hand free from his grip. I didn't like being touched. People only touched me when they wanted something in return. "That was a long time ago." How could he think we could pick up where we left off after so many years? After we'd changed so much? "We were just kids. You don't know me anymore."

"But I *want* to."

"You don't."

"Then why are you here, Dyl?" His words were laced with frustration as he stood up, running a hand over his face. "What do you want from me?"

"I-I…I'm sorry. I'll go." Picking up my jeans from the floor, I dragged them up my legs before standing to fasten them. I couldn't believe I'd been so stupid. *I shouldn't have come here. Stupid! Stupid! Stupid!*

"Dylan, stop," Cameron urged as I sat back down to pull on my trainers. I ignored him, bending to tie my laces, but then he knelt in front of me, grabbing my wrists and bringing my hands to my lap. "I said *stop*. Stop running, Dylan. There must be a reason you keep coming back. You said you needed help and I'm offering it, but I can't do it if you won't tell me what you need. *Please*, Dylan. *Please* talk to me."

A tear which I fought so hard to trap inside leaked from the corner of my eye, rolling sorrowfully down my cheek. "I don't know what I need. I just…I…"

"Then we'll figure it out. Together. But you *have* to stay. Promise me you'll stay."

"I can't." God, I wanted to so badly. I wanted to be fourteen again. I wanted to be happy, untainted by the shit life I'd been given. I wanted to be *good* again. "I can't bear for you to hate me. Not you."

"Why would it matter if I hated you?"

I risked a glance at his face, confused by the knowing glint in his eye. "What kind of stupid question is that?"

"I want to know. Why would it matter to you?"

"Because you're important to me! I loved you!"

Cameron smiled, and I suddenly I knew the point he was making. "Do you get it now?" he asked, resting his hand on my knee. "I'm going into work now but only to sort out cover. Then I'm coming straight back. If I really *am* important, then you owe it me to be here when I get back. Will you do that for me?"

A lump formed in my throat, too thick to let any words past, so I gently nodded. What the hell was I doing? Making promises I didn't know if I could keep. I felt sick, and not just because of the boulder of guilt and shame rolling around in my stomach. I was in withdrawal. The tremors had begun in my hands, and I hoped Cameron put that down to me being emotional. If I waited for him, I'd be in physical pain by the time he returned home, far worse than I was now.

Unless I scored, and quickly.

"I'll be a couple of hours, tops," he said, staring with eyes that pleaded with me not to let him down. "Help yourself to whatever you need while I'm gone." Standing, Cam kept his gaze trained on me while he walked backwards towards the coat hook on the door. "I'll see you soon?" It came out like a question, like he couldn't quite trust me as he twisted the Yale lock and opened the door.

"I'll be here," I said, wanting so desperately to mean it. I *planned* to be here, but a lot could change in two hours.

Sighing through his nose, Cameron nodded, and then he left. I was in the bathroom, throwing up into the toilet, just seconds later. It made me feel better for only a minute before a fresh wave of nausea hit. I couldn't do this anymore. I hurt, and it would only get worse. I needed a fix, but I had no money, so first I would have to earn some.

Daylight made finding a john more difficult, but not impossible if you knew where to look. There were certain places that only an experienced scumbag, like me, knew about. Specific bathrooms dotted around the city that men with too much money, and sexual fantasies they couldn't get fulfilled at home, loitered in. These were big game. They had standards, and thankfully after being able to bathe and borrow some of Cam's clothes, I could offer those standards today.

Within an hour of leaving Cameron's apartment, I was in a swanky hotel room being pounded into a king-sized mattress by a middle-aged man with flecks of grey running through his short, perfectly-styled hair. He wore a wedding ring, and when he removed the two fifty-pound notes from his wallet I caught a glimpse of a photo of a woman and two children. That should've disgusted me, or at least made me feel sorry for the family in the picture, but it didn't because he was nice to me. He treated me with respect I didn't deserve. He was gentle, and he asked my permission for everything he did to me. If all men were like him, I might not have hated the process so much.

But…it was a necessary evil. I had no choice.

I stayed with him for just under an hour before I left to find Dean. When I didn't find him in The Old Dog, the owner always knew where to track him. I think they had their own deal going on. Although, it would be easier, I wouldn't shoot up in Cam's apartment. That was a level of disrespect I wasn't prepared to cross, so instead, after scoring a bag I found myself back at The Old Dog, hiding out in a bathroom cubicle.

The high was instant. Healing. I sat on the floor next to the toilet for twenty minutes or so, my heart slowing, the pain melting, before pulling my sock and shoe back on after shooting between my toes. It's a myth that addicts are covered in track marks, at least if they're clever about it. Of course if you look close enough you'll see the evidence, but it only becomes really noticeable if you overuse the same site, pull out the needle before removing the tourniquet, or haven't been able to pick up a fine enough syringe. Applying pressure to the site after injecting is important, and vitamin E oil essential. I used the capsules from the chemist, piercing them with a needle before rubbing the contents into my skin.

Still, I used the vein next to my big toe just to be sure, given that I was about to return to Cam like I said I would. Also, my left arm was shot. I had an abscess which I hid under my long sleeves and would continue to do so until I'd drained it with a blade and given it time to heal. No biggie. I'd done it plenty of times.

I didn't have a watch, but I knew I was cutting it close and that Cameron would be home soon, so I jogged across town to his apartment. I felt pretty great as I did, and started to wonder if I *could* change the direction my life was heading with Cam's help. He didn't need to know I was an addict, not at first anyway. Maybe if I stayed with him for a while, had a fixed address, I could get a job. Find some stability. With a job, I wouldn't need to sell myself. Perhaps then I could get back on the methadone programme, only this time I'd have a reason to stick to it. I could get my life back.

Maybe.

Cameron's apartment block had locked doors that required a code to open, a code I didn't have. Thankfully, I only had to wait a couple of minutes for someone to leave the building and I lunged forward, catching the door before it closed. Once inside, I ran up the stairs two at a time, too impatient to wait for the lift, hoping I'd made it before Cameron.

I hadn't.

Shit.

He stood up from the sofa the second I opened the door, making my heart slither into my stomach as I tried to think of an excuse, a *lie*, as to where I'd been. I removed my sunglasses, realising I probably looked like a dick wearing them inside. It was just habit. I hid behind them. I felt like I could pass as almost respectable if I wore them out on the street. "I, uh, took the key from the hook," I said, holding it in the air. "Hope that was okay."

"I'm not keeping you prisoner, Dyl. I'm just glad you came back."

Relieved I'd gotten away with it, my pulse began to slow.

Until he spoke again… "Where've you been?"

Fuck. "Just needed some fresh air," was the best thing my stupid brain could come up with. "So I went for a walk."

"You look better for it."

Yeah. That'll be the smack. "I borrowed some clothes. Mine are in your washing machine. Hope that's okay too."

"When I said help yourself to whatever you need, I meant it."

Trouble was I still didn't know what I needed. The only thing I ever needed was something Cameron couldn't supply. I felt awkward being here with him. I was disturbing his life already and I'd only been here a day. He should've been at work, and while I understood what he was trying to do, I didn't want babysitting.

"So, what do you want to do today?"

Christ, this was difficult. It was hard to know what to say or how to act. I wasn't used to company. It'd been so long since I'd had a friend I no longer knew how to be one.

I hadn't realised I'd yet to say anything until Cameron continued talking. "We need to talk. Or rather, *I* need to talk, and you need to listen."

"Um…ok*ay*."

Sitting down on the sofa, he patted the seat next to him and, albeit reluctantly, I walked over to join him. For a few long seconds he just stared at me, making me feel self-conscious. My fingers drummed unconsciously on top of my knees, until Cameron placed his hand over them, causing my breath to falter.

"You're right," he began, gently squeezing my hand. "We don't know each other anymore, but we're not strangers. We share so many memories, and I think if you hold onto those you'll stop feeling so nervous around me. Instead of thinking we don't know each other, think of it as we've just got some catching up to do."

"Cam," I said, his name cracking on my lips.

He raised his hand, silencing me. "I don't know what's happened to you, although I can guess it's something bad. I also know you're not ready to talk about it, so I need you to know that I don't expect you to. You don't need to be uncomfortable with me, Dyl. I don't want anything from you. You asked for my help, and if all that means is you need a place to stay for a while, no questions asked, then I can do that."

"Cameron I…" I trailed off, the words getting lost in my throat.

"What I'm saying, Dylan, is that I *know* years have passed. I *know* we can't erase them, and I *know* we can't pick up where we left off. We were teenagers. Maybe it wasn't real love. Maybe it wouldn't have lasted. But I genuinely believe we'd have remained friends if you hadn't moved away."

"It *was* real." The words tumbled from my mouth without permission from my brain, but I was surprised to find I didn't regret saying them. It was possibly the first truthful thing I'd said since I'd been here. It hurt to think about that time in my life, but only because it reminded me how much I'd lost.

"I'm not telling you to forget whatever's going on inside your head, but know it's not an issue right now. Don't feel pressured, not by me. Let's just spend some time together, like we used to. If a point comes when you want to talk, I'm ready to listen. If it doesn't, then that's okay too."

"Why are you doing this?" I had to ask because I didn't understand. What was in this for him?

"Because I'm your friend."

"But-"

"But nothing. From now on we're just the same old Cam and Dyl. Okay? We're friends. We'll watch crappy TV, talk about unimportant nonsense, and take it one step at a time."

Steps towards what? What was his end goal? What did he want from me?

"Now," Cam said, slapping his knees. "Lunch. What do you fancy?"

"Ah, I'm not really hungry."

"Well *I* am. My life revolves around food. As my friend, you should help me cook."

A snort of laughter burst through my nose, taking me by surprise. The smile I found myself wearing was genuine, and I couldn't remember the last time that happened. "I can't cook for shit."

With a gleaming smile that tickled a part of my chest I'd forgotten existed, Cameron stood and held out his hand. I took it automatically, without a shred of hesitation, and I couldn't help wonder if this really could be the change I never thought I'd get. What if I actually *could* do this? What would happen if I trusted this man leading me into his kitchen? I couldn't erase all the terrible things I'd done, but maybe, just *maybe*, a time would come when I could stop repeating them.

"Hmm," Cam mumbled, scratching his head when we reached the kitchen. "Do you like omelette?"

I *really* wasn't hungry, but food meant a lot to Cameron so I felt like I owed it to him to force something down.

"Sure," I said. My answer made him smile, and that made me feel good, so I ramped up my enthusiasm. "I *love* them."

Cameron stepped up to the sink and washed his hands, so I did the same once he'd finished. Leaning into his giant American-style fridge, he took out some eggs before surprising me by going in for more ingredients. How fancy could you make a friggin' omelette? Eggs, a splash of milk, and a sprinkling of salt and pepper were all I would've used.

"Chop these for me?" he asked, handing me some green sprigs. He must've noticed the look of confusion on my face because he added, "Chives."

There was a knife block on the black granite counter, so I pulled out the first one my hand came to and started to chop.

I'd only made one cut when Cam's hand appeared on my wrist. "You'll cut yourself like that. Here…"

Taking my fingers, his body pressed into my side and making me feel a little dizzy, he flexed them into a new position, bending my knuckles. "Keep the blade flush with your knuckles as you move. It keeps the knife edge away from your fingertips."

"Ah, so that's how you guys do it so fast."

Tilting his head to the side, he looked up at me with a stare so intense I almost forgot what a bad person I was. "Speed takes practice, and a few stitches, but yes."

Heeding his advice, I carried on chopping. Then I did the same to a red pepper he'd placed next to me. I found it unexpectedly fun. It was a good distraction. It was only chopping vegetables, but it was the first time in years I'd had something to focus on.

Cameron whisked some eggs while some chunks of chicken and chorizo were cooking through in a frying pan. I felt a bizarre sense of disappointment when I'd finished chopping. It stopped me thinking for a few minutes and I missed the relief it brought already. "What can I do next?"

Cam looked over his shoulder while grabbing two plates from the cupboard above his head. "Toss the peppers in the pan and give it a stir."

"And the chives?"

"No. They'll go in with the egg."

It sounds stupid, I mean it was a fucking omelette, but I felt like I was learning so much. For years, the only things I'd thought about were money, heroin, and keeping dry. So using my brain to process something completely new to me was almost overwhelming.

Doing as Cameron said, I added the peppers, stirring them around in the sizzling oil with a wooden spoon. I wasn't paying attention to Cameron and when he came up behind me, his chest pressing into my back, I sucked in a gasp, hoping he didn't notice. The feel of him made my pulse race, and I couldn't quite tell if it was through excitement or panic.

Either way, I couldn't move, my muscles paralysed as he reached around my side, pouring the egg mixture into the pan. It spat and crackled as Cameron placed his hand over mine, controlling the spoon as we moved it together through the mixture each time it started to set in places.

Neither of us moved until the omelette was ready, and only once Cameron had stepped away did I feel like I could breathe normally again. I couldn't take my eyes off him as he plated up our lunch, a thousand thoughts and emotions going off like fireworks in my head. Being here with him created a wave of confusion, doubt and fear. Emotions I didn't recognise swam in my stomach, the feeling not dissimilar to the nausea coming down brought with it.

There was a glass dining table at the opposite end of the kitchen, and I took a seat in one of the silver chairs when he picked up our plates. My eyes widened as I took in my meal. It might've only been an omelette, but it was the most colourful and delicious-smelling omelette I'd ever had in front of me.

"This looks amazing," I said, enjoying the smile my words brought to Cameron's face more than I thought I would.

"It should. That's a Michelin star omelette you've got right there." He followed his statement with a little wink, and in that split second he was exactly the way I remembered him.

"I read about your award in that newspaper article. Now all that's left is your goal to present MasterChef, huh? Your parents must be so proud of you."

I loved Cam's parents. During school holidays I spent as much time at their house as I did my own. They welcomed me, cared for me, like I was part of their family. I think I appreciated that as much as my dad did. I had a good childhood. My dad loved me and raised me the best he could, but it was tough being a single, working father. There were days when we wouldn't see each other, when he worked double-shifts or landed little gigs to play his music, and those were the days I'd go to Cam's and spend time with my *other* family.

"They are," Cameron answered, cutting into his omelette. "They come into the restaurant all the time, show me off to their friends." He shook his head as he spoke, a coy smile tugging on one side of his mouth. "Wait until I tell them you're back. They'll-"

"You can't," I cut in. For a second it felt like my heart had stopped dead in my chest. They couldn't see me like this. I couldn't face disappointing any more people who I used to matter to. "I-I'm not ready to see them."

A quiet sigh flowed from Cameron's nose before he nodded slowly. "Do you want to tell me why?"

"No."

"Do you want to find a movie to watch on Netflix? Have a lazy afternoon?"

He said he wouldn't push and, so far, he'd stuck to it. I relaxed instantly, a grateful smile crawling onto my lips. "Sure. Sounds good."

* * *

Cameron took another day off before getting back to his usual routine. I liked to think it was because he trusted me when I said I'd still be there when he got back, but in reality it was because his friend called and chewed his arse off. Either way, I was just so fucking relieved I could escape to get another hit. I shot up *once* in his bathroom, but then felt like absolute shit about it ever since so I vowed never to do it again. I don't know if I would have. Probably. I was just grateful I didn't need to find out because he went back to work.

I hadn't seen Paul since the night I turned up at the restaurant, but Cameron talked about him a lot. He sounded like a good guy, and I was glad Cam had people in his life to look out for him, but hearing about him never failed to make me feel uneasy. I knew from our first interaction that Paul neither liked nor trusted me and, as Cam's best friend, it was only a matter of time before he convinced Cam to feel the same.

Initially, I almost wanted Paul to talk some sense into Cameron because I was too weak, too selfish to walk away. But as a couple of weeks passed, my life started to change. If I looked hard enough I could almost see a glimmer of a future and, suddenly, I hated the fact this friend of Cameron's had the power to take it all away from me. I was still an addict, of course. I was still a liar and a thief, a cheap rent-boy whose only true love was heroin. *But...* I was starting to believe that wasn't *all* I was.

Throughout the last couple of weeks I'd smiled and laughed. I'd learned some simple cookery skills. I'd eaten a little better, slept more soundly, and slowly but surely I started to remember all the things that made me love Cameron so much when we were younger. He was good, kind, smart, and funny. He was still all those things, and sometimes I wondered if I could be like him one day.

I was already using less, only scoring when I *needed* to rather than doing it because there was nothing better to do. Every addict I'd ever met used out of boredom as well as necessity, but Cameron kept me occupied even when he wasn't with me. Just the thought of him kept my mind busy, and so I convinced myself that maybe we *could* erase the last sixteen years. I *could* be the boy Cameron used to know. I *could* beat heroin. I was stronger than my addiction, better than all the mistakes I'd made.

On reflection, this was bullshit. Addicts lie, not only to others, but to themselves. I was no different. I'd used for so long I could've been considered a professional liar. I was good at it. *So* good, I believed myself.

"I'd have spat in it."

Cameron and I were sprawled out on the sofa on one of his rare afternoons off. This was the first day he hadn't been at the restaurant since the two days he took after I arrived, and even when he wasn't there it was all he could talk about. He discussed the restaurant, and food in general, with so much passion, even when telling me about an

arsehole customer who sent a meal I couldn't
pronounce back three times.

I could've listened to him forever.

"Believe me, I thought about it," Cam said,
chuckling. "But I'm pretty sure that kinda thing is
frowned up on by the Food Standards Agency."

"Bet he just wanted a free meal."

"Probably. But the customer is always
right…to their faces at least."

I shrugged. "I'd have still spat in it."

Cameron laughed as he reached out and
grabbed his glass of wine from the coffee table. It
was a beautiful sound, a *healing* sound, a sound I'd
never get tired of hearing.

"You're looking better, Dyl."

Leaning my head back on the sofa cushions, I
stared at the ceiling, studying the pretty shapes and
shadows in the beams of light coming from the
lampshade. My mind was calm, my muscles relaxed.
I had my last hit while Cameron was making lunch,
abandoning the shred of decency I had left about
not using in his home. My new vow was to ensure
he didn't find out. That goal seemed more
achievable.

"Dyl?"

The shards of light spread across the ceiling
like the rays of the sun. I found them strangely
mesmerising.

"*Dylan?*" The harsher tone of his voice
snapped me back into reality.

Fuck. I'd zoned out. I did that a lot. The
junkies I hung around with sometimes did that a lot

too. It was normal for someone like me, but it was a side effect I needed to get a fucking grip of around Cameron. "Sorry," I muttered. "I didn't sleep too well last night. I'm just a little tired."

"I said you're looking better." His tone turned serious with the subject change, almost as serious as his expression as he stared straight into my eyes.

I was certain this was his subtle attempt to find out how I was feeling, get me to open up to him. He'd made similar remarks over the last few days and every time I looked away as that familiar wave of guilt pooled in my stomach. I wasn't sure I could bear the look of disgust that would flood his face if I revealed the kind of man I'd grown into, but the longer I stayed here the more difficult it became to keep lying to him. He cared about me. Fuck knows why, but he did. He deserved more. I owed him more. Maybe I should believe in him the way he did me, believe that he'd stick with me, trust that he'd still look at me like I was a person who mattered, and not like something he'd stepped in.

"Cameron," I whispered, dragging a long breath into my lungs. "I think I'm ready to-"

Keys jangling, followed by the door to Cameron's apartment pushing open, interrupted me. When the guy from the restaurant, Paul, walked in unannounced, my racing heart began to slow and I couldn't decide if it was from disappointment or relief.

"Hey," Cam said, standing up to greet the friend who'd just glared at me like he wanted to break my jaw. "What are you doing here?"

"Well that's no way to greet your *best friend*."
The tone of Paul's voice changed and he stared
right at me as he uttered the words 'best friend.' He
had every right to hate me, but that didn't stop me
feeling uncomfortable. I wasn't here to steal
Cameron away from him. I knew he'd moved on
and found new friends, and I was grateful for that.

Paul carried the shopping bags he held over to
the kitchen, placing them on the counter. "I'm tired
of you blowing me off. I want to show you my new
menu ideas."

Ignoring Paul's comment, Cameron nodded
towards me. "This is Dylan."

"I know who he is," Paul said, never looking
up from his ingredients as he pulled them from the
bags.

Cameron muttered something but I couldn't
hear the whisper well enough to know what it was.
Embarrassed and a little angry, I got up and headed
to Cameron's bedroom, where I would stay until I
heard Paul leave. For a while I lay back on his bed
and stared at the ceiling. Then I messed around on
his iPad, playing some of the games and fucking up
his high scores, before eventually falling to sleep.

By the time I was awoken by the slam of the
front door, it had turned dark outside.

Thank fuck. Paul had left.

After stretching my arms above my head, I got
out of bed, yawning as I made my way back out
into the living room.

"Something smells nic-" My words fell away
when I saw Paul sitting on the sofa. "Oh. Hey."

Shit. My pulse galloped in my throat and my mouth dried up.

"Cam's gone out for some cans."

"Right." Standing with my hands stuffed into my pockets, I felt nauseous with awkwardness. "I'll, um…" I tailed off, cocking my head towards the hall that led to Cam's bedroom.

"Don't leave on my account. Come sit down. Cam won't be long."

I dared a glance in his direction and found him staring at me with a suspicious look on his face. I walked over to the armchair with caution, unease tickling my belly as I lowered myself down.

"So," Paul began, picking at a plate of fancy looking fish on his knee. "Why are you here?"

"Excuse me?"

"Why are you here?" he repeated. "What do you want from Cameron?"

Whoa. "I don't want anything from him."

"Are you stealing from him?"

"*What?* No! I'd never do that. He's my friend." My cheeks heated with anger. Who the fuck did this guy think he was?

"He's a good man. Trusting. Is he right to trust you?"

I parted my lips to say 'yes' but the word melted into a sigh. "I don't know."

I didn't look at Paul to see his reaction, but I imagined he'd be even more disgusted with me than he already was.

"Well, my respect for you just increased tenfold."

"Pardon?" I couldn't have heard him right.

"That was very honest of you. I respect that."

"Um…"

He swallowed another mouthful of food and then put his plate on the coffee table in front of him. "Look, Dylan. I don't hate you. I don't *trust* you, but I don't hate you. I'm just looking out for my friend. I care about him and I don't want to see him get hurt."

"I care about him, too." I said it because it was the truth. I knew I wasn't worthy of Cameron, that I'd been lying to him, and that I most likely *would* hurt him…but I *did* care about him.

"Then I beg of you, if that's true, walk away. I don't think you're a bad guy, but you live a bad life. If you care about him you'll leave before he gets hurt."

How the fuck did *he* know what kind of life I lived? The first emotion to bubble in my chest was anger. How dare he judge me when he didn't even know me?

"Does he know you're using?"

A lump appeared in my throat at his question, choking me, making it difficult to reply with the confidence I aimed for. "U-using what?"

"You're not the first druggie I've known. Cameron doesn't see it because he doesn't *want* to, but your bullshit won't work on me. So what is it? Coke? Smack? Meth?"

"I…I…" Beads of sweat rolled down the back of my neck. I felt sick. Dizzy. Ashamed.

I was about to do what I did best – bolt, disappear – when the apartment door started to open.

"Ah, you're awake," Cameron said, strolling towards us with a twelve-pack of lager. "Dammit. I forgot your Jaffa Cakes. Sorry, Paul."

"Fuck's sake, Cam. My mouth's been watering for those bad boys all bloody day."

Cameron shrugged, his expression apologetic. "I said I was sorry," he muttered, though there was slight amusement in his tone. He set the box down on the coffee table, looking at me with a wide smile that made my chest ache. "Lager?"

"No, thanks," I said, standing up and wiping my clammy hands on my jeans. "If you don't mind I'm gonna take another lie down in your bed. I've got a headache."

I didn't need to glance at Paul to see the sceptical look I knew he'd be wearing.

"Do you need drugs?" Cam asked.

Paul scoffed, and Cameron shot him daggers that made me wonder if Paul had brought up my addiction with Cam before today.

Fixing his gaze on me, Cameron added, "There're some Co-codamol in the bathroom cabinet."

"Thanks," I said, although I didn't plan to take them. There was only one drug that would take away the emotional pain I was in right now, and I wouldn't find it in Cameron's bathroom. Without another word, I turned away and walked down the short hallway.

I heard Cameron mutter, "What the hell did you say to him?" before I closed the bedroom door behind me and blocked them out.

In that moment I *hated* Paul. I hated him because he was right. I hated him because he made me realise it was time to stop pretending. I needed to give up on this hope of happiness I'd developed. It wasn't real. I didn't care if *I* got hurt, fuck, I was hurting anyway, but I *wouldn't* cause Cameron pain in the process. The longer I stayed, the harder on him it would be.

And so, as I pressed my head into a pillow which smelled like Cameron, I decided I would leave in the morning.

* * *

Hours later, I felt the mattress dip beside me. Comfortable, I supressed the groan I wanted to make, knowing I needed to get up and make my bed in the living room. "Sorry," I muttered, rubbing my eyes. "I'll go to the sofa."

I started to sit up but Cameron put his hand on my shoulder. "Stay," he said, causing a flicker of panic to rise in my throat. "I just want to talk, Dyl." His voice was reassuring, like he knew what I was thinking. He couldn't possibly, of course. If he knew what kind of things went on in my head I would've been lying on a bench somewhere right now.

"Paul's gone?"

"Yeah. I'm sorry about him. He just-"

"He loves you," I interrupted. "I don't blame him for being wary of me. He's trying to protect you."

"From *you*?"

Looking down at his hand on my shoulder, unsure of how I felt about it being there, I answered, "Yes."

"You know you can tell me anything, right?" he asked, slipping his hand to my chest. "I'm not stupid, Dylan. I know things are going on with you."

You do? Did he know *what* kind of things? Did he know I was an addict? I didn't say anything. I just silently hoped he couldn't feel my heart racing.

"Is there anything you want to tell me?"

Yes. I want to tell you everything. "No."

"Dylan…" he breathed, my name sounding painful on his lips. His fingers crawled up my chest, along my neck, before settling on the side of my cheek. The way he looked at me, his eyes filled with so much sadness, so much confusion, made my heart ache. I didn't like it. I wanted to take it away but I didn't know how.

There was only one way I knew how to make a man feel good, so that's what I did.

Leaning forward, I pressed my lips to his. I'd thought about doing this several times since I found him again, but I always thought it would be too painful. I thought it would take me back in time, remind me of everything that was taken away from me. I thought he'd feel and taste the same as he did in my memories, but he didn't. His lips were firmer now, surrounded by a rough stubble that scratched at my chin, and he tasted of lager and spice. If I closed my eyes, he was just another man, another john, which made what I was about to do so much easier.

When I slipped my hand into the waistband of his boxers, I knew he wanted me, despite all his talk about us being 'just friends.' *They always want something.* I hated the thoughts running through my head, the fact my mind had lumped Cameron into the same category as all the other punters I'd fucked, but it was the only way I could get through this. He wanted this, and I owed it to him. He'd done so much for me, believed in me even though he shouldn't, and I didn't have anything else to repay him with.

I could give him tonight, because tomorrow I'd be gone.

Curling my fingers around his hard dick, I began to tug softly, making him moan my name. Breaking our kiss, he tipped his head back and I unconsciously kissed along the side of his neck before shimmying down the mattress and pulling his boxers down his legs. Absentmindedly, I flicked his tip with my tongue before taking him to the back of my throat. It was almost routine for me as I bobbed my head up and down, knowing how to make this end faster, how to squeeze and twist my grip to make men blow their load in just a couple of minutes so I could run away.

"S-stop," he hissed, pushing his hips into the mattress.

This must've meant it was time to move onto fucking. That was *always* the next step. Kneeling up, I unfastened the jeans I'd fallen asleep in and started crawling out of them. "How do you want me?"

Pursing his eyebrows together, Cameron looked at me with a puzzled expression. For a second, I thought he was going to speak, but instead he sat up and cupped my face in his hands, tracing my lips with the tip of his tongue. Kissing me, he pushed me gently onto my back and started stroking my limp dick. I needed to concentrate, will it to grow under his touch, and it did. It was a physical response rather than an emotional one, but I was happy to see him look pleased.

I faked a few moans and gasps that I knew men liked to hear as he moved his lips down my body, stopping on my cock. He kissed my balls before running his tongue along my shaft, circling my tip before dragging me into his mouth.

One, two, three, four...

"What are you..." Cameron's head shot up, staring at my face. "Are you counting?"

Fuck. I didn't say the numbers aloud. *Did I?* "N-no," I said, the stutter betraying the conviction I was aiming for.

Sighing, Cameron crawled back up to the top of the bed. Snaking one arm under my back, he rolled me into his chest, hugging me close.

Dammit! The only thing I had to offer and I'd fucked it all up. "What are you doing?" I whispered, my pulse pounding so violently in my neck I was scared the vein might burst.

"I'm holding you until you fall asleep."

"Camer-"

"Shh. Go to sleep, Dyl. You're safe here."

I wanted so badly to believe him, but I couldn't. I wasn't safe *anywhere*. Life was hard and dangerous, full of pain and fear. I'd let myself pretend it could be another way for too long, but all I'd done was postpone the unavoidable. Eventually, Cameron would leave too, just like everybody else. It was better to leave now, go back to being alone before I got used to, or even worse *dependent*, on his company.

"I'm sorry," were the last words I spoke, before sneaking out of his hold and getting the hell out of there once he'd fallen asleep.

Chapter

Five

~Cameron~

"NO! IT'S GOING to sting!"

We were in Dylan's grandma's back garden and Dylan had just fallen from the tree we were climbing, scraping his knees on the gravel underneath. I could tell he was trying not to cry as his grandma approached his knee with a damp cloth and some antiseptic cream. We were ten years old, too old and cool to cry in front of each other, but eyeing the deep gash in his leg I doubted I'd have been as brave.

"It will, sweetheart," Granny Roberts said. "But what do we do when we're scared?"

Counting Daisies

A tinge of embarrassment pinked Dylan's cheeks, and I looked away so he wouldn't feel worse.

"Count daisies," he whispered.

I knew what that meant. He'd told me about it before we got old enough to feel embarrassed about admitting we were afraid of something. Knowing his eyes would be closed as he pictured the little white flowers, I turned back to him and watched as Granny Roberts cleaned up his leg.

I woke with a start, jumping straight up into a sitting position as consciousness pulled me from my dream. "Oh my God," I whispered to nobody. Dylan had been counting daisies. He was scared. *Why?* Why would he be afraid of *me?* "Oh, Dylan…"

I looked to the side and noticed Dylan wasn't there. Figuring he must be in the living room, I went to the toilet, threw on some trousers, and went in search of him. Alarm spread through my veins when I discovered the apartment was empty, his guitar propped up against the coffee table with a note taped to the leather case. At first, I refused to read it. If I didn't then I could convince myself he'd simply nipped out for a walk.

I knew he hadn't, though.

I knew he was gone, and when I eventually plucked up enough courage to peel his note away from the guitar case, my fear was confirmed.

Take care of this for me. My dad would want you to have it. It's safer with you. Be happy, Cam. I'll never forget you, or what you did for me. Love, Dyl.

A wave of anger rained onto my body before being replaced with inconsolable sadness. Next came worry, and finally, guilt. I thought I was being supportive by not pushing him to talk to me. I wasn't stupid. I knew everything Paul had said was right, I'd even Googled the symptoms of drug abuse, but I truly believed if I let Dylan set the pace, let him come to me when he was ready, that I could help him. Now? Now I'd scared him away. He could've been out there overdosing or getting in trouble and it would be all my fault.

"Dammit!"

I don't know what made me open his guitar case. As I stroked the polished, dark wood with the pads of my fingers I almost felt closer to him. I took it out, resting it on my knee and strummed the strings softly with my thumb. The noise wasn't pretty, but I did it again anyway, before noticing a bunch of crumpled papers tucked into the large pocket in the lining of the case.

Putting the guitar down, I scanned the papers. There must've been thirty or so pieces, all filled with scribbled notes, lyrics I believed. I started to read through them, my heart ballooning in my chest, mourning the loss of my best friend yet again. *Did he write these?* The pieces of paper were like a collection of short stories; tales of loss, pain, and wonder. They were austere, yet beautiful. Haunting. Like a small glimpse into the difficult life he led, filled with so much hurt and loneliness.

Then there were two photographs; one of Dylan's parents, before he was born, embracing in front of a house I didn't recognise. The second photo broke my heart. It was of Dylan, me, and my mum. We were nine, maybe ten, years old, and we were outside the monkey cage at London Zoo, my mum crouched down next to us. My dad took the picture. I remembered the whole day like it was yesterday.

"Dammit, Dylan!"

I needed to find him, stop him from doing something stupid. While he was here, he was safe. He could've been anywhere, doing *anything*, right now. He could've been hurt. Hell, he could've been *dead* for all I knew.

All I could think about while I rushed around the apartment, getting dressed and trying to figure out what the fuck I was going to do, was the sound of Dylan counting. *Why? Why did he count?* I never would have hurt him. It broke my heart to think he thought differently. I thought he'd made progress. Slowly but surely, I felt the bond we once had reappearing. We talked, we laughed, we even had a pillow fight one night.

Had he been afraid of me all that time?

I had no idea how to find him. He could've been anywhere in this huge city. I contemplated calling Paul for help but thought better of it. I wasn't prepared for an 'it's for the best,' or even worse, an 'I told you so,' speech. I knew jack shit about drugs or the people that used them, apart from what I'd seen in TV dramas or movies. I kept telling myself that I didn't even know for sure that Dylan was an addict, but I was lying to myself because it hurt less that way. I *knew* because I found a tiny clear pouch in his jeans pocket last week when I was doing the washing. It was empty, but had obviously contained some kind of powder at one point. I stuffed it back inside and put his jeans back where I found them, trying to convince myself the powdery remnants could've been *anything*. Or at least, that it could've belonged to someone else.

Deep in my heart I knew the truth, however, and it was time to stop pretending. I hated myself for thinking it, I didn't think Dylan was capable of stealing, but I checked my wallet for missing cash regardless. If I knew how much money he had, it might've given me a clue to how far away he'd gotten.

It was all there. He hadn't stolen from me. I shook my head, angry at myself for thinking he could do such a thing. I didn't know where he got his money to buy drugs from, but it was less painful to believe he received benefits I didn't know about from the government, so that's what I did. He wasn't a thief. He couldn't be.

Pulling up Google on my phone, I tapped in *Where to buy heroin in inner London?* I didn't expect to find anything, suppliers listed like supermarkets, but I didn't know what else to do. To my amazement, there were dozens of forums dedicated to drug use. I couldn't prevent the scowl on my face as I clicked on discussion after discussion of people talking about different types of drugs like it was *normal* or acceptable.

I found tips on how to inject, the best needles to use, ways to drain abscesses caused by overusing the same vein or reusing needles. It turned my stomach. How did these people think what they were doing was okay? Why weren't they screaming for help instead of ending their posts with LOL's and smiley faces?

I scrolled for over an hour, growing more concerned with every post I read. Did Dylan hang out with these types of people? The thought made my stomach churn. I wasn't too surprised that I hadn't found any information on local dealers. I guessed it wasn't something they advertised. If they were easy to find, they'd all be in prison.

Out of options, I did something that made me feel physically sick. I clicked on one of the members who seemed to be an active poster and messaged him. His username was Smack4Life, that alone made me consider him a disgusting human being, and London was listed under his title. Bizarrely, my mind refused to think of Dylan in the same light as these other users. These people seemed *proud* of their lifestyle, at least that's how they came across in the forums.

Dylan wasn't proud. If he was he wouldn't have tried so hard to hide it from me. That's what I told myself. To think any other way would've destroyed me.

> Me: Hey. New in town. Know where I can get any gear?

I hoped gear was the right word to use as I hit send. It's what they called it in the movies, and that's the only knowledge I had to go on. I refreshed the page every few seconds for over fifteen minutes while I waited for a reply from a person I already hated.

    Smack4Life: Depends what ur
    luckin for

Great. He was illiterate as well as a lowlife.

Shit. What *was* I looking for? Do I use proper terminology or slang? Was smack slang for heroin? Is that even what Dylan took? I knew the residue in the little bag I found was white, but that meant nothing to me. Unsure, I did another quick Google search to tell me what drugs came in white powder form. When the results showed that *lots* of drugs looked like that, I took a chance and decided, from the symptoms I'd read about, that it was heroin, although that *also* came in brown powder too. The whole thing confused me.

    Me: Brown. Can you help?

Hitting send, I prayed I'd chosen the right word from the several I found listed on the internet. I'd never heard it called *brown* before, but then I wasn't a fucking drug lord.

His, at least in my head it was a him, reply came through almost immediately.

    Smack4Life: Were r u?

    Me: Mayfair

Shit! I realised my mistake as soon as I'd sent it. A guy living in one of the most affluent areas of the country wouldn't be hitting up some random guy on the internet for drugs.

```
Me: I'm visiting someone. Need
some gear to tide me over till I
go home
```

When, after ten minutes, his reply didn't appear, I started to worry I'd ballsed it up and that my attempted recovery wasn't as successful as I'd hoped. I was just about to message someone else when my screen pinged.

```
Smack4Life: Not my area. Soz
```

Fuck. I should've known it wouldn't be that easy. After scratching at my head and expelling a handful of aggravated sighs, I messaged someone else…and got nowhere. In fact, it took messages to seven different people before I had something tangible to go on.

```
SweetLikeCandy: Try jo's pizza
palace or the old dog. Ask 4
Dean. Tell him Razz sent u. Know
where they r?
```

I didn't, but I figured my new best friend, Google, would tell me.

Me: Sure. Thanks

After Googling the locations of the places 'Razz' mentioned, it took me a couple of hours to garner enough courage to actually leave my apartment. Donning my long, tweed jacket, the one that Paul said made me look like a grandfather, I took a taxi most of the way, and then used the Maps app on my phone to walk the rest. Part of me thought I might've been sent on a wild goose chase. Razz didn't know who I was. I could've been an undercover police officer or a rival dealer. Why would he trust me with genuine information?

Maybe he thought he couldn't be traced through an internet profile, or perhaps Dean and Razz weren't their real names. Or...maybe his brain was too addled with drugs to think clearly, or even give a shit about the consequences.

The Old Dog was closest, so I went there first. It was an unsavoury building in an unfamiliar part of town and I felt uneasy stepping inside, like everyone knew I didn't belong there. I didn't intend to actually ask for Dean, but when the guy behind the bar didn't recognise my description of Dylan I had no choice. He pointed to a table in the far corner where I saw a man, sitting in a brown leather jacket, with a thick scar running along his cheek.

My heart felt like it had moved so far up into my throat I might choke on it as I walked over to him. Everything about this encounter petrified me and I started to pray I was wrong about Dylan, and that he didn't live like this, talk to these people.

"Hi," I said, holding my head up high to disguise the fact I was trembling inside.

He didn't reply. Instead he just glowered at me, his whole expression menacing as he raised a suspicious eyebrow.

"Are you Dean?"

"Who's askin'?"

"Razz sent me."

He looked around, swiping his head from left to right before leaning forward, folding his arms across the table. "What you lookin' for?"

"My friend. Dylan. I think you might know him."

"Can't help you."

What? I hadn't even described him yet. "Hold on," I said, pulling out my phone. Opening the Facebook app, I tapped on my most recent search, bringing up an old photo of Dylan before holding it up so Dean could see. "This is an old one, but you can tell it's him."

"Ah, you're lookin' for Titch. He's popular today."

Titch? What the hell kind of name was Titch? More importantly, who else was looking for him? "Do you know where he is?" Hope ballooned in my chest, causing my pulse to quicken.

"Might do." There was an expectant look in his dark eyes that I didn't understand until he spoke again. "What's it worth?"

Worth? Oh. Plucking my wallet from my back pocket, I counted through the notes inside. "Eighty. It's all I have on me."

Dean raised his hand, taking the money from me. "Leave here, turn right. Walk straight for fifteen minutes. There's an abandoned flat above the chip shop. He's in there."

Oh thank God. The relief lasted mere seconds before the panic over what state I'd find him in descended. "Thanks." I don't know why I thanked him. He sure as hell didn't deserve it. Dylan's life was in pieces because of scum like him.

"Pay him a decent rate will ya? He owes me money."

Pay him for what? "How much does he owe you?"

"Two fifty."

Jesus. Oh, Dylan. Spinning on my heels, I walked away from the monster I'd been talking to and headed straight for the freestanding cash machine I saw by the bar when I came in. I withdrew two-hundred and fifty pounds without thinking about it before marching back over to Dean and slamming the notes on the table.

Snorting a callous laugh, he stuffed it into his pocket. "Wow. Must give *really* good head."

Sick to my stomach, knowing what he was insinuating but refusing to believe it, I stormed out of the pub and set off, on foot, to the chip shop.

Chapter

Six

~Dylan~

"DAMMIT. MY VEINS are shot to shit," Bubbles said, slapping her arm.

"Here," I offered, taking the needle from her and holding it between my teeth. "So what happened?" I asked, my words muffled because of the syringe between my teeth, as I massaged the inside of her arm in the hope a glimmer of blue would pop up.

"My Aunt June got cancer. She's had it for months. She's gonna die pretty soon."

Bubbles found me this morning. I'd never been so pleased to see anyone in my entire life, which of course made me a selfish bastard. She'd been clean for seven months, and here I was about to shoot her up and I didn't even feel bad. I had my friend back. That was all that mattered. She'd been searching for me for three days, said she was about to give up when she saw me leaving The Old Dog. She'd been squatting in a flat across the road but people were already living there so she couldn't stay long. We made our way straight here. Priorities and all that shit. We'd catch up properly later.

"Shit. Sorry." Giving up on her left arm, I unfastened the belt and moved it to her right.

"She can't even get outta bed, so she called my bitch mother and my psycho stepdad for help. That was my cue to get the fuck outta there."

"Fuck," was all I could think of to say.

"Thought things were gonna be different after rehab. They got me clean, sure, but what's the point of that when you've got fuck all else to live for when you get out?"

Her statement might've sounded ridiculous, maybe even disturbing to some, but *I* understood completely. "Got one," I said, feeling rather chuffed with myself as I tapped the tiny, barely there, vein with the pad of my finger.

Her face became orgasmic before I'd even punctured the skin. As I drew back the needle, I envied the rush I knew she'd be feeling any second, despite only pushing off myself an hour ago.

"Ah, fuck that's some good shit…" Bubbles fell backwards, almost in slow motion, until she was lying flat on the floor looking like she'd just entered heaven.

Loosening the belt on her arm before pulling out the needle, I watched her as the burden of being alive melted from her face, replaced with a soft, satisfied smile. She groaned a little, like she was coming down from the best fucking orgasm of her life, and then she drifted to sleep.

At least I *thought* she did.

Heroin slows everything down – your heart rate, your breathing, your thoughts… It wasn't unusual to fall asleep right after a hit. It wasn't, however, usual for someone's chest to stop rising and falling altogether.

I shook her shoulder. "Bubbles?" She didn't move, so I shook harder. "Come on, Bubbles. Wake up."

Nothing.

Shit. Oh fuck. Shit.

"Bubbles! Wake up dammit!"

Oh my God.

Oh my God.

Oh my God.

"Dammit, Bubbles," I tried to yell but my voice cracked. "What do I do? What do I do?" This whole area was derelict and I didn't have a phone. I'd seen CPR on the telly so I attempted to replicate it, pressing her chest over and over again while praying I wasn't damaging her even more.

"Come on, Bubbles," I begged, tears scratching my eyes like grains of salt. "*Please.*" I heard a crack as I crawled over to Bubbles' head. Looking back, I briefly noted I'd knelt on and shattered my sunglasses before blowing into Bubbles' mouth like they did on TV. "Come on, girl, don't do this to me."

"Dylan?"

Cameron? Looking up and seeing him rush towards us, I felt as grateful as I did ashamed. I wondered for only a second how, or *why*, he'd found me, but I'd have to revisit that thought later. "Sh-she's not breathing."

The flash of horror on Cameron's face as he took in the scene in front of me – the needles, the spoons, Bubbles' listless body – made me feel sick to my stomach. This wasn't his world. He didn't understand. Yet still, he crouched down next to me and called an ambulance before taking over the compressions on Bubbles' chest.

I couldn't take it anymore. I couldn't stand the look of disappointment in Cameron's eyes. I couldn't bear to watch Bubbles die. And I couldn't forgive myself for the fact the only thing I could think about was wanting another hit to take it all away.

I bolted as soon as I heard sirens getting closer. Fleeing was an instinctive reaction. I needed to keep myself safe, look out for number one, because nobody else would. I didn't go far, hiding behind a wall so I could see the moment the paramedics brought Bubbles out. When they did, I stared at her body on the stretcher. With the distance, and the tears in my eyes, it was hard to tell if they'd got her back, but I chose to think the drip attached to her arm was a good sign.

As I suspected, the police showed up, too, and it worried me when Cameron hadn't appeared straight after Bubbles. I didn't know what to do. I had no reason to stay here. Cameron shouldn't have to see me this way. But I couldn't move. I *had* to know if Bubbles was okay, and the only person who could tell me was Cameron.

She could've been dying. Hell, she could've been *dead*, and it was all my fault. *I* injected her. I might've *killed* her.

Oh my God.

My legs trembled, unable to support my weight as I slipped to the ground, hugging my knees. Head down, I began to sob, rocking back and forth. How did this happen to me? What did I do to deserve this life? I used to be a decent kid, had a good family, great upbringing. I worked hard at school, made friends easily, had hopes and dreams like everyone else.

So how did I get here? Strung out on smack waiting to hear if I'd killed the only person who understood me? Was this it? Was this all I had to look forward to?

I might as well be fucking dead.

"Dylan?" I heard Cameron's footsteps before his voice, but I didn't acknowledge him. I couldn't do anything except sit there and rock, filled with such an intense hatred towards myself, and my life, that I struggled to breathe.

"She's okay, Dyl," he said, crouching in front of me. "They got her back. She's okay."

I couldn't breathe. I couldn't speak. I couldn't stay still, every muscle in my body trembling.

Cameron placed his hands on my shoulders, pulling me into his chest. "Talk to me, Dylan. *Please.*"

"Help," I croaked, grabbing onto his arms. "Please, God, somebody fucking *help* me."

Pulling me closer, he cradled my head to his shoulders. "I'm here," he whispered. "I'll take care of you."

* * *

I didn't remember getting to Cameron's apartment, or how long I'd been there before the sobs and trembles began to wane.

"Here," Cam whispered, taking my hand and wrapping my fingers around a mug of something hot.

I didn't look at him. Didn't talk. I couldn't seem to do anything other than stare at the mug while silent tears ran down my cheeks.

"Why did you run away? I didn't know anything about that girl. I couldn't even give the paramedics a name."

Bubbles. Her name is Bubbles. I doubted that was her real name, but when a friendship is based on drugs little things like names pale into insignificance.

"Why did you run, Dyl?" he asked again.

"Because I knew the police would show and…" This was it. This was the moment he'd realise what a piece of shit I was. The moment he'd finally hate me. "And I was holding."

"Holding what?" He fell silent for only a second before adding, "Oh."

"What if I killed her, Cam? What if I fucking killed her?"

Cameron took the mug from my hands, placing it on the coffee table before pressing his palms to my cheeks and turning my head to face him. "You've got to let me help you, Dylan. I'm *begging* you. Tell me what to fucking do."

With his hands on my face, I had no choice but to look at him. I searched his eyes for the disgust I expected but it never came. How could *he* stomach looking at me when I couldn't stand my own reflection? He didn't seem too shocked by my revelation. Had he known all along?

Why are you still here? Why don't I disgust you? "I need you to lock me in your bedroom and don't let me out no matter how much I beg." Palpitations rose in my chest as I spoke, knowing the hell that was coming for me. I wasn't ready, I'd never be ready, but I *had* to do this. The thought of death had never bothered me before. Some days I even welcomed the prospect, but seeing the life slip from Bubbles *petrified* me. I didn't want that. I wasn't ready to die.

"And I *will* beg," I continued. "I'll beg and I'll scream and I'll lie to you. It'll look like I'm dying, but I won't. You *have* to be strong, Cam, because *I* won't be."

His hands slipped from my cheeks, his mouth falling open. "Dylan...no. I-I can't."

I rubbed angrily at my runny nose with the back of my hand. "You *have* to. I can't do this anymore."

"I can take you to the doctors. We'll do this properly. I...I'm not qualified to help you do this."

"Been there, done that," I said, shaking my head so forcefully I began to feel a little lightheaded. "I was on methadone for ten months before I ended up right back where I started."

"So...you use heroin? That's what methadone is for, right?" The disgust never materialised, but an overwhelming look of hurt and concern did.

"You gotta do this for me, Cam. You said you'd help. This is what I'm asking for." I knew I was being selfish, that I was asking him to do something which could quite possibly be the toughest challenge of his life, but I *needed* this. I wouldn't survive without it. It was only a matter of time before I ended up on a stretcher like Bubbles. This was the first time I felt like I had something to live for, something I didn't want to lose.

"*Please*, Cameron," I begged, grabbing his hand and holding it close to my chest. "I don't want to die."

His eyes glistened with tears before he snatched his hand away. He threw one arm around my back and cradled my head to his shoulder with the other. "I'll do whatever you need," he murmured, the words shaky on his tongue. "I'm here, Dyl."

Counting Daisies

* * *

Several hours later, I sat on Cameron's bed, propped up against the headboard with fear flooding my veins. It would hit soon. Withdrawal was coming for me, and it would be brutal. It'd been thirteen hours since my last hit, and nausea already flickered in my gut. I'd gone over everything that could happen in the coming days with Cameron, feeling like the lowest piece of shit on this entire planet for putting such panic in his eyes.

But…it was necessary. If he could help me through this then I'd be able to let him get to know the *real* me, the me from *before*. I wanted so badly to be that boy again, but it would hurt like a motherfucker to get it.

"What do I do now?" Cameron asked, placing a bucket next to the bed. "Can I stay with you?"

"No," I answered without hesitation. I had no doubt that in twenty-four hours time I would do *anything* to get out of here, including hurt him. "Remember, you-"

"I got it, Dyl," he interrupted. He sounded frustrated and it brought a lump to my throat. "Don't let you leave, no matter what."

Nodding, I reached into my back pocket, taking the small baggy between my fingers and holding it there. My heart rate increased, my pulse pounding in my ears as I fought the internal battle of whether to hand it over.

It could help. The odd dab to my gum could ease the transition.

No. I need a clean break. All or nothing.

"Cameron," I said, calling him back as he turned for the door. "Get rid of this."

His breath caught in his throat when he saw the pouch of powder nestled between my fingers. He took it from me, his hand shaking, and nodded his head.

I could barely breathe through the knowledge that little bag was gone. I dragged in breath after breath, but it wasn't enough. *I can't do this.* "Get out, Cam. *Now.*"

He parted his lips to talk but closed them again before blinking a tear from his eye and walking away, slamming the door behind him.

I missed that bag already. My head hurt, throbbed with every beat of my pulse. My muscles ached. My bones felt like they were breaking. I felt sick.

I can't do this.

I should've planned this. I wasn't ready. If I'd known my last hit was this morning I would've savoured it more. I got up from the bed and rushed to the door, twisting the handle, but it was caught on something.

Just one last hit. I'll plan it better this time.

"Cam?"

He didn't answer.

"Cameron?"

Nothing.

You can do this. Go to bed. Sleep it off. One week and it will all be over.

Stripping to my underwear, I climbed back into bed, pulling the covers up to my neck. I needed to sleep, and *stay* asleep. Until that happened I planned to stare at the magnolia wall, turn over when that got boring and stare at the ceiling instead.

A few hours, or a lifetime, later, crippling pain that would only get worse descended on my stomach. I doubled over, grabbing the bucket next to the bed, heaving into it over and over again.

I can't do this.

I felt too hot, then I felt too cold. My head hurt, the slightest movement making it feel like it was splitting in half. My eyes stung, sensitive to the beads of sweat that rolled into them from my forehead. My bones ached. My skin itched. It felt like I'd been buried alive with three billion ants and they were crawling all over my body, nipping, biting, trying to burrow their way inside.

Everything hurt, *everything* throbbed, right down to my toes.

Help me.

Please, God, help me

Falling back onto the mattress, I closed my eyes and pictured my grandma's back garden.

One, two, three, four…

Chapter

Seven

~Cameron~

PACING THE LIVING room, I ripped through my hair with my fingers. I'd set up the sofa-bed but I didn't plan on sleeping. The things Dylan had told me to expect were terrifying. I didn't think I'd ever been so frightened. How could I sleep? What if he choked on his own vomit? Or hurt himself somehow? I'd left him with the basics like he told me to, but there was a mirror in my en-suite that he could smash and cut himself with. Or cleaning products he could sniff or swallow.

You're overreacting, I told myself. Maybe I was, but how the fuck was I supposed to know what he'd do if he got desperate enough? I didn't have a clue what I was dealing with, so why was I doing it? I could've been doing more harm than good, taking the word of an addict. But he wasn't an addict to me. He was Dylan. *My* Dylan. And when he said he didn't want to die I would've done anything he asked.

At some point during the night I must've drifted off because I woke up, fully clothed, on the couch. I'd not even opened my eyes fully when I heard frantic cries coming from my bedroom.

"Oh, God," I groaned, not knowing what the hell to do. I considered calling Paul for help before realising how stupid that would be. He'd call the police. I knew he would. Not out of malice, he'd be worried about me, but his reasons didn't matter. Thinking about him, however, made me remember I had a life I needed to sort out. A business. Being with Dylan made me forget about the whole world. He consumed my every thought, every fibre of my being, as he lay just feet away from me, audibly wrestling his demons.

Picking up my phone, I walked outside my apartment and into the public hallway to call Paul, unsure what I would say when he answered.

"Hey," I mumbled.

"Well you sound like shit," was his reply.

"I am. Been throwing up all night. Can you cover the restaurant for a day or two?"

"Sure. No problem. What the fuck have you eaten?"

"Think it's just one of those viruses," I said, forcing a convincing croak into my voice.

"Ugh. Well stay the hell away from me. Unless you need anything. Do you?"

"No. I'm good. Thanks, Paul."

"I'll call you later. Make sure you're not dead or anything."

I'd have laughed if there was any humour left in the world, but there wasn't, so I hung up instead. Back inside, I hovered outside my bedroom door for a few minutes, holding my palm flush against the wood, as if he'd be able to feel me, but not brave enough to open it. Dylan's wails - deep, primal, *haunting* screams, flooded my ears, injecting me with such deep emotional pain that I had to run to the bathroom and turn on the shower to drown out the sound.

He told me not to go in, that he'd try and leave if I did, but I couldn't sit on the closed toilet with my head in my hands, ignoring the pain he was in for the rest of the week.

"Fuck it," I said aloud, shutting off the shower and taking the two steps across the hall to my bedroom. Sliding the chair away from the door, I opened it slowly, my heart in my throat. The smell hit me instantly; a putrid mix of vomit and diarrhoea that made me feel sick. *What the hell was I thinking when I agreed to this?*

"Dyl?" I called his name when I saw the empty bed.

"Cam!" he shouted, his voice strained and hoarse as he rushed out of the en-suite.

"Oh my God…" I hadn't meant to say it out loud, or to gasp in horror, but the shock registered like a kick to the stomach. His eyes were dark and bloodshot. His nose ran, snot and spit smeared across his cheeks. And his body… He was so thin. Every one of his ribs protruded through his damaged skin. There were scabs and bruises all over his pale flesh, and a huge, raised scar on the side of his abdomen that I didn't even want to imagine how it got there.

He stepped right up to me, gripping both my shoulders with his weak hands. His touch was ice-cold on my skin, yet beads of sweat seeped from his every pore. "Cameron. You gotta let me out now. It's over. The shit's outta my system."

My breaths were short and shallow as he pleaded with me with an eager smile on his face. It couldn't be right. He told me it would take days.

"Let's get you in the shower," I said, peeling his hands from my shoulders. I'd never smelled anything quite as intense as the foul odour pouring from his body and I had to breathe through my mouth to stop myself being sick.

"I-I will," he stuttered. "I'll shower. But I need, uh, I need to go out first. Um, I, um, I need to check on Bubbles."

Bubbles? Who the hell is Bubbles? I thought, scrunching my nose in confusion before realising he must've meant the girl who'd OD'd.

"No, Dylan…" My words were low, mournful, before they trailed off into a heavy sigh.

"Didn't you hear me? I said I'm good. It's over." He picked his dirty clothes up off the floor before attempting to walk past me.

"I said *no*." Grabbing his arm, I pulled him back, positioning myself in front of the doorway. I *had* to do this. I'd promised him.

The smile he wore morphed into anger and he stared me out like he'd never hated anyone as much as he hated me right now. "I said let me the fuck *out!*"

Dropping his clothes, he shoved my chest but I didn't move, even when he started punching me with the strength of a five year old. Grabbing his wrists, I held his arms away from me, my heart shattering into a thousand pieces as he struggled and tugged to get away.

"It *hurts*! I'm *hurting!* Is that what you want? You fucking *enjoying* this?" He kicked out with his legs, using all the strength his sick body could summon, yet barely brushing my shins which he aimed for. "How could you do this to me?" he whimpered, his voice breaking along with my heart. "Why do you want to see me like this? You used to *love* me." He sounded like a helpless child, and even if he recovered from this, I wasn't sure I ever would.

I still do. Goddammit, I still did. *That's* why I was doing this to him. "Dylan look at me," I begged, my eyes clouding with tears.

He didn't. Instead he fought until the little energy he had depleted and sent him falling to his knees. My breath came in stuttered spurts as I watched his frail, naked body crawl into a crumpled heap by my feet.

I couldn't handle this. I thought I could but I couldn't. I needed to get out. *What the fuck are you doing, Cameron? You're not strong enough for this.*

I turned for the door but Dylan's hands locked around my ankle, almost tripping me over. "I'm sorry." His words were strangled by the sobs that caused his tiny frame to shake. "*Please*. I'll do better. *Please*, Cam. Please don't leave me like this."

Bending down, I prized his fingers from my leg, my tears dripping onto his back and mingling with the sweat that rained from his flesh.

"No, no, no," he whimpered. "I'll come straight back, I promise. Don't do this to me. *Please*. I'm *begging* you, Cameron, *please*."

Dragging in a stuttered breath and holding it there, my lungs paralysed, I backed out of the room, closing the door and shifting the chair back in place under the handle.

As I crept along the hall, my feet shuffling along the floor because I didn't have enough energy to lift them, Dylan's cries were replaced with the sound of furniture breaking against the walls. Each crash made me jump but I kept on walking until I'd reached the couch in the living room. I sank straight past it and onto the floor, burying my head in my knees.

When the banging ceased in the next room, the wails resurfaced, growing louder and louder to the point I feared they would be the only sound I ever heard for the rest of my life. Every so often he would call out for me, plead with me, but I ignored him.

"I'm not worth this!" he yelled. With my apartment being so small I could hear every word as if he were sitting right next to me. "You don't want me here!"

He was right, I didn't. In this moment I couldn't help wishing he'd never come back so I didn't have to see him like this. My memories of our childhood were quickly fading, superseded with hurt, worry, and anger. A part of me hated him. Hated him for doing this to himself. Hated him for changing who I was. There was no way I'd ever be the same man after this. It felt like he'd taken away my innocence, my view on the world, my happiness.

Thinking such things made me feel so selfish, and I knew I didn't really mean them. If I did, I would've turned my back on him, but I couldn't. I didn't hate *Dylan*. I hated what the drugs had done to him. I couldn't explain why I needed to help him, to *save* him. All I knew is that I didn't have a choice. I *had* to hope this was worth it, that he'd be okay, that *I'd* be okay. If I didn't hold onto that hope, if this was all for nothing, I worried it would make me resent ever knowing him.

"You wanna know how I pay for my skag?"

No. No I don't. Please stop talking. I shook my head as if the movement would mute his words. I didn't want to hear any more. I knew I wouldn't be able to handle it. I was already breaking. Was that what he wanted? To see me suffer along with him?

"I let guys fuck me for money!"

Stop it. Stop it. Stop it.

"You hear me? I suck their dirty dicks so I can shoot up!"

Putting my hands over my ears, I pressed hard. "Stop it," I tried to yell but managed little more than a broken whisper. "Please, God, stop it."

"I'm a fucking thief, too! I take from shops, people I meet. I've even broken into houses before! Still want me here? Huh? *Do you?*"

My tears fell so fast there was no point trying to wipe them away. "Why are you doing this to me?" Again, my voice was too quiet, too sorrowful, for Dylan to hear me. I tried to tell myself it wasn't Dylan saying these things. It wasn't *him* trying to hurt me. It was the heroin. The desperation. The thoughts didn't stop my body shaking with the most painful tears I'd ever cried, however. They didn't stem the furious sobs scratching at my throat, because I knew, I just *knew*, whatever his reasons for telling me, the words he spoke were the truth.

Oh, Dylan…

"I'm sorry, Cam." He changed tactics, which I knew was even more dangerous than him yelling at me. If he started to beg again, I didn't know how much more I'd be able to take before I gave in.

Don't let me out no matter how much I beg. His words echoed in my mind. He told me how difficult this would be, and I heard, but I was starting to think I hadn't actually *listened*.

"Let me out, Cam. I won't take anything I swear." I heard him tug at the door handle and part of me wanted to go and open it, let him out and hope he never came back. But that was the weak part of me, and I needed to be strong like I promised.

And so I stayed where I was, on the floor with my hands over my ears. *Just a few days,* I reminded myself, praying to a god I didn't even believe in that he would give me the strength I needed.

Hours passed, I've no idea how many, it could easily have been a full day, and when the apartment descended into silence I went to check on Dylan to see if he was okay. If he was *alive.* Pushing the door open, I took a deep breath before walking inside.

Dylan sat on the floor in front of the window, his naked body shivering. I approached him cautiously, treading ginger steps before dropping down in front of him.

"It hurts, Cam," he whimpered, his glassy green eyes boring into mine with so much pain and sadness I felt a piece of me die inside. "Hurts so fucking much."

Folding my arms around him, his icy skin stinging my flesh, I held him tight. "I know it does, baby. I know."

"I want the methadone," he said, curling into a ball in my arms, his flimsy muscles trembling. "Please, Cameron. I need it. I'm in too much pain."

What do I do? He told me to refuse anything he asked. *I'm out of my depth.* "No, Dyl," I whispered into his damp-with-sweat hair. "You said no. You can do this." *You* have *to do this.* "I've got you."

He clung to my shirt, his knuckles turning white. "Make it s-stop."

"I…I don't know how."

Fuck this. Fuck heroin. Why the hell would someone do this to themselves? I'd never seen this level of pain before that hadn't resulted in death, and even that was only on TV.

Dylan sobbed into my chest and I held him while he did. My arms were all I had to offer. He remained so cold despite my palms rubbing up and down his back, and he was dirty, too; dried up vomit sticking to his skin and hair. I'd never felt so helpless in all my life.

Needing to do something, *anything*, I climbed to my feet, lifting his body with me. "Come on," I encouraged, struggling to take his weight on my own. "Try and walk for me."

He whimpered and mumbled but made little effort to move. So, sliding one arm behind his thighs, I scooped him up like a baby, carrying him towards the bath. He clung to my neck, his grip weak, while I turned on the water. I turned the temperature down to barely warm, worried the heat might burn his shivering skin, before lowering him into the bathtub, under the fine spray of the shower.

His muscles twitched and his eyes closed as he hugged his knees to his scrawny chest. Taking a sponge and some shower-gel, I scrubbed softly up and down his trembling body, gently manoeuvring his arms and legs when needed so I could clean every inch of him.

"I'm tired, Cam," he barely whispered, dropping his head to the side.

My heart ached, like it was trapped inside a vice that was trying to crush its ability to beat, as I lathered some shampoo into his fair hair. "You can sleep soon. Nearly done."

I tried not to cry as I massaged his scalp. I wanted to be strong, but I'd never felt more vulnerable. Removing the showerhead from the hook on the wall, I hovered it over his head, rinsing away the tea-tree scented suds, before doing the same to the rest of his skin. After shutting the water off, I grabbed a large towel from the heated rail next to the toilet and rubbed it over his skin in the bathtub before lifting him out and doing the same to his back.

"I-I can't d-do it anymore," Dylan cried as I wound my arm around his waist, urging him to take a step.

"You *are* doing it. It's almost over." I had no idea if my words were the truth, but I had to hope they were for both of our sakes. Honestly, I felt like *I* couldn't do it anymore either.

It took over five minutes to get him through the short distance between the en-suite and the bed, and when I did he curled up into a ball on the mattress. After what could've been forever, his exhausted body gave into the urge to sleep and I pulled the duvet up from the floor, draping it over him. For a while, I sat with him, watching him sleep, seeing the lines of pain melt from his face, and I used my last shred of hope to pray that this moment meant it was almost over.

Darkness drew in hours ago, but I had no idea what time it was when I eventually tiptoed from the room. Stumbling through the dark, I blindly felt for the light switch along the wall when I entered the living room.

"*Oh!*" I squealed like a fucking pig when I saw Paul sitting on my couch. I pressed my hand against the centre of my chest, certain my heart had leapt straight through my skin. "Fucking hell, Paul. What are you doing here?"

"I tried to call but you didn't answer."

Shit. Dylan. Paul couldn't know he was here.

"Sorry, I was sleeping."

"With Dylan?"

Dylan's name on Paul's lips caused my breath to falter. "*What?* No. W-why would you think that?"

"Because he's not here," he said, patting the couch. "And I thought he was staying with you."

Right. Shit. I hadn't told him about Dylan leaving.

"Um…Dylan left."

I waited a few long seconds for an *I told you so* but it never came. "I'm sorry. I know you won't like me saying this…"

Then don't say it.

"…But it's for the best. The Dylan you knew is gone, Cam. Some people are too far gone to be saved."

"Yes. I know. You're right."

"What?"

"I said you're right. It's for the best."

Paul's eyebrows knitted together like he was confused. I agreed with him. What more did he want from me? Getting up from the couch, he walked over to me, using his arm to push me out of the way.

"Wait. What are you..."

Ignoring me, he turned up the hall, heading straight for my bedroom.

"Paul, stop."

Dylan's voice bled through the gap at the bottom of the door before Paul could open it. "I'm so sorry, Daddy. I'll be a good boy. I'll do better."

Shit. I'd hoped he would sleep for hours.

"Left, has he?" Paul muttered, glaring at me.

"Daddy *please*..."

"Who's he talking to?" Paul asked. "You said his dad was dead."

"I-I don't..."

Paul kicked the chair away, looking at me with a puzzled expression before reaching for the handle. I tried to stop him but he shrugged out of my grasp.

When he saw Dylan inside, knelt on the floor and pleading with someone who wasn't there, he let out a frustrated sigh before closing the door again. "You're detoxing him. *Here.* On your own." His words came out like accusations.

I scrubbed my face with my hands. "He needs help."

"Damn right he does, from a *professional.* What the hell are you thinking?"

"I...I..."

"You don't know shit about addiction! This is so dangerous, Cam. Are you really this fucking stupid?"

"He begged me. I…I didn't know what to do!"

Raking his fingers through his short blond hair, he blew out a long puff of air through tight lips before lunging forward and wrapping his arms around me. He held me close, crushing my chest into his, and I was sure his strength was the only thing keeping me from collapsing.

"You know what you should've done?" he asked, keeping his grip on me tight. "You should've fucking called me. We're a team. We don't do stupid shit on our own."

Releasing me from his hold, he pushed me back a step, keeping his hands on my shoulders. "When was his last hit?"

"Yesterday, I-I think," I stuttered, scanning my scrambled memories. "Yesterday morning. Or the day before. I don't know." I didn't even know what day it was anymore, or how long I'd been listening to Dylan's cries.

Sighing in resignation, Paul nodded. "Then the worst should be coming to an end in the next couple of days. We need to make sure he has something to eat tomorrow. Something bland."

Paul knew about this stuff because of his cousin, John. I'd never met him, but I remembered the day Paul found out he'd overdosed and died, not long after we met. That could've been Dylan. If I didn't do this for him, he wouldn't make it. The thought made me want to cry but all my tears had dried out.

"*We?*" I repeated, pursing my eyebrows.

"You can't do this alone. You're not a fucking superhero."

"So...you won't call the police? I know you don't like him but-"

"Jesus Christ, Cameron," he muttered, his tone exasperated. "Do you really think that little of me? That I'd be petty enough to have him arrested out of spite?"

"No. I just thought... What about the hospital? Will you call them?"

You can't. I promised him.

"No. *You* will. In a couple of days."

"Why not now?" As much as I didn't want to break my vow, I half-hoped Paul would do it, end this, for me.

"It's almost out of his system. Might as well finish carrying out your stupid fucking idea now we're here."

"Then...why would-"

"Why would he still need help?" Paul cut in, finishing my sentence. "Because he gets clean. Then what? Have you even thought about that? Why does he use in the first place? What's going to fill that void he'll feel when he's sober? Being an addict isn't just a lifestyle choice, Cam. It's not as simple as just a poor decision. People turn to drugs because they're running from something scarier than a needle. *That's* why this was a bad idea. *That's* the part you're not qualified to deal with. His head's gonna be fucked when he's over this phase and he's gonna need more than someone to hold his hand and mop up his vomit. He needs professionals, and that isn't you."

Damn. I hadn't thought that far ahead. I hadn't thought about fucking anything. As much as I wanted to help Dylan, be there for him, I wasn't enough.

Walking into the living room, I fell back on the couch, pinching the bridge of my nose in an attempt to ease the pounding in my head. "I don't know what I'm doing anymore, Paul. A few months ago I knew where life was going. I was going to marry Kevin, earn myself another Michelin star. I was even considering opening a new restaurant. But now? Now I have no fucking clue about anything. Dylan had been my past for such a long time, and now...he's all I can think about."

Paul joined me on the couch but didn't say anything. He put his hand on my shoulder, squeezing gently, and I stacked my own hand on top of his.

"I know you think he's worthless," I began. "But-"

"I don't think he's worthless," he interrupted. "I just know how fucking hard it is to love an addict. With John, we had no choice. He was family. So, yeah, if there was ever any chance you could've walked away from this then that would've always been my preferred option for you. But if you can't, and it's looking that way, then I'll support you the best I can."

"I...I don't know what to say. I was expecting you to say I told you so, or at least be angry with me."

"Well, that makes you an arsehole. You should know me better than that."

For several minutes, we sat in silence, that easy kind of quiet you can have with someone you know so well. Leaning back in my seat, I planned to close my eyes for a while, but Dylan's voice cut into the calm like a blade.

"Cam?" he called.

Exhaling a tired sigh, I started rising from the couch.

Paul put his hand on my chest, stopping me. "I'll go."

"No," I protested, shaking my head. Dylan asked for *me*. "He doesn't know you very well. He won't want you to see him like that."

"Cam, listen to me." He stood up, bending to place his hands on my shoulders. "Right now he doesn't love you. He doesn't need *you*. He just needs *somebody*. You're exhausted. You stink. Take a shower, make up a bed, and let *me* be his somebody for tonight."

I considered arguing for only a second before realising I didn't have the energy to bother. Paul was right. I *was* exhausted. Physically and emotionally drained. As much as I wanted, *needed* sleep, he was also right about the fact I stank, so I clambered awkwardly from the couch and followed Paul down the short hallway.

I veered into the bathroom as Paul entered the bedroom, and I couldn't stop myself from hovering by the open door to find out what Dylan needed. My bedroom was opposite, and because Paul didn't close the door behind him I could see Dylan clearly, lying on the hard, laminate floor, covered in his own filth. *Again.*

Watching the scene in front of me felt like someone had tied a band around my heart, pulling and squeezing to the point I feared it would burst any second.

"Where's Cam?" Dylan asked, his voice weak and his expression twisted into fifty different types of pain. He was no longer clean, fresh faeces smeared up the small of his back. He was thirty years old, in his prime, yet he looked so withered and feeble, unable to take even the most basic care of himself.

"Busy." Paul's tone was clipped and to the point. I didn't like it, but I also suspected it might be just what Dylan needed. Paul had no emotional attachment to Dylan. No memories of him. He was stronger, able to say no easier, than I was.

Paul bent down, winding his arms around Dylan's small waist, and pulled him up to his feet. "Come on, buddy. Let's get you in the shower."

"I...I can't walk," Dylan croaked.

"Sure you can." Supporting Dylan's weight, Paul dragged his limp body across the room, disappearing into the en-suite.

My whole body was frozen as I continued staring into the empty bedroom. My chest of drawers was in pieces, the contents strewn across the floor. The bed sheets were soiled, the cream rug stained, the smell completely overwhelming even from across the hall. I didn't even notice the chaos when I showered him earlier. All I saw was Dylan, a scared and hurt little boy.

When you read about celebrity addicts in the press, it almost seems a little glamorous. You read about the big, swanky rehab centres that look like tropical island resorts, or see pictures of them looking a tad thinner but still glitzy. Watching Dylan recovering from the effects of these drugs, however, was *nothing* like anything I'd ever read about, nothing like the movies.

It was a real, living, horror story that I wished and prayed and *begged* to wake up from every second of the day.

I didn't even feel myself slipping to the floor, and I didn't know how long I'd sat there staring when I saw Paul bring Dylan out of the en-suite, wrapped in my dressing gown, with their elbows linked. Dylan looked like an old man, so small and frail as he stood fidgeting with his fingers while he watched Paul strip the dirty sheets from the bed.

"Come on," Paul said, cocking his head towards the bed after dressing it with clean bedding. "Get in."

Dylan did as he was told without protest, climbing onto the bed and looking completely lost on the king-sized mattress as he curled up into the foetal position.

"We good?" Paul asked, placing a gentle hand on Dylan's shoulder. "Do you need anything?"

Seeing Paul taking care of Dylan made me feel guilty for doubting him. He was a good man, loving and affectionate, but I'd forgotten that. I'd forgotten *everything* because all could think about was Dylan.

Dylan shook his head, just a little, but he winced as if the small movement caused him physical discomfort. "No thanks." He looked right at me as he answered Paul, and I felt a pull deep in my chest, so intense I couldn't ignore it. Getting up off the cold bathroom floor, I walked through the gap between our doors, the pull, the *ache*, easing with every step I took.

"What are you doing?" Paul asked.

Without looking at him, my gaze fixed on Dylan, I answered, "I'm staying in here tonight."

I expected some opposition as I crawled onto the mattress, lying down behind Dylan, my chest to his back, but the argument never came.

"I'll be in the living room if you need anything," Paul said before turning for the door and leaving us alone.

"You don't have to be here," Dylan whispered as I snuck my arm under his, draping it over his waist.

"I'm not going anywhere." I pulled him a little tighter into my chest, burying my nose in his shoulder. "Ever."

* * *

The next day, I'd expected Dylan to be doing better, which I guess he was, just not as much as I'd hoped. He'd stopped shaking, his skin had dried after dripping with sweat for the last sixty hours, and he was sat up in bed rather than crawling on the floor. But he still looked sick. I was still more afraid than I'd ever been in my life.

After tidying my bedroom and stacking the pieces of broken furniture to one side, I made him some buttered toast in the morning which he threw back up ten minutes later, but he managed to keep down the chicken soup I made for lunch so I took that as a good sign. Paul covered the restaurant for me again and came straight back after closing. I couldn't have got through this without him. He was my best friend and I loved him with all my heart, and after the last few days I'd never stop telling him how appreciated he was.

The following days were spent pretty much the same way, and by day six Dylan was finally ready to leave the confines of my bedroom. It was late afternoon and we were sitting in front of the TV, staring at the screen but not really watching it.

"Do you want to go anywhere?" I asked. "Get out of the apartment for a while?"

"No," he answered without hesitation.

"You must be sick of being inside these walls." I knew I fucking was.

"Cam…" He said my name on a sigh that left me quietly terrified. "I want to score. I want a hit so fucking bad it's all I can think about. My muscles

140

ache for it. My mouth waters for it. My veins feel like they're on fire and the only thing that will cool it is a needle filled with sweet, beautiful heroin."

Whoa…

"If I go out, I'll get it. I won't just think about it, I'll go straight out and fucking get it. So, no, I'm not sick of these walls. Right now they're the only thing keeping me alive."

"Oh." What else could I say? I didn't know how he was feeling, and I most certainly didn't understand how he could describe heroin as *beautiful*. The only words I could possibly associate with it were fucking *evil*. Soul destroying. Life shattering.

I assumed once the drug had left his system he wouldn't need it anymore, that the addiction would be gone. That made me naïve, but it wasn't really my fault. I didn't even smoke cigarettes so how the hell would I know?

"Have you thought about making a doctors appointment?" I asked, hoping that's what he intended to do. Before Paul got involved I hadn't given any thought to what happened *after*, but he talked a lot of sense. I imagined Dylan didn't take drugs for the fun of it. He must've had demons that encouraged him to take that first hit, or to continue doing it over and over again. Some of the things he'd told me, *screamed* at me in an attempt to get me to let him out…

Fuck. How does a person cope with that? He sure as hell couldn't do it alone, and the fact my eyes stung every time I thought about it meant I wasn't really in a position to help him either.

"I think you should talk to someone who can help you through this," I added when I received no reply.

"There's nothing to talk about. Been there, done that, went back to smack."

"You've had counselling?"

Dylan shrugged. "Kinda. Drugs counselling. They told me ways to deal with the craving. I don't need to hear it again."

He couldn't give up so easily. I didn't help him because I wanted anything in return, but I couldn't help thinking he owed it to me to try harder this time. I couldn't go through this again.

"But what about, you know, the *other* stuff?"

He turned to face me, knitting his eyebrows together. "What other stuff?"

"Taking drugs isn't the only harmful thing in your life, Dyl. The things you told me, the stuff about how you get your money…"

"Stop," he said, raising his hand. "I…I shouldn't have told you any of that."

Does he not remember? "Is it not true?"

I knew by the look of shame on his face, the way he squeezed his eyes closed, that it was. "It's…I just…I shouldn't have said it."

"Why?" I pressed. "I said I wanted to know *all* of you and I meant it."

"Because you're the last breathing person in this world who's ever given a shit about me!" he barked before leaning forward, resting his elbows on his knees and blowing out a calming breath. "I know how disgusting I am. I can't bear you seeing me that way, too."

Scooting closer to him, I placed my hand on his knee, the warmth of his skin seeping through his jeans and into my body. He'd flitted between icy-cold and feverish all week. "I don't think you're disgusting, but I do think you need help. What you've been doing isn't healthy or safe. You need help to heal, Dyl. Physically *and* mentally."

Silence followed, a thick, uncomfortable quiet filled with so much pain it felt like I was drowning.

"You were counting daisies weren't you?" I asked, tightening my grip on his knee. "The night things turned sexual between us. You were counting daisies because you thought of me as one of those…*men*."

Dylan swallowed, a forced action that caused his Adam's apple to bob very slowly up and down. "Y-you remember the daisies story?"

"That's not an answer."

"I…" He swallowed again, rubbing his hand over his flushed face. "Those men are all I know."

I gasped a rush of air into my lungs like I hadn't taken a breath in hours. Just when I thought my heart couldn't break any more, another piece of it fell away.

"I wanted so badly to give you something, to thank you for not throwing me out."

"Christ, Dylan…" My words dissolved into a sigh. "I don't want, or expect, anything from you.

Especially not sex. Dammit, Dyl, you don't *give* sex to anyone. It's about *two* people. Together."

How did I not see? I should never have let things go so far that night. "Has anyone ever loved you, Dylan? Since your dad, your grandma. Have you ever had anybody?"

Again, he simply shrugged, and the already overbearing weight on my shoulders increased. I, a man he barely knew anymore, was all he had. That was the moment I knew what true sadness felt like. I'd been down before, same as anyone, but until this second I'd never been truly, stomach-churningly, utterly fucking *sad*.

Instinctively, like I couldn't stop myself even if I tried, I grabbed his face with both hands, forcing him to look at me. Positioning my nose a mere inch from his, I spoke softly. "*I* love you. *I* care. *I* am here for you. You're going to get through this. We're going to get through this together."

"Cameron…"

"I'm your friend," I said, stopping him from interrupting. "I'm your friend and I *love* you. You don't disgust me. You haven't disappointed me. When I think about what you've been through, the way you've been living, it terrifies me…but it doesn't make me regret knowing you. It makes me want to hold you, help you. It makes me want to love you even fucking harder."

"I'll always be an addict, Cam. You can't fix me."

"I don't want to *fix* you. I want to be your friend. Will you let me do that?"

Dylan's lips twitched and the edges of his eyes reddened. When he tried to speak all that emerged was a quiet croak, so he threw his arms around me instead, pulling me so close to his chest that I struggled to breathe, but I didn't care.

"Thank you," he whispered, the two tiny words cracking on his lips. "Thank you."

Chapter

Eight

~Dylan~

One week later...

STANDING OUTSIDE THE GP surgery after my appointment, my restless feet tapped incessantly against the pavement. It'd been a struggle to keep still the last few days. It wasn't a case of having too much energy - I felt like shit that'd been repeatedly trampled on - it was more impatience as my body anxiously awaited the hit that wasn't coming.

The GP drew some blood as part of my 'health check', which translated to me being screened for

HIV and other diseases I'd put myself at risk for. Then he referred me for counselling before telling me the waiting list was approximately two months long. I wasn't a priority because I was clean. That didn't surprise me. No one was in a rush to help the junkies when there were people dying from diseases beyond their control. And why should they? My problems were self-inflicted. Rationally, I knew it all came down to money and budget cuts, like everything else on the NHS, but as I always did, it was easier to believe people just didn't give a shit. If I needed help sooner, he jotted down the number for the local community drug services team. Finally, he gave me the address of the local sexual health clinic and told me to visit them as soon as possible.

So, that was my plan for tomorrow.

I told myself the results would come back negative, refusing to think of the alternative because that would make me hate myself even more than I already did. So, for now, I just wouldn't think about it at all.

After fifteen minutes I was still standing in the same spot, willing my feet to turn left to go back to Cameron's apartment while fighting my mind which was telling me to go right and in the direction of The Old Dog. That's another thing about heroin. The withdrawal never really ends. Sure, the physical pain had lessened, but I still wanted it. Right now, all that excruciating pain, the sickness, the violent cold-sweats the memory of literally shitting myself in front of Paul – a guy I barely knew, wasn't enough to stop the craving. The feeling of withdrawing cold-turkey felt like I was living in a kind of hell ruled by a far more sadistic bastard than the devil. It made me want to die, sparked visions of me slicing into my wrists, my neck, anywhere that would help me bleed out faster. Yet, right this second, I'd have risked doing it all over again for just *one…more…hit.*

Left. Right. Left. Right.

"Hey!"

Blinking my eyes back into the real world, I looked up and saw a black car with white racing stripes parked on the opposite side of the street with the engine still running.

"Get in!"

The midday sunlight made it difficult to see the driver, and it was only when I crossed the road I noticed it was Paul. Jogging to the passenger side, I climbed into his sports car without question.

"How'd it go?"

I raised my eyebrows, feeling a little confused and a lot suspicious. Is that why he was here? Had Cameron asked him to check up on me? Make sure I'd gone to my appointment like I said I would?

"Did Cam send you?"

"No," Paul said, eyeing up his mirror as he pulled the car away from the curb. "He trusts you. I don't."

Fair enough. I didn't trust me either. "Well I had bloods taken. He referred me for counselling. The usual shit."

"You gonna go?"

"For the counselling?"

"Yeah."

"Sure. I said I would."

Paul nodded. "Good. That's good. So how're you feeling?"

"Fine." I shrugged.

He looked over to me for just a second, his eyebrow raised, before turning back to the road. "Now for the honest answer."

Paul was a very different man than Cameron, perhaps because he didn't care about me in the same way. He wouldn't accept my bullshit, and he had no qualms telling me what he thought. He was bossy, firm, and sometimes an absolute arsehole. It felt like I should hate him, but I didn't. I appreciated his honesty. I didn't know if he was looking out for *me* or for Cameron, but the semantics didn't matter. He'd been supportive so far and I was grateful. Cameron needed someone to take care of him because I sure as shit couldn't.

"Would you have scored if I hadn't arrived?"

I let out a quiet groan. There was no point in lying. For a reason I couldn't fathom, I knew Paul would see through it. "I don't know. I thought about it."

"You always will."

Shifting in my seat, I turned to face him, curiosity twisting my expression. "You seem to know a lot about this stuff?" My statement came out like a question and I hoped it wouldn't piss him off. *But…* if he expected honesty then if felt right that I could want the same from him.

He gave me a swift glance before returning his focus to the road. "I had a cousin. John."

"*Had?*" I interrupted, my voice quiet as unease filled my stomach.

"He died. He was an addict for seven years, clean for three. Then he OD'd. We can only assume when he used again he didn't take into account the fact his body wasn't tolerant to it anymore and took too much. I like to think his death wasn't intentional, but I guess I'll never really know."

"Shit. I'm sorry." And I *was* sorry. Sorry that people like me existed. People that caused their loved ones so much pain and worry. People who loved heroin more than those who cared about them.

My thoughts took me to Bubbles and I started to wonder how she was doing, whether she was even alive. Without knowing her real name, or who she really was, I guessed that was something I'd never know either.

Paul shrugged, turning the car into a direction which didn't lead to Cameron's apartment. I'd have asked where we were going but he started talking first. "It's not your fault. The only person to blame is John. If you fuck up what Cam's trying to do for you, *that* will be your fault."

That right there is the quality I admired most in this man I hardly knew. He was harsh, straight forward, but I needed that. Cameron was too forgiving, too accepting of the shitty things I'd done in my life. Right now, I loved that about him, but with my addict brain that forgiveness is all it would take to make me reach for a hit if I were to wobble. He'd still be there afterwards. He'd put up with any crap I threw at him. That makes me sound like a lowlife bastard, and that's because I was one.

"Where are we going?" I thought I knew the answer when I saw O'Neil's come into view through the windscreen, but I didn't understand why.

"We're going to work."

Um…okaaaaay. "Oh. Guess I can walk back to Cam's place from there."

"I said *we're* going to work," Paul repeated, pulling into the car park behind the building.

I knew Paul lived within walking distance of the restaurant because he took me to the barber shop below his flat to have my hair tidied up last week, and by barber shop I mean a *huge* modern salon with fancy lighting and gold-framed mirrors; there wasn't a red or white stripe in sight. I looked, and felt, better for it. It'd become overgrown and straggly, some parts longer than others since I was only used to Bubbles hacking away at it. But now it was short on the sides, a little longer on top. I looked kinda…respectable.

So, it seemed Paul had gone out of his way to pick me up. I just didn't know *why*. "What?"

"We need a new dishwasher. You're it."

Whoa. "I don't need a babysitter." Panic rained over my head, heating my cheeks and making my breath stutter.

"So what are you gonna do with your life, huh? You think you can sit around in Cam's flat all day every day, bored out of your fucking mind, thinking about smack, and then *not* go out and score a bag to relieve the pressure?"

Fucking hell. My throat felt tight and I started to tug at my collar as if that would ease the tension. "I...I can't go in there."

This was too much too soon. I'd only been clean for thirteen days for fuck's sake. I wasn't ready. "I don't want people staring at the junkie like I'm some kind of circus freak, waiting for me to fuck up so they can laugh."

"Have you told them you're a heroin addict?"

"What? Of course not. I don't even know anyone in there."

"Then that makes me, you, and Cameron the only people who know. Your life is nobody else's goddamn business."

Christ. I couldn't do this. *Could I?* "I...I dunno. I don't know the first thing about kitchens."

"Can you put a plate in a dishwasher?"

"I guess so."

"Then come on," he said, clicking off his seatbelt. "Get your arse outta the car and get to work."

It felt like all my blood had rushed to the vein in my neck as it pounded with anxiety. "Does Cam know?"

"He will soon."

Nodding weakly, my stomach fluttering with nerves I hadn't felt since I was cast as Joseph in our primary school nativity, I did as I was told and got out of the car.

"Oh, by the way…" Paul span on his heels, the gravel crunching beneath his feet as he turned back to face me. "Your wages come in the form of a roof over your head and food in your belly. Cam would never take anything from you, but he should."

Weirdly, instead of pissing me off it actually made me feel a little positive. I hated that I had nothing to offer Cameron, that I couldn't repay him for his kindness. This felt like a start. "Sounds fair to me."

"Good. Now, follow me. I'll show you around before the rest of the guys arrive."

"Yes, sir."

Stopping in his tracks, Paul glowered at me. "Don't ever call me that again. I ain't no fucking pensioner."

Grinning, I tilted my head, looking up at him through my eyelashes.

"Oh, and don't you *dare* call me Twinkle either, no matter what Derek tells you."

Twinkle? Derek? Walking into the restaurant, one thing was certain; today was going to be interesting.

I'd been inside before, but my memory didn't recognise it. Not surprising, given that the last time my brain was strung out on skag. Paul showed me around, giving me a tour of the dining room first. There were two levels to it, with a steel, spiral staircase in the centre of the large room. The black, silver, and glass theme ran throughout, with artwork on the walls offering splashes of colour. Chandeliers dropped from the ceilings, and there were several silver trees, which twinkled with clear fairy-lights, dotted around both levels. It was sophisticated. Elegant. Extravagant.

There was a downstairs kitchen, a *prep* kitchen, that I didn't even know existed. It was *huge*; everything steel or white, under a canopy of artificial light, and completely spotless. Paul pointed out all the equipment, telling me what they were, before giving me a white uniform to put on and then showing me how to operate the biggest dishwasher I'd ever seen in my life. I nodded a lot, absorbing the information. I might've only been a dishwasher, but I was determined to give it my all. Paul didn't have to do this for me, I sure as hell didn't deserve it, but he'd put his faith in me and I wanted so badly to not let him down.

Then he took me back up to the service kitchen that I'd been in once before. This one was even bigger, with clearly defined sections for preparing different types of food. There were dishwashers up here, too, so I wasn't sure which ones I was supposed to use.

"Hey, Paul! You in here?" Cameron shouted through the kitchen, returning from a meeting with his accountant. He told me all about what the meetings entailed last night, but I didn't really hear a word. Numbers bored the shit out of me. Always had. "Have you seen Dy…" He cut himself off when he saw me. "Oh. You're here."

"Yep."

Puzzled, a deep crease appeared on his forehead. "Why are you wearing that?"

I opened my mouth to answer but Paul got in there first, clapping my back. "He's here to work. Dylan's our new dishwasher."

"Yeah?" There was a glimmer of excitement, possibly hope, in Cameron's eyes. It made me feel good, which felt strange in itself. "Are you ready for that?"

"Guess I'm about to find out," I said through a nervous smile.

"Well everyone's great here. I think you'll like them."

That wasn't my issue. I was more worried about what *they* thought of *me*.

Back upstairs several minutes later, people started filtering into the building. It surprised me just how many people Cameron employed. I expected five-or-so, but there must've been fifteen bodies, all dressed in black trousers and white jackets, scurrying around the kitchen in perfect harmony with each other. Nerves bubbled in my belly. I felt out of place, like I didn't belong here and everyone knew it.

"Oh! New face," one of the guys said, standing right in front of me.

"Derek," Cam said. "This is Dylan, our new busser. Dyl, this is Derek, head of pastry."

Derek proffered his hand. "Good to meet you."

I took his hand and shook, wishing I'd wiped my clammy palms on my trousers first. "You, too."

Glancing around, I watched everyone get to work. They all had their own individual roles, all knew what they were doing. Me? I just stood there like a fucking idiot.

Cameron disappeared, doing his chef thing, shouting out orders, but Derek stayed behind. His stare seemed curious as he looked me up and down, and I could almost feel it crawl over my skin. "You can 'elp me prep."

"Uh…" I didn't know how to cook a boiled fucking egg, let alone Michelin star desserts. "I think I'm only supposed to clean stuff."

"Well, there's nowt to clean till we dirty it," he said. His accent was familiar, took me back to living up north. If I had to take a guess at his roots, I'd have chosen Manchester. "You interested in cookin'?"

I could be, I supposed. I *did* enjoy helping Cameron make things in his apartment. "Sure. Doubt I'll be any good at it though."

"Oh, sugar, wi' a teacher as great as me, you'll be knockin' out award-winnin' millefeuilles in y'sleep."

His use of the word sugar surprised me a little. Derek was tall and broad. He had colourful tattoos peeking out of one of his sleeves, black and grey under the other. He seemed very masculine with a deep, gravelly voice. Yes, I'd judged him before I even knew him. It's human nature, and *that's* why I worried about others judging *me*.

"I don't even know what that is." And I certainly couldn't have pronounced the fancy word back to him.

Blowing out a chuckle, he cocked his head, signalling for me to follow him. So I did. I trailed behind him as he led me downstairs through the service lift to the prep kitchen, then followed his lead, washing my hands when he did, keeping track of every movement he made.

You can do this. Just breathe.

"Okay," Derek said, rubbing his hands together. "D'ya know where the fridge is?"

Scanning my memory, I tried to remember everything Paul showed me earlier. "Yeah. I think so."

"Grab as many bottles o' milk as your arms can carry, then go back and do the same again. I want you to burn it."

"*Burn* it? The *milk*?" *How the fuck do you burn milk?* More importantly, why would you *want* to?

Derek nodded. "It's for the ice cream."

"Ice cream's made with burnt milk?"

"This one is. Go *now*," he ordered. "If we don't get it in the blast chiller wi'in the next hour it won't be set for service."

"Right," I muttered, already walking away. I picked up my pace when I saw the speed everybody else worked at. Everything was so fast. No one stood still even for a second. It was difficult to keep up when heroin had made me spend the last ten years of my life in slow motion.

When I returned with the second lot of milk, Derek nodded towards some humongous metal roasting dishes. "Fill each one 'alf way," he began, not looking up from the brown batter he was whisking. "Then add the sugar I've weighed out f'you and put 'em in the oven. I've already set the temp."

Nodding, I carried out his instruction, terrified I would fuck it up somehow. "How will I know when it's burnt?" I asked after closing the oven door.

I expected him to look at me like I was a moron, but he didn't. I decided I could end up really liking this guy.

"It'll dry out, turn brown, and stick to the sides o' the pan. Stop worryin'. You're only helpin'. I don't expect you to take over my section."

"Right," I mumbled through a nervous chuckle. It seemed like the only word I was capable of saying lately, which didn't help the fact I already felt stupid.

"Rule number one," Derek said, adding more flour to whatever he was making. "Never stand still in a kitchen. There's *always* summat needs doin'."

Shit. Ummm…

Derek pointed to the dirty bowls and instruments on his station.

"Right." *Fuck!* "I mean sure. Okay." I'd turned into a bumbling dickhead and I rolled my eyes at myself before loading my arms with dirty pots and taking them to the dishwasher. Then, using my initiative, I walked around the other sections, both upstairs and down, cleaning up as other chefs created mess. It wasn't much, it was my job after all, but I felt a small sense of pride that I did it without needing to be asked.

When I eventually wound back at Derek's station, he was taking the milk, which no longer resembled milk, out of the oven. As I approached, one of the two female chefs barked, "Yes, chef!" at Derek and, honestly, I found the whole thing confusing. I'd already heard someone call Cameron, Paul, and a guy working a wood-burning stove, chef. Did they all call each other chef? Did *I* need to call them chef? I didn't get it.

"Hey," I said, leaning into Derek so he could hear me over the noise of the kitchen. Fuck, it was a *loud* place. "Do I need to call everyone chef?" My question felt a little stupid, but I didn't have a fucking clue what I was doing.

Derek started chipping away at the burnt milk before handing me a knife as if I should start doing the same to the other trays. "It's an authority, a respect thing. You call the 'ead section chefs, chef. And, o' course, Cam and Paul because they're above all of us."

Hmm. I didn't know who was head of where yet.

"You'll pick it up. You're not gonna be extradited for callin' someone by their actual name," he said, chuckling.

I almost said *right*, but stopped myself, nodding instead. Mirroring Derek's hands, I started chipping and scraping at my tray of milk. It wasn't technically milk anymore, but I didn't know if it was classed as something else with a fancy name now its state had changed. One thing's for sure, it did *not* look appetising.

"Get right in there. Chip it all from the sides."

I couldn't prevent my nose scrunching. "People don't actually *eat* this part do they?"

Derek's mouth twisted into an amused smile. "Trust me. I'll let you 'ave first taste when it's ready. It'll take a few hours. This batch is for evenin' service."

I wasn't sure I wanted to put this crap in my mouth, but I nodded anyway.

Once we were finished, Derek emptied the burnt bits, along with the sludgy milk that hadn't quite dried out, into a machine that held a runny mixture inside. He pressed a few buttons before going on to do something else, and I got rid of the oven dishes, loading them into one of the dishwashers before emptying the one that'd just finished its wash cycle. "Service in ten!" Cameron's voice boomed over all the other noise and the sound tickled something in my chest.

A furore of *Yes, chef*'s erupted, people started making their way upstairs, and something told me things were about to get a hell of a lot busier. I was exhausted already, my body and mind completely wiped. I started to doubt whether I *could* do this after all, especially once a bout of nausea kicked in. I wondered if I was hungry, I still wasn't eating properly, or just overtired. I hadn't been on my feet this long, or had so much to think about, in years.

"Hey." Cameron's hand appeared on my waist from behind when I took a minute to hide behind the dishwashers.

Never stand still in a kitchen. Derek's words echoed in my mind and I thought Cameron had come to chew my arse off. But I *needed* this minute, this brief respite. I didn't feel well.

"You okay?"

Turning to face him, I sighed. "I'm just a little…overwhelmed. I'm sorry. I'll be fine in just a second."

"Hell, Dyl, I've been in this game for years and I still get overwhelmed. Don't apologise. Do you need to go home?"

"No, no. I can do this. I'm fine, I promise."

"There's a staffroom next to my office. There's a fridge inside stocked with sandwiches and water. Take five minutes. Eat something."

"I'm okay, really."

"That's an order, Dylan." He leaned into my ear, the closeness making my pulse race. It was an unfamiliar sensation that, in all honesty, confused me. "You've been through something major, something traumatic on your body *and* your mind. Don't push yourself. You'll make yourself ill. Things are about to turn pretty crazy any minute now. Go. Refuel. Don't come back in here until you're one hundred percent ready."

Blowing out a long, stuttered breath, I nodded. "Okay. Thanks."

Cameron smiled, a bright, reassuring expression as he patted my shoulder. "Doesn't matter what I'm doing during service, how busy I look. If you need me, *find* me. You hear?"

Again, I nodded. I seriously needed to find alternative methods of communicating instead of spouting 'right' and nodding like a sea-lion on acid.

"Hey, chef!" a young chef, younger than me at a guess, interrupted while jogging over to where we stood. "The blast chiller's not working upstairs."

Cameron's face twisted into frustration. "Oh for fuck's sake!" he yelled, and then he disappeared, leaving me alone as I gathered enough strength to haul myself forward towards the staffroom.

* * *

At the end of an excruciatingly long day, I cleaned down after service, then I stayed behind while Cameron balanced his books. I might've told Paul I didn't need babysitting, but truthfully I knew I did. Especially tonight. As service drew to a close and weariness invaded every nerve in my body, I was in physical pain. I ached *everywhere*, and all I could think about was how a tiny bag of magical heroin would take it all away.

It was after midnight when we got back to Cameron's apartment and, after hanging up my jacket, I collapsed immediately onto the sofa.

"Tired?" Cam asked, joining me on the sofa.

"So tired I can't feel my legs."

Cameron chuckled, patting my knee. It felt weird sometimes that I no longer flinched when he touched me. I couldn't remember when I'd stopped. I just knew that now I felt completely comfortable with it. I think I even *liked* it. "You did great today."

I didn't feel great, but I smiled anyway.

"How'd you find it? Do you like everyone?"

"Derek's great. He let me help make some stuff, *and* taste it. Holy shit, it felt like heaven had melted in my mouth."

"He's a good guy, and an exceptional cook."

"Is he gay?"

Cameron looked a little staggered by the turn of conversation. "Gayer than a rainbow dipped in unicorn shit. *His* words, not mine," he said, grinning. "Why?"

"And he and Paul are together?"

Cameron's eyes widened, looking altogether astounded. "*What?* Hell no. Some days I don't even think they like each other."

"Oh." I might not have had any personal experience with it, at least not recent enough for me to remember, but I knew what lust looked like, and Derek *definitely* had the hots for Paul.

"What on earth made you think that?"

"Just the way Derek looks at him." I shrugged. "I must've read it wrong."

"You have, I've no doubt. Besides, Paul only recently broke up with his girlfriend."

"So Paul's *not* gay?"

"He's bi, but *definitely* not into Derek." He started to laugh like it was the most ludicrous thing he'd ever heard.

"I'm grateful, you know," I said, changing the subject. "For everything you and Paul are doing for me. I know I don't deserve it but-"

"Stop right there. I don't want to hear that shit, because that's what it is. Bullshit. You're not a bad person, Dyl. The drugs made you do bad things but, underneath, that's not who you are. If it was, you wouldn't feel so ashamed."

Ashamed didn't even begin to cover how sickened I felt about all the terrible things I'd done. I expected screwing johns would be the thing most people found repulsive, but the only person *that* hurt was myself, and I could live with that. Stealing, lying, and saying unforgiveable things to the people trying to help me were the parts of my life that continued to haunt me. I'd hurt so many people, people I didn't even know. I'd stolen from them, treated them like shit, taken whatever I wanted. *That* was the thing I doubted I'd ever forgive myself for.

Conversation eventually turned to my doctor's appointment. It was awkward and I felt embarrassed discussing it, but nevertheless I knew it was something we *needed* to talk about. If I was going to allow Cameron to help me through recovery I owed it to him to be honest, keep him informed.

He seemed shocked, but mostly concerned, by the fact counselling services carried such a long waiting list. I tried to reassure him that I could cope until then, even if I didn't quite believe it myself. When two AM rolled around, Cameron went to bed and I made up the sofa-bed. Stripping out of my clothes, I folded them neatly and placed them in a tidy pile on the coffee table. I didn't remember him being so tidy when we were younger, but nowadays perfection and order followed Cameron everywhere. They seemed like qualities you'd need in his profession so I guessed that's where he'd picked it up.

When I lay down, I stared at the folded up clothes for a while. Cameron had offered to buy me some new stuff, seeing as the few things I owned were tatty and old, but I couldn't accept any more of his charity. I knew I wasn't getting paid for my job in cash, so I didn't know how I'd supply my own things yet but I'd figure something out. Maybe if I offered to work through my days off, assuming I wouldn't be expected to work seven days a week, he'd agree to pay me a little something. I'd have even accepted the condition that he accompanied me to the shops to make sure I chose new jeans over a bag of smack. Sure, I'd have probably felt like a child, but that was my own fault.

I *wasn't* trustworthy, and I couldn't help wonder if I ever would be.

Thankfully, for now, Cameron's clothes fitted pretty well. They were a tad baggy, but we were a similar height so they didn't look too ridiculous on me. They were, however, a constant reminder of everything he'd done for me, and the fact the only way to repay him was *this*. Staying clean. Getting stronger. I *had* to do this for him as much as myself. I had nothing else to offer the world. My existence seemed futile.

If I didn't do this, there really was no point to me being alive any longer.

* * *

One month later…

"Holy shit!" Bubbles said, her words muffled with breathlessness. "You think we lost 'em?"

Doubled over, my hands on my knees, I caught my breath. "Pretty sure."

Bubbles was seen lifting a bottle of whiskey in the supermarket, stuffing it inside her coat. We bailed as soon as the alarm sounded, followed by two security guards who kept chase for three streets before fading into the distance. Seriously, it was more good luck than good management that we hadn't been arrested since we'd known each other.

Now, we were in a flat that belonged to a friend of Bubbles, about to get high.

"Did you see his face?" Bubbles laughed. "He went so fucking red I thought he was gonna combust!"

My laugh was weaker. I was getting antsy and restless. "You wanna push off first?"

"It's your turn," she said, smiling in anticipation. It's almost as addictive watching another person take a hit as when you take one yourself.

We sat on the floor, crossing our legs Buddha-style, while I plucked the gear from my pocket. Fuck I needed this. I hadn't had a decent hit in days. Our usual dealer skipped town so we were forced to score whatever the hell we could get

our grubby hands on. Amphetamines, morphine, benzos...
If it was classed as a drug, we'd take it.

Bubbles set up the spoons and syringes while I wrestled
out of my jacket and tied a shoelace around the top of my
arm. My belt snapped the day before, but anything flexible
did the trick. My foot tapped impatiently against the stained
carpet as I watched Bubbles through eager eyes while she
sparked the lighter under the discoloured spoon.

"Easy, boy," she said with a half smile. "It'll be worth
the wait."

Fuck yeah it will. *"How much did you make last*
night?"

We took turns finding tricks and then shared whatever
we scored with the money. She was the closest I had to a best
friend and I didn't even know her real name. Names just
never came up. Nothing of any importance ever came up in
fact. That's what was so great about our friendship. We
distracted each other, made it easier to forget about our pasts.
We shared just two passions – heroin, and having fun along
the way.

"Eighty. Should keep us going for a few days." That
meant we'd likely spend the next few days inside this flat,
pushing off, sleeping, and laughing. Perfect.

"Here we go, Titch. You ready?"

"Fuck yeah." Straightening my arm, I bit my lip,
eagerly awaiting the phenomenal pleasure that would come
from the needle approaching my vein...

Then I woke up.

"Ugh," I mumbled, rubbing at my eyes. "Dammit."

These dreams were becoming more frequent. They were all based on memories, and *always* ended just as I was about to push the delicious warmth I missed so much into my vein. The feeling of being brought back to consciousness was almost soul-destroying. Absolute, unadulterated, torture. *Fuck*, I missed using, but what I had now was better. That's what I told myself anyway. Some days I'd have given everything that mattered to me up just to feel that delectable hit one last time.

I could only hope that those 'some days' would eventually fade into never.

"I'm leaving soon. Will you be okay?" Cameron asked.

Today was my day off, and holy crap I needed it. I doubted anyone who'd never worked in a professional kitchen could ever even imagine how busy it is. It's hard work. Challenging, even for a lowly skivvy like me. The atmosphere is super charged. The work never stops. It's hot, sweaty, and by the end of the day you feel so exhausted that you're only a yawn away from death. But...it's also strangely brilliant, and I enjoyed being part of it.

"I'm going to sleep, eat ice cream, and watch telly. I'll be fine," I assured him, knowing 'will you be okay?' was code for, 'are you strong enough to stop yourself going straight out to score a bag?'

My answer wasn't a lie, but I did omit a few details about my plans for the day. Even though I wasn't a chef, I'd learned so much in the last few weeks, especially from Derek who'd kinda taken me under his wing, and so tonight I planned to put my newfound skills into practice. Yes, I was going to cook for Cameron.

Me, cooking actual, edible food.

I laughed out loud at my own thoughts once Cameron left for work. It was a strange feeling, this desire I felt to please another person, to make them smile. I was so used to only looking out for myself, only doing things that made *my* life easier. If I could turn out a dish that was even a quarter as decent as the stuff I'd seen the guys at the restaurant produce, I'd be pretty damn chuffed with myself.

Until then, I needed to keep my mind occupied. Just a minute of boredom would result in me thinking about heroin, which in turn would make me feel anxious. Anxiety brought with it a slurry of thoughts that quickly turned to guilt. Guilt would morph into anger, and anger never failed to make me want to forget everything that was wrong with my life, and there was only one way to do that.

Drugs.

So, yeah, I had to keep busy. I started by cleaning Cameron's already pristine apartment before doing the washing. I even ironed for the first time in my life. Even before I discovered the joys of smack I never ironed my clothes, so I was rather pleased with my first attempt, despite burning a hole in one of Cam's shirts. I threw it in the bin and hoped he never noticed it was missing.

Next came Netflix. I picked the first box-set in the recommended list – Pretty Little Liars – and watched half the first season in one sitting. I thought the plot was a little ridiculous, and it seemed like a show designed for teenage girls, yet it was too addictive to stop watching. I only turned it off when I got cramp in my right leg.

I needed to move before I got bedsores on my numb arse, so, I went to wank off in the shower for the second time today. Sex drive is another thing on the list of many that gets supressed when you're using heroin. When I say drugs is the only thing you think about, I mean it. Nothing else compares to it. Anything that's not heroin becomes uninteresting and unnecessary. There's no joy in sex, food, or conversation, so you just don't do it. You *can* if you *have* to, you simply don't want or need to do anything except get high.

So, once the shit leaves your system…*boom!* It's like you've been born again. Everything feels new and exciting. Your senses propel into overdrive and you need to experience *everything* the world has to offer. Food tastes better, colours are brighter, music tingles in your veins. And your sex drive? Let's just say I'd spent the last few weeks wanking off like a teenage boy watching his first porno up to four times a day. That first time, that first orgasm after withdrawing, felt like I came so hard my dick might burst. It took mere seconds to achieve. I'd barely brushed over the tip with my thumb before I shot all over the bathroom tiles, and I was ready to go again almost immediately.

After showering, wanking, and drying off, I stared at my naked body for a minute or so in the mirror, running my hands along my firmer chest. I looked better. I'd put on a little weight, concealing the ribs which, just a few weeks ago, protruded beneath my pale flesh. My skin was pinker, less sickly looking, and my face almost looked like the man I used to be. For the first time in fuck knows how long, I didn't feel revolted by my reflection.

Aware that Cameron would be home in a couple of hours, I dressed quickly in some joggers and a T-shirt that I'd bought, along with a few other things, last week. I didn't feel comfortable discussing money, or the possibility of being paid some actual wages with Cameron because I knew he'd give me anything I asked for. I also knew that was dangerous. I didn't trust myself yet, so he shouldn't either. With everybody else, Cameron was firm and authoritative. At work, he took charge. He had no problem giving orders or losing his shit when someone fucked up. I'd even seen him call Paul out on his bullshit a few times.

But he wasn't like that with me. I was his weakness, and it worried me that my addict brain would use that to its advantage if I ever felt myself slipping. That's why I went to Paul. He wouldn't take any shit from me. I needed that. And so, he agreed I could be paid for any overtime I accrued, before taking me out to buy some new clothes. I assumed Cameron knew about it. It was *his* restaurant after all. But he hadn't brought it up with me so neither did I.

I guess you could say Paul had become our intermediary, a 'go to' guy for the both of us. Sounds kinda pathetic, that Cameron and I couldn't

171

talk about the serious stuff together but, for now, it worked.

In the kitchen, I took out the ingredients I needed and stared at them for a few minutes, trying to remember what to do with them. Cameron told me last week that his favourite thing to eat was seafood. We got into the conversation after somebody asked me to fetch some langoustines. I felt too stupid to ask him what a langoustine was so I found Cam and whispered the question in his ear instead. Smiling, he told me to look for something that resembled a big-ass prawn. *That* was the kind of terminology my limited food knowledge understood, although I was learning more every day. I could even pronounce some of the fancy pastries with French names that Derek produced in the hundreds every week.

So now, I stood at the granite counter, having a staring contest with the dead langoustines in front of me. I swear they were giving me the stink-eye. Alongside those, I had baby squid, mussels, and some turbot which Paul filleted for me before bringing it round, with some other ingredients, this morning after Cameron had left. I began with the mussels, cleaning them and removing the sticky stringy bits around the edge. That's called de-bearding, and yes, I felt a little chuffed that I'd remembered the correct term for it.

I hadn't actually made this dish myself before, but since I found out about Cameron's love for seafood I'd been paying extra attention to Anna's section as I worked, hovering over her shoulder whenever I got chance. Her special last week was the seafood risotto, and that's what I decided to try and replicate tonight.

Not only was tonight a way to say thank you, it was also to tell him that my test results came back negative yesterday. When the words left my doctor's mouth, the breath that followed felt like the first one I'd taken in years. My lungs felt bigger, my head lighter. I'd been a lucky son of a bitch. My addict brain told me I was safe because I used condoms, but my recovering brain knew that was bullshit. I didn't make punters wear condoms when I sucked them off. There were also times when I was so junk-sick after not being able to score for a few days, that I probably wouldn't have fucking noticed if they'd taken the damn rubber off.

Johns aside, I'd shared needles over the years, too. You care about this kinda shit in the beginning. You seek advice on harm reduction; use clean needles, don't use alone, stick to low doses. The first piece of advice is usually to *smoke* it, but I'd already bypassed chasing the dragon, diving straight into intravenous use on my first try. That wasn't the norm. I'd never met anyone else who'd began their relationship with heroin through a needle. But by the time I started, I was already somewhat of an experienced drug taker, so ignoring the advice to stay away from syringes, I sought out the best, safest, ways to inject instead.

You tell yourself you've got this, that you'll never let yourself get so desperate for a hit you'd risk fucking up your health. And that works really well…until you run out of smack.

I cooked the mussels first before draining them and mixing the cooking liquid, along with a little saffron, into some fish stock. While that heated to a simmer, I fried off some shallots and garlic in a separate pan, happy that, so far, I was rocking the shit out of this meal.

I noted the time on the clock next to the fridge as I reached into the cupboard for rice. *Shit.* Cameron could've been home any time now if he left the locking up to someone else. I must've been glowering at the langoustines and their beady little eyes for longer than I thought, earlier.

Crap! I hadn't prepped or cooked the langoustines yet. "Oh for twat's sake," I grumbled, scouring my face with my hands. My confidence began to wane. Time was running out and I'd forgotten to cook one of the main in-fucking-gredients. "Focus," I told myself, twisting and pulling at the first langoustine to separate the head and body from its tail. I repeated the process with all ten of the ugly little bastards before removing the meat from the tails. I tried to do it like they did at the restaurant, cracking the shell with my fingers, but it was fiddly and, quite frankly, I was shit at it. So, I ended up using scissors instead.

These fuckers were expensive, according to Paul, and it seemed like a whole lot of money and pissing about only to be left with a tiny piece of meat you could actually eat. After tonight, I decided

I hated langoustines. They looked evil and they pissed me off.

They better at least taste nice, I thought, blanching them in a pan of boiling water. Once they were cooked and drained, I started the rice. According to Gino D'Acampo, a celebrity chef who I watched on the telly last week, this was the hard part. In a much politer and television-friendly way, he basically said risotto was the easiest rice dish to fuck up. But…I was confident-*ish* as I added the stock to the rice one ladle at a time.

After twenty minutes of adding and stirring, I knew the only way to know it was ready was to taste it, seeking that *bite* in the centre. "Ugh," I mumbled, swishing it around in my mouth. I'd either just discovered I didn't like risotto, or I was a really shit cook. Still, the texture seemed correct, so I tossed in the langoustines, salt, pepper, and some grated lemon zest before pan-frying the turbot while the risotto simmered a little longer.

"Pan-frying," I said aloud, chuckling to myself. Check me out, sounding all professional. I always wondered why chefs said 'pan-fried'. What else would you fry shit in other than a fucking pan?

Cameron's key twisted in the lock as I chucked the mussels into the risotto and turned off the heat. I'd done it! I'd actually fucking done it! *Get in!*

I was about to look round to the opening door when I spotted the baby squid sitting untouched on the counter. "Oh, *dammit!*" Seemed I hadn't actually fucking done it after all.

"What's wrong?" Cameron asked, his voice panicked and flustered as he rushed over to me. His eyes scanned the kitchen, a curious half-smile pulling on the corners of his lips. "You cooked?"

"I tried. Forgot the fucking squid." I blew out a frustrated huff. The slimy little fuckers had been sitting right in front of me the whole time. How did I forget them?

Cameron popped the lid on the pan, sneaking a peek at the risotto. "Wow," he breathed, getting his nose up close and personal to the rice. "I'm impressed."

I shrugged, deflated. "It was supposed to have squid in it. Paul said you love squid."

"Paul's very right," he said, backing away from the stove and pulling a knife from the wooden block. "It takes a minute, literally, to cook. Heat up some olive oil and butter."

"So I haven't ruined it?"

"You will if you don't hurry up," he said, smiling.

Nodding, I bounced around like an excited toddler, heating a frying pan like he said while he did his Super Chef chopping thing.

When he brought the sliced squid over to the pan, his gaze landed on the mess I'd created, specifically the discarded langoustine heads. "You shelled these yourself?"

"Yeah. Did I do it wrong?"

He let out a small sigh, one that confused me a little. It wasn't a sad or frustrated sigh. For some reason, it made me feel kinda wonderful. "No,

Dylan. You didn't do it wrong. I'm just…I'm proud of you."

His words made time stand still. *I'm proud of you.* I repeated it in my head. I couldn't remember the last time someone said that to me. In fact, I wasn't sure anyone ever had.

Cameron turned the gas off when, after a minute like he'd said, the baby squid was golden and cooked through. "Go sit down," I said, shooing him away with my hand.

"Waited on too?" He smiled, and it was perfect. "What've I done to deserve this?"

More than you'll ever know. Outwardly, I ignored his question as he walked away, and concentrated on the task at hand. I scattered the squid around the top of the risotto before drizzling the entire thing with some lemon juice and some chopped green crap that I was pretty sure was parsley. *That's* when I remembered I was supposed to add dry white wine along with the stock. *Fuck.* It was too late to do anything about it now so I scooped two portions into bowls before placing the turbot, which no doubt was overcooked and rubbery by now, on top.

Sucking my bottom lip into my mouth, I chewed it gently while staring at my creation. It didn't look all that pretty, but hopefully it tasted okay. At the restaurant, I'd often see servers walking around with four or more plates stacked along their arms, whereas I shuffled slowly, my face twisted in concentration as I carried just *two* dishes to the table where Cam sat waiting for me.

I placed his meal in front of him, my pulse quickening with nerves, before taking a seat opposite. Picking up our forks, we took a bite at the same time.

Honestly, I wanted to spit mine right back out. "I don't know what I did wrong," I said, chugging on a glass of water in an attempt to eradicate the disgusting taste in my mouth. *Must be the wine*, I decided. I'd hoped the lack of it wouldn't make too much difference.

"Wrong?" Cam asked before shovelling another forkful into his mouth. "It's pretty damn perfect, Dyl."

I looked at his plate, then at mine. They were almost identical, yet I couldn't bring myself to place another forkful of that shit anywhere near my tongue.

Pushing my bowl away from me, I said, "Seriously, don't feel the need to be nice. I can take it."

I studied Cam's face as he carried on eating. It didn't *look* like he was faking the small groans of pleasure that trickled from his mouth with every few bites. "Do you like seafood?"

I thought about it for a second, trying to remember any fish dishes I'd ever eaten. "I like fish fingers. Oh, and battered cod from the chippy."

"Oh, Dylan Roberts..." Cameron laughed a little. "I have so much I need to introduce you to!"

"Yeah, if it comes from the sea I think I'll pass."

Cameron shook his head like he had other ideas. "There is so much wonderful food out there. Don't give up until you've tried *everything* there is to offer, which will take a lifetime. This risotto is overpowering to someone new to seafood. With the rich stock and meaty turbot, packed with such an intense ocean flavour..." He spoke with his hands as he talked about food, like words alone couldn't accurately express just how enthusiastic he was. I didn't share his passion, not about fish at least, but I enjoyed watching the spark in his eyes, the smile on his face.

"I bet I can come up with a fish dish you'll enjoy." His words tumbled from his lips like a challenge, his brown eyes narrowing with mischief. He looked...beautiful. Those eyes were the same ones I used to dream about, long to see again. I think this was the first time it'd really hit me that this stunning man in front of me was Cameron. *My* Cameron. My best friend in the whole world.

I didn't want to, I knew he deserved better, but...I loved him.

"You okay?" His voice snapped me from my thoughts, and when he reached out and placed his hand on my forearm, my heart jumped in my chest. His touch felt special, wonderful. I could feel the heat from his skin all the way through my body.

Oh shit. My cock started to swell and I shifted in my seat. *Not now. Not here.* "I got my test results today," I blurted, changing the subject to something my dick wouldn't find interesting.

The colour seemed to drain from Cameron's face in slow motion as his head fell forward a little. Only then did I remember his last question, and that he must've taken my quietness for concern.

"Shit, no. They were negative. I got the all clear."

A rush of pent up air flew from his mouth. "Jesus, Dyl," he breathed. "Your face. You had me worried there. That's great news."

"I was lucky," I mumbled, shrugging. I didn't feel like I had the right to be pleased when I was the one who'd been careless in the first place. "I need retesting for HIV in three months, just to be sure."

With a serious expression, his lips set in a firm line, he nodded. "I'll put it in the calendar on my phone."

The simple task made me smile. He really *did* care about me. I felt like the luckiest motherfucker in the world.

When I looked down at Cameron's bowl I was shocked to see it completely empty, bar the mussel shells. It brought yet another smile to my lips, which quickly evaporated when his thumb started drawing small circles on the underside of my arm. My flesh broke out in goosebumps, and the tiny hairs on the back of my neck stood to attention. There was no way he couldn't have noticed, and so I snatched my arm away, forcing a cough to clear the lump clogging my throat.

"Better start clearing up," I muttered, my voice awkward and timid as I picked up our dishes, carrying them over to the sink.

The legs of Cam's chair screeched in protest as he pulled away from the table, and soon enough he stood so close to me I could feel his breath on my neck. "Thank you, Dylan," he whispered directly into my ear. "The meal, and your company, was perfect."

You're welcome. I planned to say it aloud but my lips wouldn't work. I couldn't speak. I could barely breathe with his body so near mine. I didn't understand what was happening to me.

Turning my face, my heated cheek became flush with Cameron's. He stood behind me, his hand on my hip, and I almost moved his fingers to the front, wondering what they'd feel like pressed against my cock. I was hard, of course I was. I'd been permanently horny for weeks now. Touching myself, however, was one thing. Letting someone else…

"I don't know what's happening here," I whispered, my lips so close to his I could almost taste them. I felt a little dizzy. My heart raced, my mouth dried. "I…I feel…"

Pushing on my hip, Cameron turned me around to face him. He cupped my cheek with his palm, his gaze travelling up my face, to my hair, before landing back on my eyes. Leaning in, he pressed the tip of his nose to mine. "I feel it, too," he breathed, sliding his hand to the back of my neck.

"I-I don't know what to do." My words stammered along with my breath. It felt like my heart was trying to crawl into my throat.

"Whatever you want. *You're* in charge here, Dyl."

Me? I didn't have a clue how to be in charge. I knew how to please him, how to make men feel good. *Is that what he means?*

"Can I kiss you?" Cameron whispered, his lips mere millimetres from mine.

Too breathless to speak coherently, I simply nodded.

He began by feathering gentle pecks onto my closed lips before running the tip of his tongue along the seam. I opened my mouth for him instinctively, my pulse thudding in my ears as I reached up to cup his neck. He flicked my tongue with his, before licking and tasting every corner of my mouth. It felt so new to me. Kissing wasn't something I'd had much practice with since being a clumsy fourteen year old. The only men I'd ever been with were only interested in shoving their dicks in my mouth or my arse. They didn't savour me. They didn't *care*. I was little more than a breathing blow-up doll for them to do whatever they wanted to.

This kiss was unlike anything I'd ever experienced. It didn't take me back to being a teenager. Kissing Cameron *now* was much different. His skin was rough against mine, his lips firmer. He tasted phenomenal even with traces of the seafood lingering in his mouth.

This felt… incredible. Warm. Gentle. Passionate. This kiss made me feel like I *meant* something.

Cameron smiled into our kiss before pulling back, the loss of his touch making me sag in disappointment.

"You wash, I'll dry," he said, turning to the dirty dishes.

What? That's it? He didn't want anything else?

I stood, frozen, my mouth slightly agape as I ran the pad of my finger along my lips. They were tingly and a little numb. It felt bizarrely brilliant. Cameron's cock was hard, I'd felt it rubbing against my own through his trousers. So why didn't he need me to relieve it for him? Was I no good? A bad kisser?

Am I not enough for him?

My questions were internal, but the battle must've been visible on my face because he leaned back into my side, pressing his lips to my cheek. "One step at a time," he murmured.

I wasn't sure how I felt. I thought I should be happy that he wasn't pushing me, but I couldn't help wondering *why* he wasn't. Was that kiss meant for *me*, too? Why didn't he want more? They *always* wanted more.

"They won't wash themselves," Cameron said with a teasing smile, snapping me back into reality. It seemed we'd moved on.

I'd obsess over what that kiss meant later.

Chapter

Nine

~Cameron~

"HE'S DOING WELL. Don't you think?"

Paul and I were in my office after evening service. Dylan was out in the kitchen with some of the other guys, cleaning and prepping for tomorrow.

"Seems to be," Paul said. I didn't like the lack of sincerity in his eyes, though.

"You don't look convinced."

"It's only been a few weeks. He's not had his counselling yet, so who knows what's going on his head."

"So you think he still thinks about it? About using?"

"I've no doubt." He looked at me like I was stupid. "He'll *always* think about it, Cam."

"Hmm." I knew this was something I needed to talk to Dylan about, but I'd been too afraid in case I pushed him before he was ready. "I kissed him last night."

"Yeah?"

"Yeah? That's it? You're not going to yell or tell me I don't know what I'm getting into?"

Paul snickered, and I almost wanted to punch him in the face. "After what you've been through, the things you've witnessed over the last few weeks, I'm pretty sure you know exactly what you're getting into."

I smiled, grateful that he understood, that he was my friend.

"So you *just* kissed?"

"I won't push him any further until he's ready. Not after-" *Shit.*

"After what?"

"N-nothing," I stuttered. I was a crap liar and both Paul and I knew it. *Dammit!* Dylan's secrets weren't mine to share, but suddenly, the things I knew started gnawing away at my insides. I flexed my fingers as tension built in my fists. I knew so much about Dylan, things that made my heart feel like it could burst. I needed to get it out – the pain, the burden. I needed somebody to tell me Dylan would get past these things, that he'd be okay.

"After *what*, Cameron?" Paul's tone was low, saturated with concern, and I realised it was because there was a silent tear trickling down my cheek. I quickly swiped it away, blowing out a puff of air.

"Dylan was, hell I don't even know what the right term is… A rentboy? A prostitute?"

Paul's back stiffened in his chair. "Holy fuck. I'm not overly shocked, but holy fuck."

"You're not?"

Paul shrugged. "Addiction makes them desperate. I know John used to steal. Hell, he spent more nights in a police cell than his own fucking house. Maybe he did more, I'll never know. I'm not justifying his behaviour, but on some level I understand how they get to that point."

"I don't," I admitted. I'd tried, but I couldn't even imagine something having so much power over me. "Sometimes, I look at him and think *why*. I know I shouldn't but I can't help it. I can't help imagining him with those…*men*. I feel like I should be angry with him. Disgusted. But instead I just *hurt* for him. I want to keep him safe. I want, *need* him to know I'd *never* want or expect anything he isn't ready to give me. So, yes, we just kissed, and that's all we'll do until *he* wants it to go further."

A knock sounded on the door just as Paul opened his mouth to reply. It was Dylan, and the sight of him made my cheeks redden as I prayed he hadn't overheard our conversation.

"Um, Derek wants to know where his palette knives are."

Paul's lips twisted into a mischievous half-smile, while I just shook my head. I felt like a father rather than a friend to these two guys sometimes.

"Does he now? Well why can't the old man ask me himself?"

"It went something along the lines of, 'if I go in there I'll end up ramming my fist so far down his throat it'll exit through his arse.'"

"I'd like to see him try," Paul said, laughing. "Tell him I haven't seen his precious knives."

He had. He knew it, *I* knew it, and Derek knew it.

"Grow up, Paul," I said, grinning.

Ignoring me, Paul continued to chuckle as he stood up and walked over to the coat hook by the door, grabbing his jacket and pushing his arms into the sleeves. "I'll see you tomorrow, guys," he said, smirking as he bent down to pick up his bag that almost certainly had Derek's knives inside.

Rolling my eyes, I watched Paul walk away before standing up to approach Dylan. "Good day?" I asked after pecking his cheek with my lips.

"Great," he replied through a wide, genuine smile. "Derek taught me how to make the pastry for his millefeuilles today."

"Hey! You pronounced it perfectly!"

The excitement on his face made my chest swell with pride. I wasn't sure why Derek had taken a shine to Dylan. Cookery wasn't something Dylan had been employed to learn, although it made me ecstatic to see his interest in pastry growing. He wasn't a junior chef. It wasn't Derek's job to teach him. It made me wonder if Paul had told Derek more than he should have, though it didn't seem like something he'd do. I trusted Paul with my life.

Honestly, whatever Derek's reasons, I didn't really care. It made Dylan happy. It helped him heal. That was all that mattered to me.

"So, are you interested in pastry?" I asked, eager to hear his response.

"Dunno. Could be. Derek makes it look interesting. And sweet Jesus, his stuff tastes amazing. *Nothing* like that fish shit I served you."

"For the fortieth time, that risotto was near perfect."

"*Near.* Exactly. The fact it tasted like shit stopped it hitting perfect."

"*No.* The fact it was a tad under-seasoned and you forgot the wine made it imperfect, but it was pretty damn close. Still tasted divine." Honestly, I think he believed me and just enjoyed being praised.

"So, um, what should I tell Derek about the knives?"

"Leave 'em to it," I said. "Derek will take something of Paul's, then Paul will do something else to annoy Derek…it's a never-ending cycle."

Dylan grinned, then looked a little confused. "Why doesn't he just use the other knives? This kitchen has more utensils than I've ever seen in my life."

"Because they're not *his* knives. Every chef has their own quirk, things they hold dear."

"Like my lucky pencil?"

With those few words it felt like Dylan had started singing. He rarely mentioned the past, and if *I* did he'd either close down or quickly twist the conversation onto something else. I let my mind wander back to that pencil, remembering it vividly. It was blue, chewed around the end, and he took it to every test we had. "Yeah. Just like your pencil. Do you still have it?" I figured he didn't, seeing as he came to me with only a small holdall and his father's guitar.

"Nah. I imagine the council trashed it with all my other stuff after my grandma died."

I often wondered about those missing years, the things he did after he moved away. I assumed he didn't end up a drug addict the same day, so I was curious about the in-between. Maybe one day I'd find the courage to ask him to fill in the gaps.

"My thing is a tea-towel," I said. "It's embroidered with the college logo. I took it by accident when I was a culinary student, walked home without noticing it was still draped over my shoulder. It's stained and worn, but it's followed me through my whole career. It's in my desk drawer. Thankfully, Paul's only interested in riling up Derek."

"That's because he's into him."

He'd said this before yet, again, I'd never heard anything so ridiculous. Paul was like a brother to me. I'd have known if he liked someone that way. *Wouldn't I?*

Shaking my head at the ludicrous notion, I pulled mine, then Dylan's coat from the rack. "Ready to go?"

"Almost. I just need to set up Derek's section for the morning. He's coming in early to try out some new ideas."

"Don't let him use you as his personal slave," I said. "That's not why you're here."

"I don't mind. Really, I quite enjoy helping him actually."

That made me feel...happy. Relieved. *Hopeful.*

"I won't be long," he added.

"No problem. Anna's locking up so I'll wait in the car."

There was something oddly domesticated about this moment, like we were a real couple, living the life we used to dream about up in my bedroom together. Truth is I didn't know what we were. There wasn't a label for what we had. I figured the term *best friend* would suffice. That's what I was to him. It's what I'd always been, what I always *would* be, regardless of whether anything romantic happened between us.

My best friend was back. *He's here.* The thought made me smile.

* * *

I was still awake a couple of hours after climbing into bed, so I got up for a glass of water. After pulling on some joggers, I crept through the apartment so I didn't disturb Dylan, but as I filled my glass, his sleepy voice danced into my ears like a beautiful song, making my heart thump in my chest.

"Can't sleep?" he asked, patting the empty side of the foldout mattress.

I took a sip of water and put the glass down on the counter before padding across the room to join him. Dropping to my knees, I crawled onto his bed and sat up next to him, pulling the duvet up to my waist.

"Brain won't switch off," I said, enjoying the warmth of his bare arm against mine. He was almost naked, only dressed in his boxers. My gaze travelled down his skin, admiring the dusting of light hair on his forearm. But then I saw that faded scar, just above his hip, again. "What happened?" I asked, my voice gentle as I pointed to the raised silvery line.

"I was stabbed." He said it so matter-of-factly, like it was no big deal.

My jaw dropped open. "W…how…" I couldn't even think of words, let alone translate them into speech.

"I got into a fight. My own fault. A guy sold me some gear cut with fuck knows what. It made me really sick, so I took him on despite him being four times the size of me. Let's just say…I came off worse."

"I can't even imagine dealing with memories like that." I hadn't meant to say it out loud, but I had, so decided I might as well continue. "How do you cope with that?"

"Don't have much choice. It happened. Can't take it back. Can't take any of it back."

Instinctively, my hand reached out for his, curling my fingers around it. "Do you wish you could?"

"Course I do. When I think about how things might've been if my grandma hadn't died when she did...well, it hurts. So I don't think about it."

"I'd like you to think about it." I rushed the words out before I had chance to change my mind. "I want to know all about you, about your life after we were separated."

Dylan sighed, tipping his head back to stare at the ceiling. "You know the important stuff."

"I know about your addiction, about the things surrounding your addiction, but that's not all you are, Dyl. You're *not* heroin. You're so much *more,* and I want to know about it."

Dylan didn't speak. I'd told him I wouldn't push until he was ready but I needed *something.* Anything.

"What happened with your foster family?"

"I was a bastard, that's what happened. I had four sets of foster parents. The first weren't so bad. They were nice enough, but they were only temporary. They had a whole house full of foster kids. The second lot were only in it for the money. The dad, Pete, he was a nasty piece of work. Used to knock us about, blame the bruises on sports we didn't even play, feed us his leftovers, that kinda shit."

"Didn't you tell anyone?"

Dylan shook his head.

"Why not? They would've took you out of there, surely."

He simply shrugged, concentrating on his fingers as he pinched at the duvet. "I was scared. He was a grown up, and he held a hell of a lot of weight behind those fists. Anyway, by the time I moved in with my fourth family I didn't want to be with them. I wanted my Granny Roberts, I wanted my dad, I wanted *you*. So I made their life hell. I stole from Jenny, my foster mother, to buy cider. I'd go out all night, get drunk all on my own. Sometimes I'd disappear for days at a time. We got into an argument one day when she caught me nicking from her purse. I trashed the whole living room in temper, smashed up their TV. I pushed her too far that day. She had other kids to worry about. I've always told myself they got fed up of me, abandoned me, didn't try hard enough, but I do that because it's easier than admitting I was a selfish, violent bastard."

He went on to tell me about all the years that followed; the jobs he had, the friends he made and lost, and how he got into drugs. I did nothing except listen, hold his hand, *hurt* for him. My heart must've broken over twenty times while he spoke, but when he finished and smiled at me, a *real* genuine smile, it put all the shattered pieces back together again.

"So what about you?" he asked. "I'm guessing you didn't walk right out of high school and straight into your first Michelin star."

I chuckled. "Not quite. I became one of the youngest chefs in the country to have a star by my name, but I worked *hard* for it. After you left, I kept my head down, worked hard towards my GCSE's, then I applied to study culinary arts."

"Who did you hang out with? I often wondered that. We never really bothered with anyone else at school."

"No one, really. I kept to myself. Didn't really make any new friends until I went to college. That's where I met Paul. From then on, we kinda stuck together. Went on to work in the same restaurants. My parents helped me raise the capital I needed to open O'Neil's, which is the only reason I owned my own restaurant before he did. He's more than capable of running his own business, and he's a phenomenal cook."

I was lucky to have successful parents who could help me out. They didn't sleep on sheets made from fifty-pound notes or anything, my mum owned a florist and my dad owned a car lot, but we'd always been comfortable as a family. Growing up, Dylan lived on a council estate in a really rough part of town, whereas my parents owned, through a mortgage, their own four-bedroom house just outside Chelsea.

From birth, my life had always been on a better course than Dylan's, for no other reason than pot luck. His dad worked just as hard as mine did, but he didn't reap the same benefits. Life just isn't fucking fair.

"But you guys never got together?"

A rush of laughter burst through my nose. "Oh, hell no! Never even came close. I think of Paul like my brother. My very immature little brother."

"You must've been with other people though?" His tone was laced with sadness and regret, and I understood why. I always thought I'd lose my virginity to Dylan, and I knew he felt the same. We used to talk about it all the time, even planned how it would happen when we both felt ready.

"I have. Nobody significant. I've only had one serious relationship, but it didn't work out." Kevin still texted me, though the frequency was thankfully declining. I'd stopped replying as soon as Dylan came back into my life. He didn't make me happy, not really. Being together simply became convenient. Kevin was a lying cheat who wore too much cologne. He could go to hell for all I cared.

"Sorry," Dylan muttered. "So…" he trailed off, as if trying to decide how to change the subject. "How'd your parents take you coming out? Remember when we used to plan what we were going to say?"

I smiled at the memory. "Yeah, I do. Didn't quite happen like we planned though. My mum found a gay porn DVD under my bed when I was fifteen."

Dylan laughed, throwing his head back. "Oh, God! What did she say?"

"She said, and I quote, *I hope you didn't waste a fortune on this. I know a fella on the market who sells 'em*

195

for a fiver." Just the memory of that conversation made me cringe. "And that was it. That's my coming out story. From then on it was never an issue. I told her I fancied someone at school and she automatically asked who *he* was."

"That's probably the most perfect coming out story I've ever heard. If I'd ever had the chance to come out, I'd have wanted it to go down just like that."

The smile melted from my face and my heart felt heavy, like it could slip into my stomach. I felt desperately sad for him in this moment. When you realise you're not straight, that you weren't born with the default setting society assumes you will have, coming out becomes a big deal. You plan the conversation over and over in your head. You hope you'll be accepted, yet imagine how you'll feel, how you'll cope, if you're not. It's the pinnacle moment when you've accepted who you are, who you were born to be, and you're ready for the ones you love to embrace you on your journey. It's a day you never forget.

I found it devastating that Dylan never got the opportunity he deserved, that he didn't *have* anybody to come out to.

"Come out to me," I said, shifting my arse on the makeshift bed so I could face him.

He pursed his eyebrows in confusion. "*What?*"

"You never got the chance to come out. It's like a right of passage. Do it now, to *me.*"

Dylan laughed, an adorable snort flowing from his nose. "You *know* I'm gay, Cam."

"Dylan, have you had a good day? Got a girlfriend yet?" I asked, ignoring his protest.

"This is silly," he said, a cute blush pinking his cheeks. "Do you have a DVD I can strategically place for you to find?"

"It's 2016. All my porn is on my laptop." I nudged his shoulder with mine before continuing. "Do it like you planned. Get it out."

Shaking his head, yet still smiling, Dylan let out a loud exhale. "There's something I need to talk to you about," he began, looking me right in the eye. "I want you to know that I'm sure, that I've known for a long time. I'm happy with who I am, and I hope you can be too."

"You're not getting a motorbike, not as long as I'm alive, young man. I won't watch you become a heart and lungs for someone."

Dylan's nose scrunched. "What are you doing?"

"I'm being Granny Roberts. That's who you were going to come out to first, right?" I was kind of offended he didn't recognise my impression. "Whenever you had news for her she *always* thought you were going to get…*one of those death traps*." I mimicked her voice again, pleased with the smile it brought out on Dylan's face.

"She did." He smiled a sad smile. "She used to say I'd end up covered in tattoos and dead by twenty-five if I went near one of those monstrosities."

"I'm going to pretend you've said it's not the bike. So, what it is it, sweetheart? What's bothering you?"

"It's Cam. We're not just friends anymore. I...I love him. Grandma...I'm gay."

Grinning, I widened my eyes. "Well I can't say I blame you. That Cameron is a sexy son of a bitch."

He ripped the pillow from behind his back so fast I didn't see it coming until it hit me in the face. "She would *not* have said that!"

"Course she would! Your gran thought I was the bomb!"

"She thought you were a nice lad, but I'm pretty sure she'd have been arrested for thinking her *fourteen* year old grandson's friend was sexy."

"It's true though. I'm hot, right?" My teasing brought the most precious smile to Dylan's face and I wished I could stare at it forever. He had a real toothy smile, so bright and wide. It illuminated his whole face, made his green eyes sparkle. He looked...happy.

Just for tonight I told myself everything was going to be okay. We were the Cam and Dyl we were supposed to grow into. I loved him, and he loved me. Just for tonight...the last sixteen years never happened.

Dylan's smile eventually faded and he just...stared at me. His face inched closer to mine, so slowly I didn't notice it happening until his lips grazed mine. A tiny gasp leaked from my throat as every nerve in my body buzzed with anticipation, and I had to fight against the urge to pin him down and take him. This couldn't be about *me*, or what *I* wanted. I needed Dylan to take the lead, let him guide me, *trust* me.

When his tongue stroked over my lips I parted them, allowing him entry into my mouth as my hand reached up to cup his cheek. Smoothing my thumb over the fine gathering of stubble coating his skin, I tangled our tongues together, licking, sucking, savouring every moment of this beautiful kiss. Everything about this moment was incredible, the feel of him almost overwhelming.

Tucking one hand behind my neck, his other travelled lower, slipping into the waistband of my joggers.

Breaking our kiss, my fingers clamped around his wrist before he had a chance to go any further. "Is this what you want?" I whispered. "Do you *want* to touch me?" I had to be certain he wasn't doing something he thought was expected of him.

A look of embarrassment heated his cheeks. Suddenly, he seemed nervous and awkward. I didn't want that either. *I've ruined it.*

"*I* want you to," I said, combing my fingers through his hair. Holy hell I *wanted* him. My swollen cock ached beneath the material of my trousers, desperate to feel him. "Please don't think I don't want you, Dyl. I *do*. But know I don't want you to do anything just for *me*. This is about *us*. You're in charge here." I'd said it before, and I would keep saying it until he understood, until he *believed*.

His brow crumpled, like he felt a little lost, like he didn't *know* to take control. Like…he didn't know *why* I wanted this to be about him. "I…" His words fell away as he swallowed. "I *want* to touch you."

If I didn't know better, and honestly I wished I didn't, I'd have thought this was his first time. His touch was gentle and unsure as he explored all the bumps and ridges of my cock with the pads of his fingers.

"Take your joggers off," he said, his words splitting as they left his mouth.

Never taking my eyes off his, I shimmied out of my jog-pants, my cock bouncing off my belly, and lay down flat on the foldout mattress. At first, he simply looked at me, raking his gaze up and down my naked body, sucking his bottom lip between his teeth.

I have no idea how long he watched me for. Time became immeasurable. After what could've been seconds or hours, his hand stuttered above my cock before he held it in limp fingers, as if gauging the weight, the feel of it. I tried not to buck my hips, not to force myself deeper into his fist, but I couldn't help it. In a lot of ways this felt new to me too. I'd never wanted, *needed* anyone so badly.

"Do you like that?" he whispered, his grip tightening around my shaft.

"Yes. Oh, God, yes." I forced myself to focus on Dylan's face, on the curious expression he wore, on the tiny freckle under his eye, rather than the sensations exploding in my dick. It'd been too long since anyone had touched me this way, and I was sure if I didn't tune out I would shoot all over his hand with just two more strokes.

I grabbed the back of his head, pulling him down into a kiss, needing the pleasure of his lips to distract me from that in my cock. "I want to touch you, too," I said into his mouth. "Can I do that?"

He pulled his head back. "You're...you're *asking* me?"

"Yes, Dylan. I'm asking you. Asking if you're ready, if you want it, want *me*."

Swallowing slowly, he nodded.

Rolling onto my side, I pulled on his shoulders, encouraging him to lie down with me. His hard cock tented his white boxer shorts, and I tugged them down, letting it spring free, before running my flattened fingers down his chest. I kissed along his collarbone, then down his stomach, before settling on the scar above his hip. I kissed the raised flesh while sliding my hand down to his balls, massaging them gently between my fingers.

Dylan sighed with a hum as I explored every inch of his cock. I dragged my fist up and down, my rhythm slow and steady, and somehow I felt each stroke in my own cock, my tip throbbing, my balls aching with need. Desperate to taste him, I lowered my head, hovering my lips over his bulbous tip.

"No." Dylan put his finger under my chin, raising my head. "Not until I've had my HIV screen repeated. I'm not putting you at risk."

The irresponsible, horny-as-hell part of me wanted to argue, but I knew he was right, so I was careful not to let the disappointment show on my face.

Smiling, I rolled onto my back. "What we do next is up to you."

"Oh."

In an attempt to ease his obvious nerves, I reached out and took his hand. "I'll take whatever you're prepared to give me." I pulled his hand onto my chest. "You can touch me *anywhere*. If you want *me* to touch *you*, just take my hand and guide me."

Kneeling, he stared at me for a moment like he did earlier. Then, he crawled to the bottom of the mattress, positioning himself between my legs.

I watched his face as he ran his hands over my thighs, slowly inching towards my cock. Pressing it flush against my belly, he smoothed his palm from tip to root, along my balls, then onto my arse. Spreading my cheeks with his fingers, he seemed to study my hole with a look of intrigue in his eyes.

I was completely exposed to him, willing him to do whatever he wanted, take whatever he needed from me.

He didn't make eye-contact with me, keeping his focus on the task at hand as a drizzle of spit rolled off his lips and between my arse cheeks. The sight alone made my cock throb, and I gripped it firmly at the base to stop me bursting onto my stomach already. With one finger, he drew tiny circles over the puckered skin, rubbing in the moisture before plunging inside. "D-do you…never mind." His voice was low, hesitant, as he pulled his finger from my body.

Pulling myself up just a little, I curled my fingers around his forearm. "Say it, Dyl."

"I, uh…" He dropped his head a little before gazing up at me through his eyelashes. "Do you bottom?"

Excitement pooled in my stomach. I *did* bottom. I'd always considered myself verse, but if I *had* to choose a favourite, bottoming would win outright. "I do," I said, but then my smile faded. "But only if you want to."

"I do." He looked uncertain, which unnerved me a little. "But, um, I've never done it before. Topped, I mean. I don't know if I'll be any good."

I tried not to be surprised, tried not to think of the…*things*… Dylan had admitted to doing to fund his addiction, because those thoughts made me feel staggeringly sad. But…here I was, thinking of it anyway, wondering how it was possible he'd never topped while hoping it didn't show in my expression.

I pushed the thoughts away. I *had* to before it consumed me, ruined this magical moment I was spending with him. "Dyl," I whispered, sitting up further so I could stroke his cheek with my thumb. "You have no idea how hard I've been fighting the urge to come since the moment you started touching me. It's impossible for *anything* you do to me to feel anything less than incredible."

Dylan's lips twisted into a coy smile and he turned into my touch, kissing my palm. "Are you sure you want to do this with…with *me?*"

Pressing my nose to his, I whispered, "I've wanted to do this with you since I was fourteen years old." I kissed him softly with lingering lips before clambering to my feet, gutted I had to break our intimacy while I jogged to my bedroom to grab a condom and some lube.

I was back, holding him in my arms, within seconds. I held his face close to mine as I kissed his lips until my own felt a little numb. Then, I peppered kisses along his jaw and neck before slowly lying back down. Reaching out, I took his hand, dripping lube onto his fingers before guiding them towards my hole. He let me push two fingers inside and I held his wrist, encouraging him to work them in and out of my body over and over again.

He watched his hand, studied his fingers and what they were doing. His gaze was inquisitive, maybe a little unsure, and every so often he would look up to my face as if to check I really felt okay with this.

"I need you, Dylan," I said, my voice a breathy whisper.

Acknowledging my plea, he nodded and slid his fingers free from my hole, and from my gentle grip around his wrist. He seemed to roll the condom down his length in slow motion, but that could've been due to my impatience. I wanted, *needed* the closeness, the feeling of us connecting as one person.

Taking the lube, he squeezed a generous amount into his palm before stroking it over his cock, the clear liquid glistening in the faint trail of light coming from the lamp. "Are you ready?"

My breaths were short and shallow. "I've been ready for this moment forever."

With his hands on my thighs, he crawled into position, using his hand to guide his cock to my entrance. He pushed in slowly with a deep, guttural sigh, making my breath stop in my throat. I was tight around him, a little *too* tight at first, but I breathed through the sting, watching the lines of tension evaporate from Dylan's face with each gentle thrust.

Holding his shoulders, I pulled him forwards so I could kiss him, hooking my legs around his waist. Small, thinner than I, he was light on my chest as I wound my arms around his back, gripping him close to me. Breaking our kiss to gather air, I buried my face into his neck, kissing and licking the sweat that misted his soft skin as he started to move faster and harder inside me.

"Fuck, Dylan..." I groaned in-between pants. "I love being this close to you."

His stomach rubbed against my cock as he moved, causing pressure - delicious, heavy pressure – to build in my balls. The base of my spine tingled. Blood buzzed in my ears. I was close. I didn't want to be, didn't want this to end, but... "Oh, my...*fuck!*" I ground the words through gritted teeth, ribbons of hot cum spurting between our bodies.

The slickness made his chest slide effortlessly against mine as he gripped my shoulder and drove into me so hard the couch started to move. Heat crept across his neck and cheeks, and his lips attacked mine with more passion than I'd ever experienced in my life, before he cried out into my mouth. "Holy shi…I love you, Cam."

My chest ceased rising mid-breath, and the second Dylan's orgasm dwindled a look of shock registered on his abruptly pale face. "I-I'm sorry. I didn't mean…I mean you don't-"

"It's *okay*, Dylan," I interrupted, placing a finger over his lips. "I love you, too. I've *always* loved you."

"I just…" He took a deep breath. "You give me a reason to be better. You make me think that I *can* be better."

Taking his face in my hands, I kissed him.

"And are, well are you…*okay?* Do you need me to leave you alone for a while?" he asked, avoiding eye-contact.

Oh, Dylan. He didn't get it. He still didn't fully understand what we just did, what we'd shared together. Is that how he usually felt…*after?* Did he want to run away, forget it as soon as he could?

Of course he did.

Wordless, my chest aching, I brought him in for another kiss; a slow, sensual, savouring kiss that lasted for what could've been hours, before we eventually drifted to sleep in each other's arms.

* * *

The next day I woke up in a slight panic when I felt the cold, empty pillow beside me. It only intensified when I saw a note on the coffee table. Dylan's notes never led to good things in the past, and I couldn't help wondering if I'd taken things too far last night, if he wasn't ready.

With a racing heart, I reached out to take the paper.

Gone to work early. Derek's showing me how to make panna cotta. Love, Dyl.

Clutching the paper to my chest, a sigh of relief flooded the air. The unexpected interest he'd taken in pastry made me smile, and I started to wonder how I could help him develop his knowledge. I guessed it was too soon into his recovery to start thinking about college and apprenticeships, but his enthusiasm was wasted as a busboy. He was so smart at school, smarter than *me*. He'd get A's in tests without even having to revise, whereas I had to stay up until two AM studying my arse off. He used to gloat all the time about having a brain that absorbed information really easily, usually accompanied by a wicked grin that made my permanently-horny teenage-cock stiffen instantaneously. I missed those days. I missed that grin.

As I got up and took myself off to the shower, I decided I'd talk to Paul about Dylan's options before work. He could be a phenomenal chef if he put his mind to it. I always knew he'd be great at whatever career he chose, he just never got the chance to find one.

I got to Paul's around an hour later. As usual, I walked into the flat unannounced, quickly regretting that decision when I caught him balls-deep in a guy I'd never seen before on his kitchen floor.

"Oh crap," I said, turning straight back around and out into the hallway that housed the stairs which led to the street outside. The walls in this building clearly weren't as thick as Paul thought they were, and I heard laughter followed by an encore of moans and grunts.

I can't believe he's finishing! There's no way *I* could have, knowing my best mate was standing just feet away. I removed myself from earshot, walking over to the stairs and perching my butt on the top one. Paul's arse was firmly burned into my mind and I literally shuddered as I tried to shake the image away.

I sat there for almost twenty minutes before the flat door opened. "I'll call you," Paul said before kissing the guy's cheek. As I stood up to let the lad past, I glowered at Paul, becoming even more annoyed when I got a smirk in return.

"I can't believe you actually finished," I said, purposely knocking into him as I stomped into his flat.

Paul shrugged, a smug smile dancing on his lips. "What can I say? He felt too good."

"Ugh," I grumbled, striding over to his black leather couch and plopping myself down. "And in the *kitchen?* You prepare food in there!"

Again, he shrugged, before pulling a T-shirt over his head. "I'll mop the floor."

"Who is he anyway?"

"Dunno. Met him on Grindr last night. Darren…or David. Or was it D-"

"Grindr?" I interrupted. "Since when has *Grindr* been your thing?"

"Since relationships always end in me being miserable."

Damn. Now I felt sorry for him and his stupid puppy-eyes.

"I just want some fun before I get old and shrivelled. Is that so bad?"

"Guess not. As long as you're being careful."

"Yes, Dad. I'm being safe I promise."

Arsehole. "Anyway, I came to talk about Dylan."

"Ah, so I'm not the only one who got laid last night, huh? Thought you were walking funny."

"*What?*"

"It's written all over your face," he said, joining me on the couch. He flipped the recliner and sprawled out with his head on the back cushions.

"No it isn't." I rolled my eyes. "That's not what I came here to talk about."

"How was it? Good, I'm guessin', seeing as you can't say his name without getting the same dreamy look in your eye that I used to get wanking off to my Patrick Swayze poster."

"You wanked off to Patrick Swayze?"

"I was thirteen. I wanked off to everybody. Anyway, you didn't answer my question."

"Yes, okay? It was mind-blowing. Satisfied?"

He chuckled, and I hated him as much as I loved him. "How's he doing?" he asked, his tone turning serious. "He looks to be doing well at work, but how is he *really?*"

"Good. Great, I think. He said I'm a reason for him to be better. So that's good, right?"

"Are you telling me or asking?"

Umm. I wasn't quite sure anymore. His expression made me think I wouldn't like his opinion, and usually when I didn't like what Paul had to say it was because he was right. I just didn't want him to be.

"Because if you're *asking* me," he continued when I didn't reply. "Then I think that sounds a little dangerous. You can't be his only reason, Cam. He needs to do it for *himself.*"

"He *is.*" *I think.*

"Well good. I hope you're right. Still, I think he'll benefit from his counselling."

"Yeah," I agreed because I couldn't think of anything else to say. My mood had slipped by a thousand percent and I couldn't help huffing in frustration. Why did Dylan have to go and get himself hooked on drugs? Would we *ever* have a happy, *normal* relationship, without so much worry and fear? I had no idea, and that just made me sad. There was *so* much sadness lately. I'd never experienced such turbulence until I reconnected with Dylan.

"So what *did* you come here to talk about?"

I let out another sigh. "Nothing. It can wait." Wait until when, I wasn't sure. Until he'd had therapy? Until he'd been clean for X amount of months? Years? Until he was *ready*?

What if he's never *ready?* What if he'd been through so much crap in his life that he'd never be able to dig himself out of it completely?

What if...what if I *wasn't* a big enough reason?

Chapter

Ten

~Dylan~

"IT'S ALL IN the wobble," Derek said, twisting the plate that held one of his panna cottas from side to side. I'd followed the process of the dessert in front of me from start to finish, and I found it oddly fascinating seeing the finished product.

Evening service was in full swing so I didn't have time to stay and watch him make it look all fancy on the plate, but he said he'd let me have a go at making a batch myself in the next few days. I didn't think for a second he'd serve my efforts to paying customers, but I appreciated the opportunity all the same.

In fact, I appreciated *everything*, and everyone. For years, I saw no future for me. I always imagined I'd be found dead in an alleyway after overdosing or getting the life literally kicked out of me over a debt I'd stacked up with a dealer. Yet, here I was. Clean. Employed. I had friends. I had Cameron. I didn't need drugs when I had him. Sure, I craved them from time to time, but I didn't *need* them.

I'd even told Cameron I loved him. That was a *huge* step, but I wasn't completely sure if it was true. I didn't know if I was even capable of love. I thought I was, he meant *everything* to me, but that made me feel guilty. My love destroyed people. It pushed them away. Whenever I loved someone they fucking died on me. *I shouldn't have said it.* Even if I meant it, Cameron didn't deserve my love. He deserved so much more.

No. I pushed the bad thoughts out of my head. I'd done it. I *had* this. That part of my life was over. I had people, and interests, to keep my mind occupied, distracted. Never in a million years would I have thought those interests would include cooking. I remembered poking fun at Cameron for wanting to be a chef when he grew up like it was just this morning. But it was so much *more* than simply cooking. Anyone can whip up a meal, but the things the men and women in Cameron's kitchen produced were works of art.

The thought made me think of my dad. He was an artist too, in a sense. He played and sang stunning pieces of music. Maybe he'd passed some of that creativity onto me. Maybe I could finally make him proud.

"Service!" Andrew, who I didn't really know yet, was heading the pass tonight, and his loud bark snapped me out of my untimely thoughts.

Throwing my tea-towel over my shoulder, I got back to work, weaving my way through the stifling heat and picking up dirty pots along the way with a smile on my face.

Right now, life was really fucking good.

* * *

I spent the next few weeks working as much as I could, using all my spare time to practice the things Derek had shown me, before spending each night in Cameron's arms. Making love to Cameron felt surreal at times. It wasn't just sex. Sex was something I used to do to please other people. Sex, for me, was quick and dirty. It was the reason I'd never topped another man before Cameron. Sex made me feel seedy and disgusting and I doubted I'd have been able to keep an erection long enough to see the job through.

But I didn't have sex with Cameron. I made love to him, and he loved me right back. He took care of me. He savoured me. He made me feel like what we did together was a beautiful thing. Special. Cameron was *it* for me. I could spend all my time with him, I *did* spend all my time with him, and never get bored, never need that hit.

He was my hit.

My appointment came through this morning for my counselling, along with another date for cognitive behavioural therapy. The first appointment was three weeks away and, honestly, I didn't think I needed it anymore. But…I'd do it. I'd go. For Cameron's sake.

It was late evening on a Thursday, and Cameron and I lay tangled together in his bed after spending a rare day off work together. Cameron spent the morning trying out new recipes and getting me to taste them, then he took me to the cinema in the afternoon. It felt like a *real* date, like the kind you see in the movies. It was an experience I never thought I'd have again, and nothing like when we used to go as teenagers. Back then, the place was packed with people. Today, there were only two other people sharing a screen with us. Oh, and back then Cameron didn't used to feel up my dick in the darkness either.

Nobody stared at me. Nobody frowned at my scruffy clothes or sunken eyes, because I no longer had them. I didn't need to look for exits or security cameras. I was just… *normal.* A decent member of society. I felt like I belonged, like I had as much right to be there as everyone else. The whole day was perfect. Ordinary and natural. I felt fucking amazing.

"So," Cameron began, twiddling a strand of my hair between his fingers as I rested my head on his chest. "I have to go away tomorrow. Just for one night."

It felt like my heart had stopped dead in my chest. My throat felt tight and my body too hot. "Why? Where?" I hated the panic in my voice but I couldn't prevent it. *Why is he leaving?* What would I do on my own?

"I have a meeting about proposals for a new restaurant up in Edinburgh. I've been thinking about it for a while now."

Edinburgh? Is he leaving me? "W-why do you have to go on your own?"

"I'm not. Paul's coming too."

Paul? Why not me? "Oh." I rolled onto my back, needing the distance to breathe properly and cool down.

"It's just one night, Dyl," he said, shuffling onto his side to face me. "You'll be okay, right?"

No. I need you. The only reason I'd come so far was because I hadn't been alone. "Sure."

He placed his hand on my chest and I stared at it, almost mourning it knowing it wouldn't be here tomorrow. "Are you mad?" he asked. His voice sounded puzzled.

"So are you moving there? To Edinburgh?"

"No!" He chuckled and it frustrated me. I didn't find it funny. I needed him and he was leaving! "The restaurant will bear my name and I'll make regular trips to oversee everything, but I'll be employing a team to do the day-to-day running."

Regular trips. Bet he won't take me on those either. I couldn't stop myself repeating everything he said in my head, twisting his words, becoming more anxious.

"You know if you need me I'm only a phone-call away." Reaching up, he brushed my cheek with the back of his thumb.

I forced a smile. "Sure."

But I *wasn't* sure. I wasn't good on my own. I didn't do good things.

"It's just one day, right?" I said, willing myself to believe it, believe I'd be okay, that I wouldn't fuck everything up without Cameron taking care of me. I *had* to believe that…

But I didn't.

When he left the next day it took all my strength not to fall to the floor and cling to his ankles. I was scared. Terrified. Afraid I wouldn't cope. I went into work as usual, but it felt different without Cameron. It felt like everyone knew I was *nothing*, like they expected me to fail without him to fall back on. I tried to disguise how I felt with fake smiles but I realised I hadn't done a good enough job when Derek approached me.

"Y'okay, mate?" he asked. "You seem a little distracted today."

I carried on stacking the dishwasher in the prep-kitchen, unable to look at him. If he looked into my eyes he'd see who I really was; a weak and clingy sorry excuse of a man who didn't know how to function alone.

"Headache," was all I said.

"I've got some Co-codamol in my bag. They're the good stuff. Prescription strength. I get 'em off my mum."

The mere mention of painkillers had me thinking of a whole different drug entirely. I pushed the thought out immediately, refusing to give it ground to grow on. "I'm good. Thanks. I'll be fine after I have something to eat. I missed breakfast."

"If y'sure."

"I'm sure."

"Fancy honin' your pipin' skills later? I 'ad plans wi' Paul until Cam dragged him away for the night and ballsed it up."

My initial reaction was *no*, especially after being reminded that Cameron had gone, but what else would I do with my night? I wasn't working evening service, and seemingly neither was Derek. If I went back to Cam's place alone I'd no doubt have spent the night feeling sorry for myself and my pitiful existence.

"Sure," I agreed.

"Great. We'll 'ead straight to my place after service."

I forced another smile. "Great."

Did this mean I could officially count Derek as a friend? I liked to think so, Paul too, but they were *Cam's* friends first. If he kept leaving me and I fucked up, they'd side with him, and I'd have nothing and nobody. *Again.*

Maybe I did need fucking therapy after all. I was a grown man, bumbling around, not knowing how to live on my own like an abandoned child. He'd only left for one fucking night. The rational part of my brain *knew* that, yet my addict brain was getting louder with every hour that passed.

My addict brain felt like he'd abandoned me. My addict brain told me he didn't care, that he could never love someone like me, that he deserved better. My addict brain knew I couldn't trust anyone, couldn't rely on anyone. It made me believe that this was just the beginning, that Cameron would keep leaving more and more often, stay away longer and longer, until he disappeared altogether.

My addict brain was a twisted cunt…but one that usually won.

Everybody leaves. Heroin doesn't.

"Yo, Dylan!" My name brought me crashing back into the real world and I turned towards the voice to find a very angry-looking chef glowering at me. "It's fuckin' pilin' up over 'ere! Sort it out!"

Crap. Blowing out a controlled breath through pursed lips, I started jogging towards the untidy section. "Yes, chef."

* * *

Early evening, my jaw dropped open a little when we arrived at Derek's house. Nestled in the centre of a long row of magnificent Georgian terraced houses, it was a white building, guarded by black iron gates with six steps leading up to the front door. This kinda place would cost a bomb in *any* part of the country, but in the heart of London we were talking a fortune of epic proportions.

"Holy shit," I said, stepping into Derek's home. It looked average size on the outside, but once he opened the door it was frigging *huge*. "You never told me you lived in the fuckin' Tardis."

Derek chuckled, shrugging out of his coat before hanging it inside a tall cupboard in the elongated hallway. I followed him past the stairs and into the living room; a *great* room, longer than it was wide, filled with white and monochrome. Very modern. Very bachelor pad-esque.

"You live here on your own?" I asked, craning my neck as I admired the intricate coving bordering the ceiling. They looked original, as did the decorative ceiling plasterwork, and a little out of place with the rest of his contemporary furnishings. Still beautiful nonetheless.

"Yep."

"You must be fuckin' wadded."

Again, he laughed. "My parents more-so than me. But I guess you could say I'm pretty comfortable," he added with a smirk.

"Why do you bother working?" I couldn't help asking. It made no sense to me. Being a chef looked exhausting, and he clearly didn't do it out of necessity.

"Because I love what I do." His tone sounded almost incredulous, like I'd asked a stupid question.

"You can't love being bossed around. With this much dosh you could open your own place."

"Nah. I love to cook, not manage, not crunch numbers and frit away 'alf my life on paperwork. I'm already livin' my dream. I don't need nothin' else."

"That must be nice." *Shit*. I hadn't meant to say that out loud, or sound so fucking sorrowful. I waited for his reaction but other than a brief look of curiosity, maybe even concern, it didn't come.

Instead, he fixed his winning smile back in place. "So," he said. "Pipin'!"

"Right." I nodded. That's why I was here.

Derek led me through an equally grand dining room and into the kitchen. *Fuck me*. This place was breath-taking, like the show-homes you see in glossy magazines. Everything was black and stainless steel, and his cooker alone was bigger than the whole back wall of Cameron's kitchen. I felt like I should've offered to take my shoes off, but he still wore his so I didn't.

"So what do your parents do?"

"My mum's a barrister. Dad's an investment broker; 'as 'is own firm."

"Wow. Clever family then."

"Oh yeah. I'm a fuckin' genius." He winked and it made me laugh. "I think they expected me to study law like my mum, but it's always been about food for me."

Derek started gathering equipment and ingredients from the high-gloss black cupboards while I perched on a breakfast-stool and continued questioning, getting to know him. "How did you know?" I asked. "The food thing. How did you know that's what you wanted to do?"

"Wasn't like an epiphany or anythin', if that's what you're waitin' for," he said, his tone teasing.

I think I *was* waiting for that. A sign. A spark. A magical awakening where I suddenly knew exactly what I was supposed to do with my life. That would've been easier than trying to figure it out for myself.

"I guess I enjoyed watchin' my nan cook when I stayed with 'er as a kid. Then, turned out I was pretty good in food-tech in 'igh school. Didn't think much of it until I saw people eatin' what I'd made, watched them enjoy it, clear their plates. It kinda spiralled from there. When I applied to college it was a literal toss-up with a pound coin whether I'd take art and design or culinary arts. Food won."

"Do you think anyone can do it? You think I have what it takes?"

"No, I don't think *anyone* can do it. It takes a lot of 'ard fuckin' work, dedication, and natural flair."

"Oh." Mood deflated, I looked down at my knees.

"Not everyone 'as that flair, but from what I've seen o' you so far, I think *you* do."

My head jerked back up, an eager smile taking over my lips. "Yeah?"

"You gotta work for it though. It's gotta be all y'think about. You need to live, breathe, dream, food."

Well, that was me out. I couldn't dedicate all my thoughts to food because most of them were already occupied with Cameron and smack.

"Does it matter that I don't like half the stuff they serve at O'Neil's?

Derek's mouth curled into an 'O'. "You don't like my food?"

"Oh hell no! I didn't mean yours. I'm yet to taste one of your desserts that doesn't feel like my tongue just orgasmed. I mean the fish shit. And that, dammit…" I clicked my fingers as if the action would help me remember the word. "That fatty duck liver crap."

"Foie gras?"

"Yes! Ugh. Just the thought of eating it makes my stomach roll."

"All chefs, regardless of their speciality, know about *all* food. You need a good palate. You 'ave to work on recognisin' flavours, learn which foods and taste combinations compliment each other, but you don't necessarily 'ave to like 'em. And it *is* possible to concentrate on pastry from the start, dependin' on what courses you take."

"Courses? Like…*school*?" Sod that for a month of Sundays and three fucks a day. "Can't *you* just teach me?"

"Not if you want to work as a professional chef. At least, not if you want to work in anywhere even close to the calibre of O'Neil's. If your dream is to work in a country pub, sure."

I fell silent, feeling like shit yet not really knowing why. I'd felt so fucking great lately. So positive and optimistic. I thought I'd *cracked* this. What the hell was wrong with me?

"Get off your arse," Derek said, cocking his chin to where he stood. "Mix that." He shoved a bowl towards me, filled with icing sugar, cream, and vanilla essence. I stirred, while Derek melted dark chocolate on the stove. I knew this recipe. I'd seen him do it countless times, so I knew without being told when to add the cocoa-powder next to me.

When ready, Derek stuffed the mixture into a piping bag, explaining the different nozzles to me as he did. I thought it would be as simple as squeezing and relaxing the bag between my fingers, but I was wrong. After my fifth failed attempt, and five squashed blobs, Derek covered my hand with his, guiding me, showing me how to hold the bag, how much pressure to apply and when.

After a couple of hours, I had several sheets of baking parchment filled with various beads, ribbons, and peaks that actually looked pretty impressive. Seemed a shame they'd all be going straight in the bin. Maybe we should've baked some cakes first.

The lesson had taken the edge off my sour mood, but the fucker returned once we'd finished. Normally, I'd have asked if we could try something else, he'd been teaching me so much lately, but tonight I just couldn't be arsed.

"Wanna go out somewhere once we've cleaned down?" Derek asked.

"Where?"

He shrugged. "A club. Bar. Wherever you fancy."

"No thanks. I don't drink." Alcohol would've weakened the faint shred of resolve to stay away from drugs I seemed to have today.

I've done so fucking well! I mentally reminded myself, my subconscious severely pissed off. *What's changed today?*

Also, places that served alcohol also served heroin. They, the owners, might not know it, but dealers were always there, most of whom I knew. If I saw someone I recognised, a dealer, a fellow junkie, I didn't trust myself not to give the signal and meet them in the bathroom.

"Pizza then," Derek suggested. "It's Friday night. I'm too fuckin' young to spend it inside!"

"How old are you?" I asked out of simple curiosity. He didn't look much older than Cameron and I, but he was definitely taller and more well-built. I imagined he had a pretty fine body under his clothes, which surprised me at first, given his passion for sweet foods. But then I learned that in order to eat as much as he did, he spent two hours at the gym every single morning. Even at weekends.

"Thirty-five on the outside, forever twenty-one in my 'ead."

Grinning at his playful tone, I nodded. "Pizza sounds good."

So, that's what we did. We went out, ate great food, and talked until they threw us out at closing time. He told me kitchen gossip, funny stories about Cameron and Paul – mostly Paul – and I told

225

him about the Cameron from my past, stopping right before my grandma died.

It was a good night with a great friend. My mood improved, my addict brain quietened, and I felt like I *had* this all over again.

Until I got back to the apartment and I was all on my own again.

* * *

I didn't sleep well last night. I tossed, turned, and wanked off a couple of times, before getting up at four AM and continuing my Pretty Little Liars marathon with a giant bag of Doritos and an energy drink I found in the back of the cupboard. The can tasted like pure melted sugar as it dripped sluggishly down my throat, but it perked me up so I decided I'd go buy some more when daylight hit.

Damn, I missed Cameron. I spoke to him last night on the house phone and I couldn't seem to stop myself being curt with him. I wasn't mad with him, not really. I was more angry with *myself* for needing him so much, and I took it out on him because I was a prick. While I lay awake afterwards, regretting the way I'd spoken to him, I wished I had a mobile so I could text him and apologise. I hadn't owned one in years, didn't need one, but now I did. Although it didn't always feel like it, I was a respectable member of society now. I lived a *normal* life like everybody else and so I *should* have a mobile phone.

Counting Daisies

After showering and dressing for the day, I counted the money I'd been saving from my weekend shifts at the restaurant. I didn't have a bank account so Cameron paid me in cash, which I kept in a shoebox under his bed.

"One twenty," I said aloud, tucking the notes into my pocket. I'd spent a lot recently on new clothes and shoes, but there was enough left to buy myself a cheap pay-as-you-go phone and some energy drinks. So, off I went, without bothering to have breakfast first.

I wasn't expecting my pulse to quicken when I walked into the first shop. I was a legitimate customer. I had money in my pocket, yet I felt like everyone would stare, like they'd *know* who I really was; a worthless junkie looking to steal from them. I was sober, I had meat on my bones, I wore smart clothes...but inside I *felt* like him. Like the *old* me. I still had his eyes, I still thought like him sometimes, and so I instinctively averted my gaze away from anyone who glanced in my direction.

Focused on the floor or the shelves, I never looked at another person. I grabbed several energy drinks, hoping they'd ease the anxiety crushing my chest, and a couple of chocolate bars too. Nausea whirled in my stomach and it felt like someone was pulling on a thick rope tightened around my throat as I joined the queue at the checkout. I didn't understand what was happening to me. I'd been doing just *fine*. I'd been out in fucking public before. I'd paid for things in a fucking shop, all the while functioning like a normal human fucking being.

Since I'd been clean, however, I hadn't done any of those things alone. How had this happened? How had I become so damn needy? More importantly, *why?* It was almost like the heroin still taunted me, reminding me what life by myself was like, telling me that loneliness wasn't something I coped well with, and that it was still here for me if it all got too much.

No. I said the word in my head almost as if I were talking to it, to the smack, as if it were a living entity capable of understanding me. *I don't need you. You ruined my life.*

"Sir?" The voice coming from behind the counter startled me. I hadn't seen my turn approach, and if I wasn't being stared at before, I sure as shit was now.

"Sorry," I muttered, handing my items over to him, silently willing him to take my cash so I could get the hell out of there. I paid as quickly as I could before practically jogging through the store and back out onto the street.

The air was cool, the slight breeze whipping my cheeks. I needed that. For a few long seconds I just stood there, tipping my head towards the sky while I dragged in some controlled breaths. I felt…lost, vulnerable, out here on the busy street, surrounded by people – decent, honest people – living their lives around me. I wasn't one of them. I was a druggie, and I always would be.

Once you become an addict, you're one for life. The second you become hooked on your substance of choice, you're left with only three ways to describe yourself.

Using.

Recovering.

Dead.

There is no in-between. You can't ever go back to life before drugs. They're part of you now, whether you use them or not, they're there. Always. In your head. In your dreams. Life becomes a constant battle. The moment you let the shit take hold of you it never lets go. You've signed up to a never-ending war without even realising it. Sometimes you'll win, sometimes the skag'll win, and that fight is lifelong, only ending the day you draw your last breath.

You can do this. Pull yourself together. My mental pep-talk worked long enough to get me to the phone shop, barely. Once inside, I plucked the first one I saw in my price range off the shelf, not caring what features and functions it had. I just wanted to text Cameron. I *needed* him.

My addict brain kicked in at the sight of the security tag on the small blue box. Those tags were the reason I never stole from shops like this in the past. I had to look at things a different way then, assess the threat level for nearly everything I did in my life. Nothing was simple. I had to *plan* things. Life was dangerous. Every single day I put myself at risk of being arrested, beaten, infected, *killed*...

I detested those memories, but right now I felt grateful for them. They reminded me of all the good things I had now, all the hard work I'd put in to get them. They propelled me to carry on, keep fighting, and to stop being such a whiney pussy about Cameron leaving for *one* fucking night.

Chuffed with my new gadget, my *only* gadget, I headed back home.

Home.

It was the first time I'd referred to Cam's apartment as home and, honestly, I didn't know if I had the right to do so. *No*, I told myself. *You don't.* I'd hardly earned my place there. I'd caused Cameron nothing but hassle and pain. I didn't pay my way. I didn't contribute to anything. I know I worked for him, but I saw that as an opportunity for *myself* more than him. I *couldn't* pay him back. I had nothing. I *was* nothing. And just like that, my mind slithered into darkness once again.

* * *

Several hours later, the sound of the house phone ringing woke me up. I must've fallen asleep on the couch after I lay down earlier, too frustrated to bother setting up my new mobile.

Jolting upright, I grabbed the handset from its cradle, hoping it was Cameron. "Hello?"

"Oh," the woman's voice replied. "I'm calling for Cameron. Is he there?"

The air lodged in my throat mid-breath. It'd been so long since I'd heard her sweet voice, yet I recognised it instantly. Body frozen, a peculiar ache panged deep in my chest. "Mrs O'Neil?" It came out like a question even though I already knew the answer.

"Yes. Who's this?" She sounded confused, maybe even flustered.

"It's, um, it's Dylan. Dylan Roberts."

There was a slight pause before a shallow gasp entered my ear. "Dylan? Oh my goodness…*Dylan!* Is that really you?"

Her gentle, familiar tone relaxed me instantly. "Sure is. How've ya been, Mrs O?"

"When did you get back? Where've you been? Why the heck didn't Cameron tell me? How are you? Are you well?"

"Steady on, Mrs O," I interrupted, coughing out a chuckle. "I can't keep up."

"Sorry." I could hear the smile in her voice. "I just…Dylan Roberts. I thought we'd lost you forever. You were a big part of our family."

My eyes began to water, tears stinging as they clawed their way to the surface. "It's good to hear your voice again," I said, raw emotion clogging my throat.

"I need to see you. Can I see you? I'm seeing you. Tell Cameron I'll be there within the hour."

Shit. I'm not ready. She couldn't see me. She'd *know*. She always could see through me, knew when I was lying. She used to say my nose twitched when I was trying to hide something. If she saw me now, she'd take one look at me and know what a terrible person I'd been. "Uh, Cam's not here. He's in Edinburgh with Paul."

"Ah. I thought that was next weekend. Oh well, doesn't matter. Get the kettle on, Dylan. I'll see you very soon."

Okay. I could do this. I loved Mrs O. I missed her. She was family. I needed as much support as I could get, even if I thought that made me weak. "Okay. In a bit, Mrs O."

Only when I'd hung up did I notice the little red light flash on the phone cradle. *Voicemail.* I dialled into it straight away, my heart fluttering as Cameron's voice danced into my ear.

"Hey, Dyl. Sorry I missed you. We're just about to go into the meeting. I should be home around nine tonight. Call me if you need me sooner. Love you."

"Love you, too," I whispered, even though I knew he couldn't hear me. Ending the call, I held the phone to my chest for a little while, repeating his message in my head. *Nine.* Nine o'clock felt like days away.

I didn't have time to feel sorry for my pathetic arse. I had to change and tidy up a little before Mrs O arrived. Despite the nerves, I smiled just thinking about her. She was the closest thing I had to a mother, and I'd not allowed myself to think about her for too long. That ended today. It was time to remember my past. Embrace it. Take back all the lost years, all the pieces of myself I threw away.

Forty minutes and two energy drinks later, a light tap sounded at the door. I imagined she had a key and knocked purely out of politeness but I was grateful, regardless, because it gave me a moment to compose myself. Standing just inches from the door, I ironed out imaginary creases in my T-shirt, dragging in a deep breath before slowly opening the door.

And there she was, Mrs O, looking *exactly* the same as I remembered her, bar a few shallow wrinkles hugging her eyes and a sprinkling of grey in her hair. Her eyes filled in front of me, glossing over with tears as her bottom lip started to wobble.

Tossing her handbag into the room, she opened her tiny arms and lunged forwards, using all her strength to hold me tight to her chest. "I can't bloody believe it," she whispered, her voice shaky.

I was a good bit taller than her, so I hunched my shoulders, lowering my head to kiss the top of her hair. "I've missed you, Mrs O."

Pulling back, she held me at arms length, studying every inch of my face. Her expression crumpled, twisting into what looked like sadness.

She knew. She *saw* me. She knew what I'd become.

"I'm so sorry, Dylan."

Sorry? For what?

"It all happened so fast. I didn't hear about your grandmother until the day after it happened, and by then you…" She broke off, sniffing in her tears. "You were already gone. We'd have taken you in. We'd have loved you. But the bastards wouldn't tell us anything."

My nose was blocked with tears so I blew steadily through my mouth. Realising the door was

still open, I backed out of the doorway, Mrs O
following my lead, and closed it behind her. I
meandered to the sofa on unsteady feet, lowering
myself onto it before my knees gave way.

"It's haunted me all these years," she
continued, sitting beside me and clamping her small
hand over my knee. "If I'd fought harder,
contacted more people…"

"Don't do that," I said. "It wasn't your fault. I
didn't tell them about you. Social Services. I didn't
tell them when they came to the hospital. Didn't
tell them anything. I just…let them take me."

"You were a child, a child who'd just lost the
last member of their family." She rubbed my knee
and sighed. "I expected to see you at the funeral. I
planned to talk to the social worker there, ask about
your options."

"They said I could go, but I didn't want to. It
was only a year after my dad's funeral. I
just…couldn't do it. I couldn't handle any more
death, any more goodbyes."

"Did they not contact the school? They
would've known how close you and Cameron were,
that you still had people who loved you."

I shrugged. "Dunno. Didn't ask questions. I
kinda just…withdrew." Maybe it wasn't the same
these days. Maybe kids got a better crack at life.
Maybe nowadays they *would* try harder to place you
with people you knew. *I dunno.* I just knew *I* wasn't
given that opportunity.

"You poor boy." She sucked in a breath and
shook her head.

Just imagining what life could've been like if I'd gone to live with Mr and Mrs O flooded my mind with such overwhelming sadness, causing a tear to spill over the rim of my eye. I could've had such a good life, one like I envisaged when I was young. I could've been a decent person. I could've been sitting here right now completely oblivious to the awful things that happened on the streets every day. Things that were firmly carved into my memory. Things that would haunt my thoughts and dreams until the day I died.

The world could've been such a completely different place.

"Cameron must've been so happy to see you again. He never forgot about you. A mother knows these things," she said with a warm smile.

I knew that, he'd told me so himself, but I didn't like how it made me feel so I stayed quiet. I often wondered what would've happened if I'd sought him out sooner. I thought about it when I first left the care system, but with four years passing since I last saw him, I knew he'd have moved on – followed his dreams, found new friends…while I was starting out with nothing.

If I'm honest, I was jealous of him. He had a family. He had people to love and love him back, and it made me angry back then. I was angry at everyone and everything and I was for a long time. It wasn't fair. Why couldn't *I* have what he had? I'd never done anything wrong. I was a good kid, so why did fate decide I wasn't good enough to have the things everybody else took for granted?

I'd never really admitted any of this to myself before, how envious I was. It was testament to how fucked in the head and selfish I was.

"How did you find each other again?" Mrs O asked. "Cameron's in so much trouble for not telling his dad and me you were back."

"I told him not to," I admitted, dragging my hands over my flushed cheeks. "I, um…I was in a bit of trouble and I didn't want you to know."

"Oh, you silly sod! Why on earth not? We could've helped you."

I tried to summon a smile but it never materialised. "I didn't want to disappoint you. My life has been a little fuc-sorry, *messed* up since I went into care. Didn't want you to see me that way."

"I thought, *think*, of you like a son, Dylan. I'd never judge you."

My sober brain believed that. She was a good woman. Kind. Compassionate. For all my sins, this woman loved me. "I'm a junkie, Mrs O. For ten years, my whole life has revolved around heroin."

Her small hand flew to her chest, shock making her jaw drop for only a second before she palmed the back of my neck and brought my head to her shoulder, hugging me. "Oh, Dylan…" she choked out on a shallow sob. She sounded almost guilty, like she really believed she should've tried harder to protect me, like she could've prevented what I became.

I went on to tell her everything. Well, not *everything*. I left out some of the despicable things I'd done to fund my habit, and I didn't mention the hell I'd put her son through while he watched me get off the junk either. Regardless, she listened to every word I had to say, offering nothing but reassuring smiles and a few tears. There was no judgement. Not disappointment. Not once did I see anything other than love in her eyes.

"Then Paul gave me a job at the restaurant," I continued. "Just a dishwasher, but Derek's been teaching me some pastry skills."

"That's wonderful. I'm very proud of you, Dylan."

"It's all on Cam." I shrugged. "And the rest of the guys. I couldn't have done this on my own. I've tried in the past. Never worked."

"To say I understand, even a little, would be patronising, but I don't think you should undervalue the strength you've shown. How are you now?"

"Okay. Some days are harder than others." I smiled a weak, hesitant smile.

"Do you think the counselling will help with that?"

Shrugging a little, I avoided looking her right in the eye. "That's the plan." It was the best I could offer. "I'm glad you called today. It's been good seeing you again."

"You say that like I'm leaving. I'm going to stick around until Cameron gets home, if that's okay with you? I need to be a good mother and interrogate you about your intentions towards my son." Her tone was teasing, her smile playful.

"You know about me and Cam? Even back then?"

"Of course I did." She waved off the question with her hand, like it was absurd. "He used to look at you like you were crafted from diamonds. I imagine he still does."

And just like that, it felt like I'd never been away from the woman I considered my second mum.

* * *

By late evening, my voice was a little hoarse from overuse. We'd talked, laughed, reminisced, and cried, for hours. She asked lots of questions about my 'missing years' and I tried to brush over them as much as I could. But now, since telling her I never really had any close friends since Cameron, all I could think about was Bubbles. My thoughts often went back to her lately. Was she okay? Was she clean? Using? In trouble? *Alive?*

"Remember when Mr O fell down the stairs and broke his big toe?" The memory alone sent me into a fit of hysterics. Finishing up our takeaway, the conversation between Mrs O and I had turned lighter, and it surprised me the old memories we brought up weren't as painful as I thought they'd be.

"Oh, stop!" she said, breathless from laughing.

Mrs O was walking down the stairs, Mr O following behind carrying a washing basket in his arms. Hearing a crash, Cameron and I darted into the hall and found his dad crying out at the bottom of the stairs with Mrs O stood over him, trying to keep a straight face while tears of laughter rolled freely from her eyes.

"*Stop, Janet! Stop!*" Back in the present, Mrs O mimicked her husband's voice, the words barely audible through her winded chuckling. "I thought it was the washing basket falling so I ran faster! If I'd known it was Stephen I'd have stopped and broke his fall. His toe's still bent to the left to this day." Wiping the tears from her eyes, her laugh dissolved into a happy sigh.

Grinning, still amused, I discarded the crust from my slice of pizza on the plate and wiped my greasy hands on a napkin, stopping abruptly when the door started to open. My pulse quickened immediately, my heart pushing against the walls of my chest as if it were trying to get closer to the man who'd just stepped into the room.

Cameron's brilliant, healing smile faded as soon as he saw his mother standing up to greet him. "Mum," he said, his face paling like he'd just been caught nicking from her purse. "What are you doing here?"

Dropping his weekend bag by the door, he walked over to his mum and gave her a cautious hug.

She pulled back, ticking her finger from side to side in front of his face. "You *should* be worried," she said, noticing his nervous demeanour. "Hiding Dylan from me. You're in big trouble, Cameron Stephen O'Neil. *Big* trouble."

"I, um…" He scratched at his head, his lips morphing into a firm, guilty line.

"I'm just teasing, honey. I understand." She patted his shoulder. "How was your trip?"

"Good. Great in fact. Looks like we could be going ahead in just a few months."

Mrs O clapped her hands into the praying position. "That's excellent! Well done, you!"

"Thanks, Mum," he said, his voice a tad coy. He looked over her shoulder as he spoke, boring his gaze into mine.

It felt like my insides were melting.

"Hey," I said, my veins vibrating with the need to feel his skin on mine.

"You boys go sit down," Mrs O said. "I'll brew up."

Cameron didn't even reply before padding closer and enfolding me in his arms. "God, I missed you," he breathed into my ear.

You did? I didn't speak my thoughts aloud but he made me feel less embarrassed about missing him so much, too.

"Have you been okay?" he asked, pulling back and studying my face. "Derek said you guys hung out together last night."

Great. So you've been checking up on me. My thoughts were unfair and I knew it, but I couldn't prevent the fucked-off scowl that appeared on my face. My addict brain had been fighting for centre stage recently, and I had to force myself to ignore it. I couldn't let it win.

He cares about you, I reminded myself. Fixing a smile in place, I said, "Yeah. He's a good guy. I really like him."

Mrs O interrupted us with cups of coffee and we sat down to drink them while Cameron spilled the details of his trip. I listened mostly, letting Cam catch up with his mum, and once my mug was empty I made my excuses and went to bed. I presumed they'd want to talk about me, and I was okay with that. They both loved me, fuck knows why but they did, and I knew Mrs O would want to ask Cameron things she couldn't say in front of my face.

So, I left them alone, curling up in Cameron's quilt and letting my mind drift back to Bubbles. Wherever she was, I hoped she was okay.

Maybe…maybe I should try and find out.

* * *

The next few days were tough. Something had changed between Cameron and I since he went away, though I couldn't figure out what or why. I knew, *knew*, it was all in my head, but I still couldn't shake it. My mind was consumed with irrational thoughts, worries about the next trip he didn't even have a date for yet. I couldn't tell him how I felt because I'd sound crazy and possessive, so I kept it all inside and let it eat away at my brain like a cancer, tormenting me, torturing me, pushing me down a dangerous slope.

"You've already had one of those this morning," Cameron noted as I plucked another energy drink from the fridge. "They'll rot your insides."

I've had three actually. I shrugged. "I like 'em," I said, my tone unbothered. The drinks kept me alert, even gave me a slight buzz if I had enough of them. Buzzing on sugar dulled the urge to get buzzed on something else, something *illegal*, and the way I saw it that could only be a positive thing.

As I took a generous swig from my can, my eyes roamed up and down Cameron's body. He had a meeting with the bank about his new restaurant, so he'd dressed in a fitted black suit, crisp white shirt, and a navy blue tie which he was currently tying into a tidy knot.

Putting my can on the counter, I stepped up to him and grabbed his waist. "You look all kinds of fuckin' hot in this suit."

A devilish grin teased his lips. "I do, huh?"

Nuzzling his neck, I kissed my way up to his ear. He smelled fucking delicious and my dick perked up in agreement. Grabbing his hand, I placed it over my crotch. "Yeah, you do."

A gruff, frustrated sigh vibrated in his throat, tickling my lips as I kissed his neck again. "Damn, Dyl," he moaned, his voice pained. "I'd love to take care of you right now..." He squeezed my cock, making me groan. "But I'll be late. Tonight though, tonight that cock is all mine."

Oh, hell yes. "I approve of that plan."

"I'm not driving to the bank at this hour. Do you want to share my taxi? It'll be going past Tesco."

I wasn't working today and planned to go to the supermarket to stock up on energy drinks and buy some razors. Cam used the last one this morning and I hadn't shaved in two days. What I hadn't told Cam, however, is that I was going to try and find Bubbles first. I knew it was a risky, possibly foolish move, but I *had* to know if she was okay. She wouldn't leave my mind. I couldn't move on with the knowledge the shit she took that day might've killed her, and *I* was the one who pushed it into her body. I needed to do this, needed to see her so I could succeed in staying clean once and for all.

"No thanks. I'm not going till later. I'll just chill out here for a bit and then make my own way."

He nodded, then kissed my cheek; such a small gesture, but one that dissolved all the tension I'd been feeling. "Okay. Well I'm going straight to work afterwards so I'll see you…" he pressed his hand against my dick again, "…tonight." Winking, he gathered his jacket and a file containing his business plan, and headed for the door.

Walking over to the shoe-cupboard, I pulled my trainers on as soon as he left, feeling like an utter bastard as I did. My chest felt weird, my stomach heavy. It felt like I was betraying him somehow, deceiving him…and that would be because I *was*. I stayed behind for ten minutes or so to make sure he'd definitely gone, and I was just about to reach for the door handle when a knock sounded on the other side.

Opening it, I started to talk. "Forgot your keys aga-" I cut myself off when my eyes met those of a man I didn't recognise. "Oh. Hey."

His gaze scanned me up and down, his face contorting into an almost disgusted expression.

What the fuck is his problem?

"Cam around?" he asked, looking over my shoulder into the apartment.

"And you are?"

"Kevin. Cam's fiancé."

I felt the blood physically drain from my face and I knew my skin would be a ghostly shade of pale. I didn't reply right away. I *couldn't*.

Fiancé? What the...

"Cameron doesn't have a fiancé." *Who the hell is this lunatic?*

"Well," he began, shrugging. "Technically we're on a break. Is he here or not?"

"N-no," I said, detesting the stutter which proved how much this cuntbag unnerved me.

"Is he still in Edinburgh?"

Whoa. How the fuck did he know about that? Did Cam *really* know this dickwad? *Is he...is he really engaged?*

No. He couldn't be. I'd been with Cameron, practically glued to his side for last few months. This arsehole was just looking to cause trouble.

"None of your fucking business," I spat, slamming the door in his fuck-ugly face. He wasn't *actually* ugly. He was almost hot, but it made me feel better to pretend I'd seen finer looking shit stains in the toilet bowl.

I heard the smug bastard laugh when I closed the door, and even though his retreating footsteps followed, I didn't leave right away. I needed a few moments to process what the fuck just happened, to compose myself and remember how to breathe in an even rhythm.

Stomping over to the fridge, I ripped open the door, so forcefully I'm surprised I didn't snap the hinges, and grabbed my last energy drink. I downed the full can in one, without pausing to take a breath. "Stupid fucker," I said to nobody, hating the smarmy twat I'd only known for two minutes.

I couldn't decide if I should question Cameron about Kyle, or whatever the hell his name was, all I heard was *fiancé*. I wanted to know who he was, but I'd been so fucking clingy lately and I hated myself for it. I didn't want to make that worse by going all Rambo on his arse over an ex. So, as with most things, I'd likely let it fester; give my addict brain something to chew on.

Shaking my head, as if the action would unscramble my thoughts, I decided I'd worry about this later. If I had any hope of getting on with my life, laying my past to rest, I needed to find Bubbles.

* * *

After making my way to the less savoury parts of the city, the areas I wanted so desperately to forget existed, I scoured all our old hangouts, disappointed but not overly surprised when I found no trace of Bubbles. There was only one option left, one that made me feel sick to my stomach, yet one that made my veins buzz with need. I would have to go find Dean.

Pushing a long, steadying breath through tensed lips, I tapped my foot against the pavement as I stood outside The Old Dog. What I was about to do was reckless on countless levels. My blood fizzed with excitement just looking at this building. I could almost taste the heroin on my gums, feel its warmth beneath my skin.

Worse than the intense craving, however, was the fact I owed Dean money and I could quite possibly, *very* possibly, be leaving here with several broken bones and some missing teeth.

One, two, three, four…

Another deep breath, five imaginary daisies in my hand, and I was as ready as I was ever going to be. Pushing open the swinging door, I stepped inside, treading over the stained red carpet to the corner Dean usually occupied. And there he was. The vile son of a bitch who was once the most important person in my life, for he supplied the only thing I used to live for.

"Titch!" he announced my name, the name he'd given me because I was a good five inches shorter than him, like we were best fucking friends. "Long time no see." He leaned across the scratched wooden table and lowered his voice. "Got some new gear. Good stuff. Real fuckin' pure. I think you'll like it."

I had no doubt I would. I *wanted* it. Right this second I fucking *wanted* it as much as I wanted my next breath. "No," I choked out, the words feeling like a betrayal to my yearning body. "I got no money on me." I pushed the words out past the lump in my throat, fighting with everything I had not to take them back. It seemed like the best excuse. No cash, no sale. Simple. If I'd told him I was clean he'd just keep pushing. He'd lure me back in and, honestly, he'd have been able to do it really easily right now.

"Your tab's been settled. I could start a new one for you."

What? "Settled by who?"

Dean shrugged. "One o' your johns I expect. Didn't catch his name."

What the... "Who? What'd he look like?"

"Fuck's sake, kid, I didn't take a fuckin' photo. Your height. Dark hair. Smart-lookin'. Rich type. Wore one o' those pansy-arse tweed jackets."

Cameron. He'd described Cameron. *How the...why...Oh, God.* The day he found me with Bubbles, he must've gotten my whereabouts from Dean. I'd never asked him how he found me, and I never planned to. Talking about that night, about any part of my revolting past drowned me in shame. I had no idea how he'd found Dean, I just knew, now, that he *had.* The realisation rolled around in my stomach like a ball of barbed-wire, making me feel sick. This wasn't Cam's world. He shouldn't have had to deal with dangerous fuckers like Dean. He must've been terrified.

"I, uh…" I shook Cameron from my head. I'd have rather died on the spot than let Dean know he'd gotten under my skin. "I'm looking for Bubbles."

An amused smile tickled his lips. "Good luck wi' that. Bitch is dead."

The words plunged into me like a hammer to the chest, making me stumble back a couple of steps. *She's dead. Dead! I killed her…*

"Found her sorry arse three nights ago, by the bins round the back o' *Rochelle's,* drowning in her own vomit. Bitch owed me money. Whatever shit she took, she didn't get it from me."

Bubbles. Oh shit, Bubbles. Tears scraped the back of my eyes but I wouldn't let them fall. Not here. Not now. I didn't kill her, but that didn't ease the pain stabbing into every nerve in my body. I was too late. If I'd found her sooner…

"Still don't want any gear?" he asked, wiggling his eyebrows. He enjoyed this, seeing me squirm, watching me hurt, trying to entice me back into my old life.

"Go fuck yourself." Turning around, I ran from the pub and out onto the street. I kept running, moved until my legs felt numb and my lungs burned. I ran, and I ran, and I didn't stop until I reached Cameron's apartment an hour later.

Inside, I leaned against the door, sliding down against it until my arse hit the floor. Hugging my knees, I rocked back and forth, wailing uncontrollably into the air. Tears stung my eyes, screams burned my throat.

"Fuck! Fuck! Fuck!" I yelled, punching my thighs. It was too much. The pain, the grief, that tosser from this morning and my insecurities about Cam leaving. Because he would. He'd leave. Eventually, he'd spend more and more time in his new restaurant, leaving me behind.

Or, he'd die just like everyone else.

I couldn't cope.

I couldn't do this anymore.

My head pounded and my chest ached. My hands trembled and my eyes felt like they'd been sliced open and bathed in salt. I'd *tried*. I'd tried so hard to beat this, but I wasn't strong enough. I never would be. It was *always* there, heroin, calling me. If that was ever going to stop, if I was ever going to defeat the motherfucker, I would've done it by now. The thirst, the *need*, would've gone away. But it was still there.

I hurt.

Everywhere.

Not *one* part of me didn't fucking hurt.

Standing up, I knew exactly what I planned to do next, but I wouldn't allow myself to think about it because that made it official. I was weak. I'd given up. In about an hour's time I would've thrown everything Cameron had done for me back in his face. I'd have let him down, let *myself* down.

Yet, that wasn't enough to stop me.

After taking a cab to the other side of town earlier, I only had a tenner left in my wallet; enough to buy the razors and energy drinks, but not enough to score a bag, not even enough for one tiny hit. I wouldn't go and find myself a punter. The thought alone made me shiver. I loved Cameron, really I did. I wouldn't ever be desperate enough to let another man's hands touch me again. I *had* to believe that. I *had* to believe this was just a temporary fix to get myself over Bubbles, and that I wouldn't let it take over my life again.

Just this once.

Just today.

It was the biggest, most frequent lie a junkie ever told themselves, yet today I believed it. Today I, Dylan, wasn't here anymore. Today, my addict brain had taken over. But it *was* just today. I'd come back tomorrow.

I wouldn't cheat on Cameron, but seemingly I *could* steal from him. I'd pay him back. Somehow. Some day.

I knew he had an older generation iPad at the bottom of his wardrobe that he never used, and I tucked it into my jacket without even thinking about it. If I thought about it, I'd feel guilty, and that was an emotion that could quite possibly kill me today. *Too much.* Everything was too much. I wasn't cut out for this life. I wasn't strong enough. I couldn't deal with tough situations the same way as everyone else.

Life was too hard. I *needed* this. I just wanted it all to disappear for a while.

Counting Daisies

Just this once.
Just today.

Nicola Haken

Chapter

Eleven

~Cameron~

I WORKED THROUGH service with a
cheesy smile on my face. I'd dreamed of expanding
for years, and it was finally happening. At thirty
years old, I was incredibly young to have such an
established career and, without wanting to sound
too egotistical, I was really frigging proud of myself.

I couldn't wait to get home and tell Dylan the
bank had approved my business loan, so when I
strolled into the apartment just after midnight I was
a little disappointed to find him asleep in bed. I'd
expected him to wake up so we could finish what
we started this morning.

After taking a shower to wash away the smell of the kitchen, and the sweat working in such a heated environment created, I climbed into bed naked, snuggling up to Dylan. He squirmed and grumbled as I draped my arm over his waist, so I took the opportunity to rouse him further.

"You awake?" I was excited and wanted to share that with him, so I raised my voice a notch higher. "Dylan?"

"*What?*" he snapped, pulling out of my hold.

Whoa. "Hey," I said. "What's wrong?"

"Nothin'," he said on a sigh. "Sorry. I was half-asleep."

I wasn't convinced. I actually felt really shitty now. "I got it. I got the loan."

"Yeah? Thought you'd have called to tell me." He sounded pissed off. Something was bothering him and I couldn't help think it was *me*.

"I wanted to tell you in person. Are you…are you *angry* with me? Have I done something wrong?"

Refusing to look at me, he stared up at the ceiling. "Were you ever going to tell me about your fiancé?"

"My wha-" *Shit.* Kevin. "Do you mean Kevin?"

Dylan shrugged, but didn't speak.

"Kevin is *not* my fiancé. He was, but he hasn't been for a long time. Who told you about him?"

Bet it was Derek. Him and his big gob.

"*He* did. He showed up this morning."

"What, *here?*"

253

Dylan replied with a single nod, his expression thoroughly unimpressed.

"He's an ex. A very persistent ex, I'll give him that, but that's all he is to me. I don't even talk to him anymore."

"Really." The single word reeked of accusation.

"You think I'm lying to you?"

"How would he know you were in Edinburgh if you didn't talk to him?"

"Um…" I hated the hesitancy in my answer but, honestly, I had no idea how he knew that. "I don't know. He could've called the restaurant. Anyone could've told him. You believe me, right? I'd never do anything to hurt you."

Exhaling a deep sigh, Dylan nodded. "Sure." He couldn't have sounded less convinced if he'd tried.

"Oh come on, Dyl! When would I have the time to cheat on you? We're hardly ever apart!"

"I know that. Don't talk to me like I'm stupid."

What the… "Dylan what's wrong with you? I wasn't trying to start an argument."

"Nothin'."

"It's something."

"Don't pretend to know what's going on in my head. You don't know shit."

Sitting up, I cupped his cheek, turning his face to look at me. "Why are you snapping? You're worrying me."

Closing his eyes, he took a deep breath. "Sorry," he said, but it seemed forced. "It's just been a tough day. Seeing your mum, remembering the past…I just feel a little overwhelmed."

That made sense, especially as his reunion with my mother was unplanned. I was glad she'd seen him though, and so was she. My parents and I were close and, although I was willing for Dylan's sake, I hated keeping things from them. Plus, I think my mum was just relieved I'd moved on from Kevin. She never did like him. Never said as much, of course, but I could tell. My mum couldn't fake a smile for shit.

"Do you want to talk about it? She didn't judge. She loves you. You know that, right?"

"I know. Honestly I just want to sleep it off. I'll be fine in the morning."

Leaning in, I brushed his lips with mine. "Put your head on my chest," I said, lying back down and outstretching my arm. This was my favourite way to go to sleep, holding him, loving him.

Doing as I said, he rested his cheek right over my heart, and I stroked up and down his back with my thumb.

"You're doing great, Dyl," I whispered, kissing the top of his head.

A reply never came but that didn't matter. He was here. *I* was here. We were together.

* * *

Dylan seemed a little distracted over the next few weeks. Distant. Edgy. He had his first counselling session last week and Paul thought that could be the reason behind the change. Dylan had a lot to work through, a lot of demons to tackle, after all. I imagined talking to a therapist would bring up all the parts of himself and his life that he'd rather forget. So, I *believed* that was why he'd started acting differently. I believed it because I *forced* myself to. I believed it because I *wanted* to. I believed it because the other suspicion pecking into my mind *hurt* too much.

Maybe the therapy would've been easier on Dylan if he'd *talked* to me about his sessions, but he wouldn't. He'd close down or gloss over the subject whenever I tried to bring it up. Life was hard. Caring for Dylan, for an addict, trying to comprehend what he was going through was difficult. Confusing. Exhausting. Supporting him was challenging, especially when he needed it the most.

But loving him...loving him was effortless.

And so I'd wait. I'd be patient. As much as it devastated me at times, I would stay strong, not push, and be there whenever he felt ready to let me in. I just couldn't fight the feeling that this was a dangerous approach, however. Dylan seemed happy, to my face at least. He told me he was grateful for everything I'd done, everything I continued to do, and that he was glad he had me to help and encourage him. Yet every time he said it an alarm bell rang in my ears.

I'd tried to research everything I could about addiction, about heroin, and about recovery, and during one of my sessions on Google I came across a meme; a meme that, lately, became all I could think about.

It said: *If the addict in your life is pleased with your help, you're probably enabling. If they're annoyed, you're probably helping the person you love more than they want to realise.*

Was I enabling Dylan? By ignoring my suspicions was I facilitating his addiction? Did the fact I'd told him I would always love him, that I'd always be there, that he could always rely on me, give Dylan *permission* to start using again?

I considered giving him an ultimatum. Heroin, or me. I'd found a wealth of information on the internet that suggested doing that very thing – making him choose. But…what if he chose wrong? I didn't think, hell I *knew*, I wouldn't be strong enough to follow through with my end of the bargain. I couldn't abandon him. How selfish would that make me? I couldn't wash my hands of him because he wasn't perfect.

Stop, I mentally scolded myself. Dylan wasn't using. I had no proof. He was trying his best, *beating* this crap, and I was doubting him. Suddenly, I felt like a bastard. I felt self-absorbed and unsupportive. This whole situation messed with my head. *Fucking drugs.* They don't just affect the user. The addict takes them, and the ones they love suffer for it.

After getting off the phone with my mum, I was rummaging through the wardrobe when Dylan got back from his latest counselling session. I went out into the living room as soon as I heard his key in the door.

"Hey," I said, stepping up to kiss him on the cheek. "How'd it go?"

"Fine." One word. I knew it'd be the only one I'd get, too.

I sighed in exasperation. I couldn't help it. I needed him to include me, stop shutting me out. He couldn't do this on his own, and neither could I. I needed *him* as well.

He walked straight over to the fridge and plucked out one of his energy drinks. I honestly didn't know how he could stomach so many of the damn things. I tasted one the other day and it was like drinking pure syrup. Derek left one here once, he drank them after his workouts, and it'd sat untouched in the cereal cupboard for months until Dylan found it.

Patience, I reminded myself. *Don't push.* "Hey, have you seen my old iPad?" I asked, changing the subject for no other reason than I wanted a conversation with him. At this point the subject didn't matter. I just wanted him to *talk* to me. I missed his voice. "My mum's one broke so I told her she could have it, but now I can't find the bloody thing."

"Uh, no," he said, popping the seal on his can of sugar. "Sorry. Have you tried under the bed?"

Huffing, I clicked my tongue. "I've looked *everywhere*. I'm wondering if I've already given it away and forgot."

"Maybe." He took a long swig of his drink. "You're always forgetting your keys and shit."

He was right, but I was *sure* I would've remembered giving someone such an expensive piece of technology. "Hmm." *Where the hell is it?* "Are you ready for work?" It was almost time for us to go in. I'd have to look for the iPad again later. "If you're not up for it you can stay home."

"I don't need special treatment because I'm seeing a junkie counsellor," he spat, his tone icy enough to chill my veins. He was in a bad mood, *again,* and I was almost done with pussyfooting around him. I couldn't take much more.

"You look tired, that's all." His cheeks were flushed and blotchy so I touched one with the back of my hand. "You're a little warm too. You might be coming down with something."

"I said I'm fine."

Fine. *He's always* fine. Me? I wasn't fucking fine. "I'll wait in the car," is all I said. I didn't have the energy to keep going, keep trying. *I'm exhausted.*

The kitchen was already in full throttle by the time we arrived. Instead of acknowledging everyone like I usually would, I stormed straight into my office and closed the door, needing a few minutes away from the whole damn world. Of course, when you had friends like Paul, that didn't last very long.

"Why'd you look like you've just been diagnosed with gangrene in your dick?" he asked, closing the door behind him.

"Sorry," I muttered, running my hand through my hair. "I'll be out in a minute."

"You're going nowhere until you've told me what's bothering you."

Sighing, I dropped my head. "It's Dylan."

Paul pulled up the chair opposite my desk, taking a seat and leaning forward to listen.

"I want to be there for him but he's not letting me. I thought things would only get better once he started therapy, yet I feel like we've taken ten steps backwards. He's been acting weird since the day Kevin showed up. Honestly, I think he's pissed off with me because I didn't tell him about Kev myself. It feels like…well it's almost like he's punishing me."

"Well that's bullshit. Kevin's a moron. You're not responsible for his actions and I'll tell Dylan as much myself."

"No, no. Stay out of it. I don't know, maybe I was naïve to think it wouldn't be this hard, that it wouldn't take him so long to recover."

Paul fell quiet, his forehead crunched like he was contemplating. "Come out with me tonight. We'll get off our faces, put the world to rights like we used to."

I shook my head. "I shouldn't leave him."

"That's exactly what you should do. You're living in each other's pockets and it's not healthy, Cam."

Hmm. "I don't know. I'll see if he's okay with it."

"No you fuckin' won't. He isn't your damn mother. You're a grown man. If you have to ask permission from your boyfriend to go out with your best mate then something is seriously wrong with your relationship."

"I didn't mean I'd ask for permission," I snapped. Although, the things he said were probably true. "I don't fancy going out," I added in a softer tone. "How about we just go back to yours with some cans?"

"Suits me," he agreed. "Now get your arse out there. Service is only an hour away."

"Sure." I nodded. "I'll be out in five." First, I needed a shot of strong coffee and several deep breaths.

I didn't get time to corner Dylan until lunchtime service had dwindled. When I approached him, he stood by the dishwasher staring into nothing, while a commis loaded the dirty dishes inside.

"Dyl?" I said, stepping up behind him.

Nothing.

"Dylan." I tapped his shoulder, startling him.

He spun on his heels to face me. "Crap. Sorry. Caught in a daydream."

His excuse didn't sit well with me, though I couldn't figure out why. "You okay?" I asked, narrowing my eyes as I assessed his expression.

"Sure. Why wouldn't I be?"

"Because *Evan* is doing *your* job right now."

Evan, my commis, tossed me a glance at the sound of his name, raising his eyebrow as if to tell me Dylan had been like this all day.

"S-sorry," Dylan muttered, taking the stack of plates from Evan's hands. He only stuttered when he was nervous.

Why's he nervous? What was he hiding?

"I, um…" I almost didn't say it. I felt like I was abandoning him when he was so obviously struggling with his therapy. But Paul *was* right. I needed this, needed a break. "I'm going to Paul's tonight."

His skin paled and he looked at me with pure hurt in his eyes. "Why? What've I done?"

"*Done?* You haven't done anything. I'm just spending a few hours with my friend."

"*I'm* your friend."

"What…why…" Confused, I leaned in closer to him, curling my fingers around the top of his arm. "Dylan," I breathed. "Something's wrong with you and it's worrying me. *Talk* to me. Is it Kevin? Are you still mad with me?"

"What right have I got to give a shit about who you've fucked with *my* past?"

My eyebrows knitted together and my reply snagged in my throat as I took a step back. "Why are you being like this? I've done *nothing* but try and support you and you're treating me like crap!"

He shrugged like a petulant teenager and I didn't know what the hell to do, what to say. I wanted to walk away as much as I wanted to hold him. "If you don't want me to go, I won't."

"I'm not your keeper. Do what you want."

"*Then what the…*" Pausing, I took a calming breath and lowered my voice to an angry whisper when I realised I'd been shouting. "What the hell do you want from me? *Tell* me and I'll do it. Let me *in*, Dyl. For Christ's sake *let me in.*"

Please.

"Hey, chef!"

Dammit. I cursed the voice calling me, interrupting me.

"There's a customer out front who wants to compliment you!"

Dammit! Dammit! Dammit! Face crumpled, I looked at Dylan and sighed, frustration gripping my heart like a vice, before turning towards the voice. "On my way!"

* * *

"Damn I needed this." My words were barely intelligible as they drowned in laughter. Three hours and countless beers into being at Paul's, and I hadn't laughed so much in months.

Relaxed back on the sofa with one ankle balanced on his knee, Paul picked at the label on his glass bottle. "See? Uncle Paul always knows best."

"I thi-think…" *Damn.* I got the hiccups. "I th-think I'm go-going to reg-regret this in-in the morning."

263

"You hiccup like a yapping puppy."

"Can-can't h-help it."

Paul passed me another beer. "Down that. Don't stop for breath."

I really didn't want another drink, my head was fuzzy enough already, but I also didn't want hiccups so I drank it anyway. When I eventually pulled the bottle from my lips, Paul looked at me with an expectant expression.

I counted to ten in my head. No hiccups. "Gone."

"Good. I was about to slap your back and I wouldn't have been gentle." Paul seemed a little more 'with it' than I was, so I suspected he'd not drunk as much as I had. That meant the arsewipe would be able to gloat while I moped around with a hangover tomorrow.

"Hey," I said. "You seen my spare iPad? Can't find it." My speech was a little slurred, making Paul chuckle.

"Have you asked Dylan?"

"Yeah, he's not…" *Wait.* He asked me that question in an almost accusatory tone. "Why'd you say it like that?"

"You said yourself he's been…*off.* I've seen it myself too. Caught him staring off into space today more times than I can count. You don't think…" he trailed off, sucking in a breath like he was trying to find the courage to voice his thoughts. "You don't think he's using again, do you?"

"*What?*" In an instant my hazy, alcohol-ridden brain abruptly cleared. "No! He wouldn't mess up all the hard work he's put in." *The work* I've *put in,* I added in my head. I *forced* myself to believe it. I *had* to. "Why would he undo everything he's achieved?"

Paul surrendered his palms and it made me realise I'd been yelling. "It was just a thought," he said. "You know him best."

"Yes," I agreed, my voice curt. "I do." At least I thought, *hoped,* I did.

"Forget I said anything. John was a liar, a good one too. I can't help comparing them."

Except I couldn't forget. I couldn't forget because I was already thinking it, and I had been for a couple of weeks. But I didn't want to be. I *wanted* to forget.

Leaning forward, Paul plucked another bottle from the crate, holding it out to me. "Another?"

"No." I shook my head. "I've had enough." I'd had enough of bloody everything. All I wanted to do now was sleep. Sleep and forget. Sleep, forget, and *pray* that Dylan hadn't let himself, let *me* down.

* * *

You don't think he's using again, do you? Paul's words echoed in my mind on a loop for the next two weeks. Every time I answered *no* in my head, but I was starting to think enough was enough. Dylan was lying to me, and *I* was lying to myself. A week ago my camera went missing. I rarely used it, didn't need to in an age of smartphones, but it'd been on the left hand side of my underwear drawer for over two years.

Now it wasn't.

The day after, cash went missing from my wallet. A twenty-pound note. Usually, I probably wouldn't have even noticed, but since my doubts about Dylan surfaced I'd been extra vigilant. I counted the money in my wallet daily, and I'd been doing so for a couple of weeks. Before then, he could've been dipping into it all the time and I'd have been none the wiser.

Two days after that three ten-pound notes disappeared. I recounted several times, not wanting to believe it. But…it was *definitely* missing. The most fucked up part of everything, is that I felt a sense of reassurance. If he'd been stealing from me, he wouldn't have needed to prostitute himself. The thought was consoling, and I knew that described how gloriously messed up this entire situation was. There should be no comfort to take from *any* of this.

Now, today, I couldn't find Dylan's guitar. Since he first arrived it'd been propped up against the wall next to the couch…now it wasn't. He never touched it, rarely even looked at it, but I always hoped, just like when we were kids, that he would eventually. But now it wasn't here, and I felt physically, violently sick. That instrument was worth *so* much more than money…

How could he?

Some days he'd even *ask* me for cash, and I'd given it to him. I didn't question him when he went out to buy 'new shoes' and returned empty handed. I didn't challenge him when he went missing for hours at a time. I didn't ask him why he was so drowsy lately, falling asleep in the middle of the afternoon. I even agreed when he asked me to drive him to the other side of town because 'his energy drinks were cheaper there'. Why did I do that? Why did I *help* him go out and score? Because I didn't want to believe it. I didn't want to confront my worst fear. I wasn't strong enough to deal with it again.

I did all those things, enabled him to keep using, because I was fucking petrified.

On top of all that, he'd been distracted at work, slipping into dazes at home. He'd had a 'stomach bug' for over a week, which was his excuse for not eating properly or wanting sex with me, and now he had a 'cold' too. The problem was, I'd seen the same puffy eyes and runny nose before, back when he first reappeared in my life. He didn't have a cold. He was *using*. I knew it deep in my heart.

I couldn't ignore it any longer, couldn't keep hoping he'd 'snap out of it'.

Why? Why? Why? I must've asked myself the question a thousand times already today and it was barely noon. Loving someone had never felt so exhausting, so painful. I was *angry* with Dylan.

Confused.

Disappointed.

Frustrated.

Hurt.

All the things he'd feared I'd be, and all the things I'd told him I wouldn't.

Why? Why? Why?

I confided in Paul, not that I needed to. He already knew. And so, he knew exactly what was wrong when I had to bow out of service.

He found me in my office and sat on the edge of my desk, rubbing my shoulder. "Did you do it?"

I nodded. I'd just spent an hour on the phone with a private residential rehabilitation facility. Whatever the NHS offered clearly hadn't worked. Either that, or Dylan hadn't attended the sessions like he said he had. Dylan needed help, help I couldn't give him, and he needed to be locked away from the outside world while he got it – away from temptation. He needed an intensive intervention and this was the only option I could come up with. Riverside View would set me back three grand a week for a six-week programme. Eighteen thousand pounds that, if it worked, would be worth every goddamn penny.

"It has to be voluntary," I said, my tone despondent. Dylan didn't know anything about it yet. As far as he was concerned, I was still blissfully unaware of what he was doing. "Needs a GP referral and an assessment at the centre to see if he's suitable. Apparently, that can all be achieved in under twenty-four hours but...well, I'm not sure he'll agree to it."

"He *has* to. Dammit, Cam, you can't go on like this."

"I don't know what to do, Paul. I feel…I feel so out of my depth. Is this my life now? Always worrying, always trying to catch him out. I…I can't do it again. I'm not strong enough for any of this." I made a weak attempt to slam my palm against the desk but the sound barely registered.

"What do I have to do?" I continued. "Why can't I be enough for him?"

"Don't. Don't do that to yourself. He's sick, Cam. He's not doing it to hurt you, not intentionally."

"Well he *is* hurting me, and I'm tired. So fucking tired. A part of me…Christ, Paul, a part of me *hates* him for putting me through this again."

Just as Paul opened his mouth to reply, a knock rapped on my office door, shortly followed by Evan popping his head around it. "Hey, chef. Umm…there's a problem in the kitchen. Derek needs you."

"It'll have to wait," I said, my tone dismissive as I shooed him away with my hand.

"It's Dylan."

I was on my feet and jogging towards the door before he'd even finished speaking Dylan's name. "Where are they?"

He didn't need to answer me. As soon as I rounded the corner I saw the commotion happening ahead.

"Get the fuck off me!" Dylan screamed, trying to wrestle free from Derek's arms. He struggled and kicked, knocking some trays off the counter and sending them crashing to the floor with an almighty clatter.

I rushed over to them, helping Derek keep Dylan still while we carried him out of the kitchen. Heads turned, eyes stared. It made my blood simmer in my veins. "Show's over!" I yelled. "Get back to work or you're out of a fucking job!"

Dylan's limbs flailed, his hand whacking my face a few times, and we lowered him down outside, by the bins. I grabbed his shoulders, staring straight into his dazed eyes. "This stops, Dyl. It stops *today*."

"I just need some money," he argued, his voice trembling. "Need money, for uh…shoes. I need shoes. But those bastards in there…" He jabbed his finger towards the back exit door of O'Neil's. "They were laughing at me, Cam. They looked at me like I was scum!"

Dropping my head, I sighed in frustration, in exhaustion, in utter fucking helplessness.

"Just a fiv-tenner. Twenty. Twenty quid's all I need. *Please,* Cam. I just need some money."

"No, Dyl. No money. I want to take you somewhere tonight, and I need you to agre-"

"*Please,*" he whimpered. "I'll beg if you want." Dropping to his knees on the dirty gravel, he clapped his hands into the praying position, tilting his head to look up at me, *plead* with me.

It broke my fucking heart.

Squatting to his level, I curled my fingers around his hand. "I've got you a place in a rehab centre," I explained, tears misting my vision.

"N-no." He shook his head.

I ignored him. "It's a good clinic. Residential. Best in the country."

"*Fuck you!*" he roared, standing up. He stumbled as he crawled to his unstable feet before bending down and shoving me in the chest, knocking me backwards onto my arse. "Fuck the lot of you!" He started to run but, reaching up from the ground, I grabbed his forearm, pulling him back.

Standing, I forced him against the brick wall, taking his face in my hands. He writhed in my hold, tried to look away, but I was stronger. "Look at me goddammit!"

Slowly, reluctantly, his bloodshot eyes, weighed down with dark, heavy circles, rolled to meet my gaze. "You have to do this," I said, my nose inches from his. "Once and for all, you *have* to do this. I'm *begging* you." My bottom lip quivered, making my words jumpy.

Dylan sucked in short, sharp breaths, his body weakening. "I can't do it," he whimpered, breathless, panicked...*terrified*. "P-please...please don't make me. I-I-I...can't do it. I'll do better. I promise. I'll be b-better for you, Cam I swear. D-don't send me away."

"I have to!" I yelled, shaking his shoulders. "You're gonna kill yourself with this shit, Dylan! I won't watch you die!" I was crying now, violent sobs rocking through my body.

"I-I've f-fucked up, Cam," Dylan cried, his legs buckling beneath him. Derek, who'd I'd forgotten was even there, jumped in to help me hold him up. "F-fucked it all up."

"Dylan…" I lightly slapped his cheek as I spoke. He looked like he was about to pass out. "Say you'll go. Nod. Just once. Nod for me. Let me help you."

His head bowed into the faintest nod before his eyes rolled back and his listless body fell into my arms.

"Car," I choked out to Derek, holding Dylan's entire weight.

"On it." As Derek jogged away, Paul came bustling out of the exit door. I wondered briefly why he didn't follow me out here in the first place, but I didn't care enough to ask.

"Shit," he said, helping me lower Dylan to the ground. He was coming around again now, mumbling something I couldn't interpret.

"Go make an emergency appointment with the GP. The number's in my phone in my office."

Nodding, Paul scurried away, leaving me alone with the man who'd owned my heart since I was a kid, the man who was breaking it right in front of me.

"Bubbles is dead," Dylan mumbled, tipping his head back against the wall. "My parents, my grandma…everyone I care about dies."

Bubbles. That girl. "Dylan," I whispered, cupping his cheek.

"I'm poison. Everybody leaves. They leave or they die."

"I'm still here. I'm not going anywhere."

"You will. Eventually…you will."

That was the moment it hit me, the moment I understood why I, alone, couldn't help him, why I'd never be enough. There was more to tackle than his addiction. Heroin was a side effect of something much deeper. Dylan was damaged, not just physically, but psychologically.

"I'll poison you too," he added, barely audible over the sound of my tyres crunching the gravel as Derek brought my car into the loading bay.

Focused on Dylan, I tipped his chin, encouraging him to look at me. "We're going to the GP," I began.

"Doesn't work," he cut in, his head falling to the side. He looked beyond defeated, and it crushed me.

Ignoring him, I continued. "It's going to be different this time. You're going to a clinic where you'll get twenty-four seven support. They'll-"

"You're sending me away." It was an accusation more than a statement.

If my heart ached any harder I was sure it would give out and kill me." "No." I gripped his face, levelling my eyes with his. "No, Dyl. I'm not sending you away. I'm sending you to get *better*, so you can come home to *me*."

He might've been living in my apartment, but he wasn't *with* me. I'm not sure he ever really was, not mentally.

"Do you trust me, Dylan?"

He nodded, *barely*, but it was there.

"Then agree. Say you'll *try*. Say you'll *live* for me. Not just exist…*live*."

"I'll fail. I always fail."

"*Try.*"

He nodded again, this time with more conviction, but the fear in his eyes was palpable. When I got to my feet, he gripped the arm I held out and pulled himself up. I put my arm around his waist, not just to guide him, to support his weight, but to keep him close.

Safe.

Reaching the car, I opened the passenger door for Dylan to climb inside before turning to Derek. "I'm sorry you had to see this," I whispered.

Derek didn't look shocked as I thought he'd be. He actually looked…remorseful. "I'm sorry. Thought I'd been lookin' out for 'im. I didn't even notice he'd slipped."

"Wait…you *knew?*"

"Don't rip Paul a new one. As the two 'ead chefs, you guys are busy runnin' the kitchen. Paul thought Dylan needed someone who could watch over 'im, 'elp 'im settle in. Guess I fucked that one up."

Goddammit, Dylan. He had no idea how many people cared about him.

"This isn't your fault," I said. "If anyone's to blame here it's *me* for not doing this sooner. Look at him." I nodded towards the car window, my breath melting into a sigh. "He's terrified. This is what I was putting off. I thought I could be strong enough for both of us, that he could love *me* more than he loved drugs. But…it's not about that, and I realise it now. He needs people who know what the hell they're doing. That isn't *any* of us."

Turning to the sound of footsteps, I saw Paul jogging towards us. "Appointment's in an hour," he said, handing me my mobile.

"Thanks." I took my phone, stuffing it in my back pocket. "I'll call you later."

"Like fuck you will," Paul muttered, opening the back door of my car. "I'm coming with you."

"This isn't a daytrip, Paul. I need you to cover service."

"I'll do that," Derek cut in. "I've got it. You guys go."

"I ain't gonna sit on the doc's lap," Paul said, rolling his eyes. "I'll wait outside."

"Fine." I glanced back to Derek. "If anyone chats shit about this in there shut them down. If he ever wants to come back here I want it to be a safe place for him. This isn't Entertainment Weekly, this is our fucking lives."

"No probs, chef."

Striding to the driver's side, I climbed inside and fixed my seatbelt before looking at Dylan, my chest tight, my stomach heavy. "Ready?"

His shattered gaze met mine for just a second before he turned away, resting his cheek on the glass. "Just drive."

* * *

We were in and out of the GP's surgery before our allotted five minutes were up. He processed the referral without too many questions, and said it would reach the rehab centre I'd spoken to within the hour. It's rather amazing how fast things move when you're paying for it.

So now, we were at Riverside View. A timid Dylan had been ushered into a private room where he would undergo a thorough physical and psychological assessment to see if he was suitable for their programme. *How can he not be?* I kept asking myself. He was addicted to narcotics, what more did they need from him?

"Commitment," Paul answered when I asked the question I'd been silently repeating in my head since they took Dylan away. "If he doesn't *want* to do this then there's no point to any of it."

"He does want to." I *knew* he did. He wanted to be the Dylan he used to be, he just didn't think he deserved to. The thought alone almost killed me. *How did I not see it?* He blamed himself. All the bad stuff, all the people he'd lost, he thought it was all because of him.

"This place is like a fucking holiday resort in the Seychelles," Paul muttered beside me under his breath.

It was certainly luxurious. Pale walls, oak furniture, large gardens. According to the brochure they even had two heated swimming pools, an extensive gym, and cable TV. I just hoped my money was paying for skilled medical professionals and not saunas and foot massages.

We waited in the small room they showed us into when we arrived for three painfully long hours before Dylan returned, escorted by a woman in a skirt-suit, carrying a tablet. "If you'd like to come with me I can take your payment details," the woman said with a saccharine, well-rehearsed smile.

Removing my wallet from my jacket, I thrust it into Paul's chest, keeping my eyes on Dylan. "He can take care of that," I told her. Paul knew *everything* about me, including all my secret passwords and pin numbers.

"Of course, sir. Dylan's doctor will be through shortly to answer any questions you may have."

With Paul and Mrs Smiler out of earshot, Dylan edged closer, grabbing my arm. "I don't think I can do this," he said, his voice raw and desperate. "M-maybe in a few days. Just give me a few days and I'll do it."

"Dyla-" I began, but he cut me off.

"How much is this costing? I can't…I'll never be able to pay you back. I'll do it myself. I'll be stronger this time. I promise. I'll be better. I'll…I'll be who you want me to be."

"You *can* do this. They're going to help you."

"Y-you can help me," he said, his voice wavering, words shaking. "I know I let you down but I'll do better!"

A smile filled with so much sadness it felt like it could kill me crept onto my lips. "No, Dyl. I *can't*. I can't help what's going on in here," I said, gently tapping the side of his head with my finger. "You need this. You need these people."

"I need *you*."

"You've got me. Always," I said, palming the sides of his neck, pulling his haunted face close to mine. "But only if you do this. I can't watch you destroy yourself, Dyl. I can't watch you die." It felt shameful to give him an ultimatum, and I loathed the words as they left my mouth…but I couldn't keep living like this. It felt like I was dying right along with him.

In that moment the door opened again. A doctor wearing a white coat over his suit joined us, holding out his hand. I shook it for longer than I planned but I already saw this stranger as some kind of saviour.

"Dylan, would you like to say goodbye now?"

No. I didn't want him to leave. Not yet. I knew by the watery look in Dylan's eyes he wasn't ready either. Heart in my throat, pulse thudding in my ears, I leaned forward to kiss his cheek but he turned away. "Bye," is all he said, before heading towards the woman waiting for him in the hall. He didn't even wait for me to return his goodbye. He just…*left*.

"Mr O'Neil?"

The doctor's voice snapped me back into the room. "I'm Doctor Collins. Dylan has signed a consent form which allows me to discuss his care and progress with you. He's also listed you as his next of kin. Are you ready to get started?"

"Yes," I answered without hesitation. I was scared, but *so* ready. Ready for Dylan to get better, ready for him to come back to me.

Doctor Collins proffered his hand towards the white couch Paul and I sat on earlier. "Take a seat." We sat at the same time, the doctor opting for the armchair opposite me.

"So you can help him?" Knotting my fingers together on my lap, I gave him a pleading look.

"Absolutely. He seems very positive towards treatment."

"He does?" I couldn't help the surprise in my voice. He didn't seem very positive to *me*.

"He's afraid, which is to be expected, but he recognises that he has a problem. That's the first step."

Good. That's good. I simply nodded.

"I'm led to believe Dylan only recently relapsed. Is that true?"

"Yes. Well, kind of. He got clean on his own a couple of months ago," I said, my voice timid, embarrassed that I hadn't sought professional help for him sooner. "Guess that didn't work out too well."

"Relapse is, unfortunately, common. It's to be expected."

I didn't like the sound of that. *How many times will I have to go through this?*

"Physical affects aside, substance abuse is a lifelong disease of the brain. In a sense his brain, his thought processes, need to be completely re-programmed, retrained to enable him to make the right choices. Once he's detoxed we'll work through the psychological aspects of his addiction with him. Here at Riverside, recovery covers physical, mental, *and* emotional rehabilitation."

"But you're saying it might not work. That relapse is common."

"It is, especially when it's done without professional support, as in Dylan's case. It's common, but *not* inevitable. Living in recovery will mean Dylan will face a lifelong process of recognising, avoiding, and minimising triggers. That's what we aim to teach here, and we have a very high success rate."

"Triggers?"

Doctor Collins was very animated when he talked, using hands and expressions to convey his passion and belief in what he preached. It filled me with confidence. "A trigger is something, an event, a visual stimulant, even a certain smell, that can mentally take a person back to a situation they're trying to combat. Different people have different triggers and Dylan needs to learn what his are. It could be something as simple as a movie containing scenes of drug use, hearing a song he once heard while using, or being in the same area he used to procure his drugs. Once he discovers his triggers, he will need to work for the rest of his life to avoid them. In cases where those triggers are unavoidable, he needs to learn how to process them, how to stop them turning into a craving, or into obsessive thoughts."

"And you can do that?"

"No. But I believe *Dylan* can do that, with our guidance once he's completed detox."

The word *detox* made the corners of my eyes sting, remembering how painful, how soul-destroying, it was last time. I still heard his screams in my sleep, and a part of me thought I always would.

I didn't know if Doctor Collins could see the fear on my face, or if the next part of the conversation would've followed regardless. "We will administer Dylan a drug called buprenorphine to alleviate some of his withdrawal symptoms. Towards the end of detox if he's still struggling physically, we'll offer lofexidine as well."

I'd never heard of the complicated drug names before. I didn't know what they did, but they sounded like they'd help his transition to sobriety easier so, to me, they sounded wonderful.

The doctor talked me through the drugs and the symptoms they treated, and the anxiety bound tight around my stomach loosened with each piece of information he offered. I wasn't stupid enough to believe Dylan's detox would be painless, but it sure sounded like it would be easier than the last time. When I witnessed his battle in my apartment, it was like watching the person I loved crawling over the burning coals of hell, and there was nothing I could do to save him. My only option was to watch, like I was trapped in a wire cage; close enough to see him burn, hear him scream, but too far away to put out the flames.

"Dylan will receive around the clock care while he's here," Doctor Collins assured me. "I should have a proposed treatment and care plan available for you within a couple of days. I should also point out, although Dylan has given consent for me to discuss his treatment with you, anything he discusses with his therapist will be kept strictly confidential. I cannot breach that trust."

"No. Of course." I nodded.

"Do you have any questions?"

Thousands. "What happens after the six weeks?"

"He'll continue to receive care here as an outpatient. We usually recommend three therapy sessions per week initially, but that can increase or decrease according to Dylan's individual needs. Those sessions include one-to-one, group, and family sessions. In order to help him, to understand the recovery process, we encourage patients to bring a chosen family member, or their partner, to some sessions with them. He'll also be assigned a sponsor, and then-"

"Sorry," I said, apologising for my interruption. "What's a sponsor?"

"A sponsor is someone who will support Dylan through recovery for as long as he needs it. He can relate to them because every sponsor has been through, and continues to live through, recovery themselves. They provide an unbiased ear to talk to, they'll help guide him through the twelve steps and beyond. Most importantly, they'll understand exactly how he's feeling because they've worn his shoes at some point."

"Twelve steps? Isn't that an alcoholic thing?"

"Recovering from *any* addiction requires a similar process. The steps are explained in the booklet Natalie, the lady on reception, will give you before you leave. We work closely with Narcotics Anonymous, who also utilise the twelve steps method, and we'll be encouraging Dylan to attend their meetings alongside his therapy when he leaves here."

"Isn't it...*religious?*" I felt a little silly, and a *lot* judgemental, but I briefly remembered something about admitting your problems to God in a movie about an alcoholic I saw once. "Dylan is an atheist." After becoming an orphan four months before his fourteenth birthday, he always said if there was a god, then he hated him.

"Here, at Riverside, we leave beliefs at the door in group sessions. The only mandatory requirement we have is that all members want to overcome their addiction. You are right, however, that the twelve steps programme derives from Christian origins, but you don't have to believe in any kind of god for you to benefit from the steps.

"If he does indeed go on to NA, they will focus on a 'higher power." He air quoted with his fingers. "Dylan can choose whatever he feels comfortable with as his higher power. Some people choose God, some choose reality. He can decide where he pulls his strength from. In essence, it's about teaching people that they're not alone. They don't have to carry the burden of their demons by themselves. In people who don't practice an active faith, we encourage them to think of the messages contained in the steps as spiritual rather than religious."

Nodding, I tried to process everything we'd discussed. I wasn't very successful. All I could think about was Dylan's face when they took him away, wondering if that's how frightened he looked when he had to go with the social worker after his grandma died.

"I can see him, right? While he's here. I can visit?"

"We ask for no contact for the first seven days. While Dylan detoxes and settles in, phone calls and visits aren't permitted. After that period, we encourage regular contact with loved ones, yes."

Seven days? The thought of not seeing his face, hearing his voice, feeling his skin, for a whole week felt like someone had taken a hammer to my chest.

"Do you have any other questions?"

"No, I don't think so." Though I imagined I'd think of some later.

"Our phones are manned twenty-four hours a day. You can call at any time with questions, or just for an update on how he's doing."

That made me feel somewhat better.

"Thank you, Doctor Collins," I said, standing and offering my hand to shake.

"You've chosen well with us, Mr O'Neil. We will take good care of Dylan. You can find details of our approach, statistics and such, in the welcome pack you'll receive on your way out."

The guy sounded like a cheesy salesman at times, but I could overlook that if he helped my Dylan get better like he said he could.

Opening the door, Doctor Collins stepped aside and motioned for me to leave first. Paul was waiting on the circle of leather chairs by reception, and I gave him a silent nod when he saw me.

"You okay?" Paul asked, joining me at the large reception desk.

"Not really." The words cracked on my lips. I couldn't elaborate or the tears burning the rims of my eyes would've spilled over.

I exchanged pleasantries with the lady behind the desk and she handed over various pieces of paperwork and a welcome brochure. Taking them, I said goodbye and got the hell out of there as fast as I could. Today's events had happened so quickly, and when I stepped outside the cool evening air blasted into my lungs like it was the first breath I'd taken in months.

"Christ," I breathed, tipping my head back to stare at the grey sky. I felt sick. Dizzy. Breathless. I was exhausted; physically and emotionally drained. "His face, Paul. When they took him to his room… He's terrified. *I'm* terrified. He thinks I'm abandoning him, I know he does."

"But you're *not*, and he'll see that when he's sober."

Maybe he would. Maybe he wouldn't. The wait to find out would be unbearable. I missed him already.

"I told him I'd only stay if he did this. How selfish is that? I practically threatened him."

"There's nothing wrong with that. He needs an incentive. He needs a reason to keep at it. John knew we'd always be there and, if I'm honest, I think that was detrimental. Dylan needs to have something to lose, or what's the point?"

I hadn't realised I was crying until a slight breeze swept over my cheeks, making the tears trickle faster down my face and feel ice-cold against my skin. Seconds later, something hard crashed into my chest, making me stumble.

Paul hugged me, clapping my back. "He's in the best place. You did the right thing."

I knew that, I *really* did, so why did I feel so damn guilty?

"Let's get you home," Paul said, releasing me.

"Actually, can I stay at yours tonight? I just…"

"No explanation needed, mate. Mi casa es su casa."

Raising an eyebrow, a grin pulled on one side of my mouth.

"What? I fucking *aced* French in my GCSE's."

"Um, that was Spanish."

Paul's eyebrows narrowed like he was deep in thought, then he shrugged. "Me llamo, Paul. What language is that?"

"Still Spanish." I couldn't help laughing, and then I felt guilty about it. Dylan wouldn't be laughing right now. He was probably crying, screaming with pain.

"Well then maybe I aced Spanish. Fuck knows. It's all the same to me."

Smile completely evaporated, I tossed Paul my car keys, and followed him to my car. I didn't feel alert enough to drive.

Counting Daisies

Stay strong, Dyl, were my last thoughts as Paul started driving, Riverside View slowly fading into the distance through the wing-mirror. *I'll wait for you.*

* * *

Eight days later…

The last week had been torture. I called Riverside twice daily to check on Dylan and each time I was put through to the doctor in charge of his care each day. As promised, they answered all my questions, even ones I feared were stupid or irrelevant. It took only four days until they started reducing his medication, which the doctor confirmed was a good thing, but now the *real* work began. Now it was time to tackle Dylan's *mind*, confront his demons, knock the evil fucker known as heroin out once and for all.

The seven day contact ban was up yesterday and I was as excited as I was nervous to see Dylan again. I hoped the visit would reassure me, that it would bring a sense of normality back into my life because without him I'd been little more than a moving shadow. Work dragged. I made mistakes. Thankfully, I had a strong team of capable kitchen staff who kept up the standards expected of them without me trailing their arses. It would be unfair to say I'd headed the kitchen like I was supposed to recently. That title belonged to Paul. I was under no illusion that my life would've crumbled without his support over the last few months.

I managed to find Dylan's guitar, out of sheer luck more than anything else. I checked out the pawn shops in the area where I found him with that girl, the girl who died, and there it was, displayed in the window for anybody to buy. The sight of it made me angry, then tremendously sad. I knew Dylan's father well, saw him almost every day when we were kids and, after Dylan, that instrument meant the world to him. I didn't really believe in heaven, and in that moment I hoped such a place didn't exist, because if Jeremy Roberts could've seen what Dylan had done it would've destroyed him. I bought it back, grateful it hadn't been lost forever, knowing if it had Dylan would never forgive himself. I'm sure I paid a hell of a lot more than Dylan sold it for, but also a *lot* less than what it was worth. Three hundred pounds, it cost me. Clearly, and thankfully, the pawn shop owner knew jack shit about classic guitars.

That same day, Kevin showed up again, offering a threat that I'd lose him forever if I didn't agree to talk things out with him. "Bye, then," is all I offered in return. It led to an angry outburst on Kevin's side, followed by some pleading, but any feelings I ever had for him had well and truly dissolved. I didn't wish him bad. If you ignored the fact he had a tendency to dip his wick in other men's candles behind my back, he was a decent guy. But he wasn't *the* guy. I'd always remember the times we shared fondly, most of them anyway, but I just didn't love him anymore.

I don't think I ever really did.

Not like Dylan, like I'd *always* love Dylan. I'd have done anything for the boy I grew up with, and I felt like I proved that every day I stuck by his side. It wasn't always easy, it was actually one of the hardest things I'd ever done, but I'd love him forever regardless. I didn't have a choice. Dylan owned me, owned my heart, and I was powerless to stop it.

When I saw him yesterday I didn't get the reassurance I looked for, but I had hope that it was coming. The fear in his eyes when our gazes met melted into the familiar shame I'd seen so often in those beautiful green irises. Shoulders hunched, demeanour timid, he avoided eye-contact with me for most of our time together. We didn't talk much. I stuck to *safe* questions, asked about his room, the facilities, whether he liked his doctor and so forth. His answers were brief, his voice quiet, but we were together. That was all I needed…for now.

He was on course, doing well. He was going to beat this. I'd get him, the *real* him, the boy that I loved and the man I would always love, back.

I had to.

I didn't know how to live without him anymore.

Chapter

Twelve

~Dylan~

THIS PLACE MUST'VE cost Cameron a small fortune. The thought rolled around in my head repeatedly, adding extra weight to the chain of guilt suspended from my neck. I told myself I wouldn't let him down again, but I'd said that so many times I couldn't help believe it was bullshit. I said as much to my therapist, Jason, who I saw for the first time yesterday. In return I received an 'it's never too late to make a change' speech. I'd heard it all before, and it was bollocks.

Cameron was coming again today. I didn't want him to, and I did. My head was fucked. He'd always insisted he'd never be disappointed in me, but I could never accept it or understand why. *I* was disappointed in me, so how the hell could he not be? I often wondered if I could be the man he deserved, and the thought usually ended up hurting when I realised I probably wouldn't.

"Good morning, Dylan."

I looked up to find my therapist standing in my doorway, and offered a brief tip of my chin.

"Are you ready for group?"

No. I'd been dreading this moment. Sitting around a circle with a group of junkies wasn't my idea of a fun time. My feelings, my secrets, were *mine*. I didn't want to share them with a bunch of strangers. Jason said I didn't need to talk if I didn't want to, not at first anyway, so what was the point in going?

I had to go, of course. I'd already pledged my commitment to the programme, to Cameron, and I couldn't back out now. I *wouldn't*. This was my last shot. If this failed then I would be screwed for all eternity. I said I'd give it my all and I meant it, regardless of whether I thought it would actually work.

"Sure," I said, tucking my notebook under my pillow. They encouraged us to keep a diary, which I thought seemed silly at first, yet I wrote in it anyway; my thoughts, my feelings, things I wasn't ready to say out loud. Sometimes I'd doodle in it out of boredom, others I'd write song lyrics I'd never sing just to get the twisted thoughts out of my head and try and turn them into something beautiful. I only started writing in it three days ago and the book was almost full, so maybe it wasn't so silly after all.

Walking into group was as daunting as expected. Hands tucked into my jeans pockets, I kept my head down and took a seat on the first empty chair I came to. Scanning the room, I noticed some people chatting, relaxed and smiling, and some who looked as nervous as I felt. If anyone glanced in my direction, I'd avert my gaze. I felt uneasy. Stupid. They all knew why I was here, how weak and reckless I was, and shame gnawed at my insides.

I wondered if any of these people were as bad as I was, if they'd done the same terrible things. I wondered if they'd let people down too, if they had friends and family who'd given them everything and they'd thrown it back in their faces. I wondered if they, if *I*, could actually leave here as different, *better*, people.

"Good morning," Jason greeted, nodding and smiling to each of us individually as he entered the room. He took a seat at the head of the circle, in front of a large whiteboard.

Here we go. Shifting awkwardly in my chair, I kept my gaze firmly on the parquet floor, praying he wouldn't call on me to speak. Last night I dreamt about standing there, feeling completely exposed and vulnerable while giving the, 'my name is Dylan and I'm a heroin addict,' speech.

I can't do that, I thought, remembering my dream. My hands were clammy and I felt pressure on my throat. I wouldn't have been able to talk even if I'd wanted to.

True to Jason's word, I didn't have to say a thing, and I spent the first half of the session counting the joins in the wooden floor, wishing it would end. But then one of the women in the room, older than me, at a guess, with dark brown hair piled into a bun on top of her head, started speaking, and every word she said resonated deep inside my tortured soul.

She explained how she didn't feel like she was addicted to heroin, but to the numbness it brought. The peace. Solitude. She said heroin *fixed* her problems by taking them away. When she was high, she didn't care, she didn't *feel*. She could've plucked every word straight from my mind. This woman, this stranger, 'got it'. She got *me*. Then she said she'd spent so many years masking her troubles with drugs that she didn't actually know how to work through them any other way. She was no longer capable of facing problems, processing emotions, or finding solutions. She was programmed to ignore them, to forget, to push them out of sight, and the only way she could stop them coming back was to keep using.

"I get it." The words shocked me as they left my mouth. Heads turned, eyes honed in on me, and a choking lump formed in my throat. Coughing, I dislodged the sudden anxiety and fixed my stare on the woman who understood, blocking everyone else out. "I'm Dylan. This is my third time in recovery and…and I get it." My voice was quiet, a little shaky, but I'd done it, I'd spoken, and I was *okay*.

Nobody gasped, nobody wrinkled their nose in disgust, nobody laughed at me.

Because they were the *same*.

They *all* got it.

They were *all* here to change.

They *all* wanted to be better.

I'm not alone.

* * *

Recovery: Week Two.

The woman I related to in group last week was called Beverly. She approached me after the session and asked how I was finding Riverside. She was in her third week here since relapsing after being sober for four years. Her story brought my addict brain to life. It tried to tell me there was no point to any of this if I would only end up back here like Beverly.

"I know what you're thinking," she said. "Why bother, right? What's the point?"

"Yeah." I considered lying, but Jason said being honest was the only way I'd succeed. I had to re-train my brain, my thought processes. I had to learn to tackle my issues head-on instead of hiding them behind drugs and lies.

"If I hadn't bothered last time I probably wouldn't have got those four years. If I don't bother this time I might not get another four. We have to keep going, keep trying. If we fall, we have to get back up. Don't know about you, but I'm not living when I'm using. I don't even remember half the crap I've done when I've had junk in my veins. All those days, months, years…wasted.

"I don't want that. I don't want to die without memories. The point, Dylan, is *life*."

It seemed bizarre that I'd never thought about it like that before. When I thought of my life, I remembered my childhood. I thought of my time with Cameron, both as a boy and, now, as an adult. I remembered my old friend, Sam, and my job as a labourer.

The ten years in between were just…lost.

I achieved nothing. Experienced nothing. I didn't *live*, merely breathed. Did I want a lifetime of lost years? *No.* No I didn't.

The point is life.

* * *

Recovery: Week Three.

Today was a bad day, a *difficult* day. I had daily sessions with Jason. The man knew everything about me, and we worked on different issues every time we talked. We'd been over my childhood, my time in care, and when I started using. We'd discussed *why* I used, how often, how much. We even talked about the energy drinks. I genuinely didn't think they were an issue. They were legal, readily available, marketed as pick-me-ups. But apparently overusing them isn't uncommon with recovering addicts, and I *was* overusing them. Caffeine is a mood-altering drug according to Jason, and dangerous territory for someone like me. In essence, I was self-medicating, trying to alleviate my stresses and triggers with something I thought of as completely acceptable, innocent, instead of heroin.

That was an enlightening conversation. An *easy* conversation. Unlike today, when the time came to discuss how I funded my addiction to heroin.

"I hate it," I said. "I'm disgusted with myself."

"Why?" Jason asked, leaning forward with his elbows on his knees. "How do these memories make you feel?"

Over the years I'd met a few people who were happy to sell their bodies. They *chose* to do it. Some even enjoyed it. They respected themselves and their decisions and I admired that, but it's not how *I* felt. I didn't *want* to do it. I felt like I *had* to.

"Angry. Ashamed. I feel like it wasn't my decision. Heroin made that choice, not *me*."

"So why not turn that hatred to heroin instead of punishing yourself for something out of your control?"

"Because I'm just trying to pass the buck. I *chose* to use heroin. Every time I took it that was *my* decision."

"But *was* it? Or was it, as you call it, your addict brain making those choices?"

I shrugged, emotion swelling in my chest. "Same thing."

"If they were the same you wouldn't differentiate. You recognise there is another part of your mind that doesn't belong to you. The part which belongs to heroin, the part which lies to you."

"Maybe." I shook my head. "I…I don't know."

"Addiction is a disease, Dylan. A disease you can't cure, but one you can manage. You can control it. You're the boss, not heroin."

I shook my head again. It felt like cheating to accept that, to pass the blame. The only person responsible for my addiction was *me*. "People get diseases through no fault of their own. I *chose* drugs, nobody forced me."

"Let's imagine somebody with lung cancer. They smoked all their lives, knowing the risk, and now they're dying. They're paying the price for their mistake. Do they deserve help? Medical treatment, surgery, chemo. Do they deserve another shot? A chance to fight, to stop smoking, to make the right decisions going forth? Or should we tell them they brought it on themselves and toss them aside?"

"That's…" He was confusing me. I didn't know what to believe, what to think anymore. "That's different."

"Why? Smoking is an addiction, one they *chose* to have. Why is that different from your own experience? Why do they deserve to live and you don't?"

"I…" Hell, I didn't know.

"It's never too late to turn around, to become what you were meant to be. You need to forgive yourself, Dylan. The only way you can achieve a successful future is to accept the past, own your mistakes, and let them go. Learn from them, but vow not to repeat them."

"I don't know if I can." Honestly, I didn't think I ever could. If I closed my eyes I could still feel those men on my skin. I wanted to hate them, *blame* them for taking advantage of me, but that wasn't fair. I agreed to every single thing they did to me, well, mostly. I *offered* myself to them. The only person to hate was myself.

"And that's okay, for now," Jason said. "There's no time limit on your recovery, Dylan. But don't tell yourself you can't achieve that forgiveness, rather you can't achieve it *yet*."

"I…I can do that." *I think*.

"You've made excellent progress. You need to own that in the same way you own your mistakes. Allow the *good* into your mind. Be proud of how far you've come. Focus on it. Give it some weight. Visualise it crushing the negative."

I fell into silence, considering his words. *Visualise it*. I could do that, like I did with the daisies. Closing my eyes, I thought about all the things I was ashamed of – the johns, the stealing. I thought of all the things that *hurt*, picturing the moment I found out my dad had died, then my grandma. I allowed myself to feel the pain that ripped through my chest when the social worker with the black hair took me away. Finally, I remembered coming off smack, the agony, the shivers, the memory of wanting to die, and I relived finding out Bubbles had died all over again.

Then I piled the *good* on top of it. I thought about Cameron, how safe I felt with him, how beautiful he was, how glorious his touch felt on my skin, how he looked at me like I was worth *everything*. I pictured the restaurant, the foods I'd tasted, the skills I'd learned. I thought of Paul and Derek, the times they'd made me laugh, given it to me straight, believed in me.

Then, when I opened my eyes, I found myself smiling. I felt…different. Lighter. I felt like I could do this. *Really* fucking do this. Right now, there were equal parts light and dark, but I had a chance to change that. I could allow that light to spread. I could add to it, make memories, *crush* all that motherfucking darkness.

"I think it's time to begin our family sessions, bring Cameron in. How do you feel about that?"

"Umm…" Damn, I didn't know. "What will we talk about in front of him?"

"Whatever you want. Whatever *he* wants. In order to support you through recovery he needs to understand not only addiction, but *your* addiction. This process, although in different ways, is just as difficult for loved ones. He needs support and guidance, too."

Nodding slowly, I said, "Okay. I'll tell him later when he visits."

"Excellent. I'll check my diary and get back to you with a time. Do you have any questions before we end the session?"

"Just one. Will it ever go away? The craving. Even though I can see my progress, I still think about it all the time. I still...I still *want* it, even though I know it only ever ruins my life."

"Honest answer? No."

Shit. I sucked in a shallow gasp. I wanted, *needed* him to say it would go away. I didn't have the strength to say no, to make the right choice, over and over again, every single day for the rest of my life.

"Just like those bad memories will never leave entirely, neither will your craving. But it *will* fade. It won't always feel like it owns you. *You* are in control, Dylan."

He kept saying that, but I didn't feel very in control. "And if something bad happens? Something I can't deal with?"

"There are lots of tools available to you. Exercise is a *great* distraction. Take a walk, go for a jog, run up and down stairs. Don't underestimate the power of *natural* drugs that your brain can produce all on its own. Exercise releases endorphins, which actually produce a similar effect on the body as opiates, morphine and *heroin*, for example."

"You're kidding me, right? My own brain can make heroin?" I couldn't help think he was talking bollocks. If people could produce their own heroin in their brain there'd be no reason for Riverside View to even exist.

"Without getting too technical and discussing neurotransmitters and pituitary glands with you, narcotic pain medications like morphine and codeine, were actually created to mimic natural endorphins. They're a natural painkiller. They also induce feelings of pleasure, euphoria, and they even increase your appetite. Your body is capable of amazing things if you allow it."

"So, won't I just get addicted to exercise instead?" It wouldn't necessarily be a bad thing, better than smack for sure, but still the thought intrigued me.

We'd talked a lot in my last session about the concept of addictive personalities. I'd heard the phrase before and always thought it was a copout, total bullshit. But…then we looked over my past, and I started to see similar patterns in my behaviour, even when I was a kid. For example, when I was eleven I wanted a rabbit. I couldn't just go out and get one, however. Instead, I researched the hell out of them. I made sure I knew every single thing there was to know about rabbits. I learned that they preferred company of their own kind, so I needed *two* rabbits.

I found out about their natural habitat, so no longer felt comfortable forcing them to live in a tiny hutch. So, I gave my dad all my savings, which wasn't much and I knew he contributed even though he never told me that, and together we built an entire bunny fucking village. I'm talking a big-ass shed with a cat-flap built into the side that opened out onto a *huge* run made from chicken-wire and wood. The creation took over the *whole* back garden.

After a few months of caring for my two new rabbits, however, I got bored and moved onto something else. The rabbits went to live with some old lady on a farm and I concentrated on cars because I was now determined to be a mechanic. It became all I thought about. I studied hundreds of manuals, learned everything there was to know. But then I got bored of that too.

I guess these were more obsessive behaviours than addictive, but they were the first steps on a very slippery road. It made me wonder about cooking. What if that was becoming my new obsession? Would that be a good or bad thing?

"No," Jason replied. "Endorphins are broken down almost immediately when they lock into the opioid receptors in your brain. There are a lot of theories out there, linking them to things such as obsessive compulsive disorder, but right now they're just theories. The difference between endorphins and chemical opiates, is that heroin, morphine, etcetera, are resistant to the enzymes that break the substance down, resulting a longer, more intense, high."

"So it's *not* like my own personal stash of skag in my brain?"

"No, but as I said, don't underestimate your brain's potential. I'm not saying it will *replace* your craving, but it will help. There is no magic cure,

Dylan. Even with all the right tools you've still got one hell of a fight on your hands."

"But exercise will help," I said it more to myself than Jason.

"And you'll *talk*. That's the point of all this," he said, motioning his hand around the room. "You're going to learn how to recognise your triggers and how to overcome them. It's very difficult to get through recovery alone, Dylan, which is exactly what you've been trying to do. You'll be leaving here with a support system in place. *Use* it. Talk. Share. Ask for help. That doesn't make you weak. It makes you powerful, stronger than heroin wants you to be. Heroin likes being a dirty little secret. It likes controlling you, making you dependent on it. Don't give it what it wants."

It sounded so simple, but I knew it wouldn't be. I also knew, truly believed for the first time, that it wasn't impossible.

Fuck you, heroin. Fuck you.

* * *

Two days later, Cameron and I sat in Jason's office, waiting for him to arrive. I was nervous. *He* was nervous. Neither of us had any idea where this session would go, what we'd talk about, and honestly, the wait was nothing short of scary.

"You look well," Cameron said. It felt a little awkward, like we didn't know how to talk to each other anymore.

I nodded. "Jason says I'm doing good."

"And what do *you* think?"

Pausing, I contemplated for a few seconds. "I think he's right. I dunno, it just feels different this time."

"That's good." He smiled and reached out to touch me, but then backed off again. "Really good."

Why won't he touch me? Had it finally happened? Had he lost his faith in me?

"So, do you like it here?" he asked. "Are they treating you well?"

"Someone needs to teach the chef how to season properly, but apart from that, yeah. Yeah, it's all good."

A wide smiled pulled on the corners of Cameron's lips; a beautiful, infectious smile that relaxed me enough to take hold of his hand. He stared at our entwined fingers for a moment, his smile growing even wider, even more stunning.

"You're still interested in cooking?" he asked, his tone hopeful. "I thought…well I figured…I started to wonder if it was just a distraction. A distraction that didn't work."

"It was, at first. But…I think I could be good at it. I *want* to be good at something."

In that moment, as I finished speaking, Jason walked in, clutching a file to his broad chest. Cameron dropped my hand, forcing a nervous cough, and it took me back to the last time we were in this situation. Back in high school, we'd been sent to the head-teacher's office for smashing a window. It was an accident, kicking a ball around the all-weather PE court, and as we sat in her office we held hands and laughed about the trouble we were in.

Until the head walked in and Cameron almost shit out his stomach over the idea someone might've seen us acting too close.

Jason dropped the file down on his desk and proffered his hand to Cameron. "Don't be nervous," he said, giving Cam's hand a firm shake. "I don't bite."

"Sorry," Cameron muttered. "I've never done anything like this before."

I took his hand again, giving it a squeeze of reassurance. We weren't in high school anymore. We weren't in the closet. If I wanted to hold his hand, I'd hold his fucking hand.

Jason sat down behind his desk, crossing one leg over the other as he relaxed back in his leather chair. "Cameron, would you like to start?"

Cameron budged uneasily in his seat. "Um, I don't really know what to say."

"Say the first thing that comes into your head."

"Um…"

"How do you feel when you think of Dylan?"

"Scared," Cameron all but whispered. "Sad. Confused. Angry sometimes."

My heart sank and I dropped my head, looking to the floor. *Honesty.* That's what this was about, I reminded myself.

"Why do you feel angry?"

Looking up, I watched Cam as he watched me. His eyes were strained, like he was asking for my permission to be truthful. I nodded, just once, just a little.

"Because I don't understand," he said, turning to Jason. "I don't understand how he could choose drugs over the people who love him, over *me*."

"Dylan?" Jason said, offering his flattened palm into the air. "Only you can answer that."

"It…it takes everything away." I talked to Cameron but I stared at the painting of a meadow on the wall instead of his face. "I can't deal with things like you can. Pain, fear…it consumes me. I feel like I was destined to be *bad*. From the second I was born, bad things happened. It feels like my mum dying was the first snowflake to fall in the storm that became my life. Ever since, it just kept on snowing, pelting down on me, harder and faster. I'm buried, Cam. Buried too deep, and it feels like I can't dig myself out."

"Dylan," Cameron said on a sigh, squeezing my hand tighter.

"I couldn't breathe, Cam. The snow, the pain, it's suffocating, and it's there *all* the time. In here," I tapped the side of my head. "The bad memories, the hurt, the guilt, they're in my head all the fucking time. Heroin takes it away. For a little while, it helps me breathe."

"You could *tell* me. When you can't breathe, *talk* to me. Get it out that way."

Nodding slowly, risking a glance at his face, a face haunted with pain, pain that *I'd* put there, I replied, "I'm going to try. I swear to you, I'm going to try."

Cameron glanced down at his knees, dragging in a deep breath before returning his gaze to mine. "Why'd you do it, Dyl? This time, why'd you go back to it? What couldn't you cope with? Was it your friend? The girl who died."

I caught sight of Jason watching me with curiosity. He knew about Bubbles, but we'd only discussed her briefly so far. "Bubbles," I said. "Partly."

Finding out about her death gave me the final push into darkness, but it wasn't the only reason. Bubbles was part of my life. She was familiar, she understood addiction, didn't judge…but I didn't *love* her. She wasn't the best friend I believed she was when I was using. Our friendship wasn't healthy. We encouraged one another to self-destruct. So when she died, it wasn't grief that forced me over the edge, it was reality. It was wondering who would find *me,* find *my* dead body curled up in a pool of my own vomit when the day inevitably came.

At least, I *thought* it was inevitable until I came to Riverside. Now? Now I wasn't so sure. Now, I thought, *what if?* What if I could change my future? What if I really *was* in control?

"Well, what else?" Cameron probed. "I thought…I thought you were doing great."

"*You,*" I whispered, guilt rising in my throat, making the word crack.

Cameron's eyes widened, hurt registering on his shocked face. It broke my heart, but I needed this. *We* needed this. *Honesty.* "You went away.

You...*left* me." I knew it sounded stupid, that it *was* stupid, but it's how I felt.

"Left you?" Cameron's forehead wrinkled in confusion. "Do you mean when I went to Edinburgh?"

"Yeah."

"But...it was just one night. It was work. I don't understand."

"I know it's irrational, really I do, but...I needed you."

"You didn't say anything. I never would've gone if-"

"I couldn't say anything," I interrupted. "Because I knew how pathetic it was. But I needed you, and you left. Everybody leaves me. *Always.* And it scares me, Cam. It scares me that I need you so much. It's like I replaced the smack with *you*. Instead of depending on drugs, I depended on you. I...I don't know how to live on my own. Whenever I've tried, I've fucked it all up."

"You don't *have* to be on your own," Cam said, gripping my hand tight with his. "I'm here."

"I'd like to interrupt here," Jason cut in, leaning forward in his chair. Cameron and I both turned our heads to look at him, to listen. "You raise a valid point, Dylan. You're *right* to be scared of your reliance on Cameron."

Puzzled, Cameron's expression twisted.

"It isn't healthy to not know how to be in your own company," Jason continued. "There will be times when you *are* left alone. Cameron has a life, too. He can't be with you twenty-four-seven and he

308

shouldn't have to be. You need to learn to cope by yourself, live, make the right choices on your own, for *you*…not for Cameron. Independence, learning how to take care of yourself, is vital to your recovery."

"I don't understand what you're saying," Cameron said. "Are you saying we should…*break up?*"

"Not at all," Jason replied. "I *do*, however, think it would be beneficial for you to live apart for a while after Dylan leaves here."

"*What?* No!" Cameron's eyes darted to my face. "Tell him, Dyl. There's no need for that!"

Swallowing the lump in my throat, I dropped my stare to my knees. "I think he's right," I murmured. "I have to be with you because I *want* to, which I *do*, please believe I *do*…but not because I *need* you."

"But…I…where would you go?" The panic in his voice, the grief on his face, made me feel like shit. "You can't afford your own place."

I shrugged a little. "Derek might put me up. He has the space." I just didn't know if he'd want to once he knew the truth. "We'll still see each other every day. At work…if I'm allowed back."

"Of course you are," he said on a defeated sigh.

"I'll still come over to your apartment. I'll still *love* you. I need to do this, Cam. For *me*, and for *us*. I have to know how to live on my own, live as an adult, without running back to heroin whenever I get scared. I've...I've never done it before, and I *need* to."

After several seconds of deafening silence, Jason cut in. "How do you feel about that Cameron?" he asked, twiddling a pen between his fingers.

"I don't like it." Cameron's voice was stern, but it melted into a heavy exhale. "But I understand. And...you wouldn't be on your own. Not really. You'd have Derek."

"But I don't *need* Derek, and he doesn't need me. His life truly is independent from mine. But, he might not even say yes. Not once he finds out about me."

"He already knows," Cam told me, causing my neck to snap back in surprise. "He has since the beginning."

"He has? And...and he still spent time with me, coached me..."

"You're not the monster you think you are, Dyl. People care about you more than you realise."

Closing my eyes briefly, I processed his words and...and I *believed* them. "Yeah."

Cameron let go of my hand for the first time since Jason arrived and raked his fingers through his hair. He drew in a deep breath, staring at the ceiling before bowing his head. His expression, his posture, everything about him told me something heavy was coming my way. "I need to ask you something," he said.

"Anything," I replied, though I wasn't sure I meant it.

"I hate myself for thinking it, but I need to know." He sucked another long breath into his lungs, boring his gaze into mine. "When you relapsed this time…did you…*sleep* with other men?"

His question hit me like a punch to the chest and scalding shame simmered in my veins, heating my skin, making me nauseous. "No. I didn't." I hadn't been with other men, and I hadn't shared needles. It was a small comfort, but one Jason told me I should be grateful for. I hadn't put myself at risk. I could have my repeat HIV test before I left here and trust the results.

"But…you stole from me?"

"Yes."

He squeezed his eyes closed, breathing steadily through his nose.

"And I'll never forgive myself," I added.

Opening his eyes, he reached out and took my hand again. "You have to," he breathed. "Let it go, Dyl. *I* have. *I* forgive you."

"You knew, didn't you? You knew all along that I was using again? That I was taking from you?"

Cam looked confused, just briefly, before sighing in resignation. "I didn't want to, but yes. Yes I did."

"Why didn't you confront me? Why didn't you try and stop me?" It was a selfish question. He wasn't to blame. The likelihood is he wouldn't have been able to stop me anyway, but I needed to know why he didn't even try. I think, at the time, I hoped he would. I *wanted* him to, even though I knew deep inside my head it was my *own* decision to take those drugs. I wanted him to give me a reason not to. I wanted him to pull me back. That's why I kept doing it. Kept taking. When he didn't notice I'd stolen a tenner from his wallet, I took another. Then I took twenty. I wanted him to fight for me, because I was too fucking weak to do it myself. But then it was too late. I'd spiralled too far and I had no fucking idea what I was doing anymore.

Now I was clean I realized how unfair that was.

His gaze dropped to his knees and he sucked a long breath in through his nose. "I was afraid. Afraid you'd leave. Afraid you'd stay. Afraid you'd die. Just…afraid. I tried to convince myself I was wrong, because it was easier. I let you down, Dyl, and I'm sorry."

"No," I said, twisting sideways in my chair and grabbing both of his hands. "God no. I've been walking down the wrong road for a *long* time, Cam. Without you, I might never have found the right turning. Don't you dare say that to me again. You're the only reason I'm sitting here right now."

Tears pricked my eyes, Cameron's too. The emotion in the room was overpowering and for a moment I wanted it to go away. I wanted to forget. I wanted…I wanted heroin. But then I looked at Cameron, saw the hope, the love, the promise in his eyes, and the pain melted into insignificance.

By the end of our session, I think Cameron had finally started to see that my relapse wasn't because he wasn't enough. He hadn't failed me. It had nothing to do with him. Nobody could save an addict. Nobody could save *me*.

Only *I* could do that.

And I *would*.

By fuck, I would.

I wanted a future, and I was going to get one.

* * *

Recovery: Week Four.

Beverly left Riverside yesterday. Her time was up. She'd completed the first steps towards the rest of her long, drug-free life. That was the aim anyway, all any of us in here could hope for, *work* for. I felt a little lost after she left, but not the kind of loss I felt when I was away from Cameron. A battle didn't ensue in my head. I didn't feel abandoned or neglected. I just…missed her. I liked everyone I'd met here so far, but I had the most in common with Beverly. I'd miss talking to her, laughing with her. She did, however, promise to keep in touch, and I hoped she did.

Jason and I had also worked on mindfulness. It sounded like some kinda hippy shit and at first I laughed at the idea. I had visions of me sitting on the floor, my hands praying, while I meditated under candlelight. But it wasn't like that at all. To be mindful simply meant to focus on the present. Jason did encourage me to straighten my back, close my eyes, and concentrate on each breath as it entered my body, but I didn't have to contort myself into any kind of weird pose.

He told me a craving was just a *thought*. It had no power. I didn't have to obey it. If I was mindful, took a moment to picture the present, where I was *now*, what I'd achieved, I could send that thought away as quickly as it arrived. Again, mindfulness, like exercise, wouldn't beat heroin, but they were tools to help *me* beat it. *I* was the only soldier in this war, and the things I'd learned were my weapons. I could win this fight. I *would* win this fight.

I'm in control.

My biggest surprise of the week was Paul and Derek accompanying Cameron on one of his visits. It was a little awkward at first, I felt embarrassed, but then they started talking to me like I was…*normal*, like I was just on holiday and not in a drug rehabilitation facility.

"It's almost worth taking drugs to get a stint in 'ere," Derek joked. "I pay seventy quid a month for my gym membership and the pool is the size of a toilet bowl compared to the one in the brochure for this place."

He made me chuckle, but Paul rolled his eyes.

"Shut the hell up, Old Man."

"Oh, *please*. You're just jealous you're not gettin' your arse pampered. They do massages and facials and shit."

The annoyance on Paul's face morphed into curiosity. "Do they?" he asked, turning to me.

Again, I chuckled. "I haven't had one, but yeah they do. It *is* kinda like being on holiday, if you don't count the emotional turmoil."

"Well, facials don't come as part o' the package when you move into my place," Derek said. "Well, not the kind they offer 'ere anyway."

"Fuck's sake, Derek," Paul whisper-shouted, swatting Derek's shoulder.

If these guys don't end up together, I'll eat my own dick.

"I asked him last night," Cameron cut in. "Told him what we'd discussed with Jason."

"And…you don't mind?" I asked, shifting my gaze to Derek. "It's not forever. Just until, well, I don't know. But not forever."

"Providin' you tidy up after yourself, wash your own underwear, and you don't fuck Cam on my settee…you can stay as long as you want."

An amused, yet grateful, smile, crawled onto my lips. "Thank you."

"Oh, and don't tell Twinkle 'ere where I 'ide my knives," he added, jerking his chin towards Paul.

Paul just shook his head and then turned away to hide his mischievous expression.

"Has Cameron explained some of the things he's learned from my therapist?" I asked Derek. "I mean, you should probably know some stuff if I'm going to be living with you for a while." He needed to know how I thought, how my mind worked. Most of all, he should know to trust *his* instincts over *my* words.

"A little," Derek said. The playful tone had vanished from his voice. "I think I know all I need to."

"And you're sure? Don't agree to me staying with you out of loyalty to Cameron."

"I can 'andle you," he said, winking. "I'm serious about the settee though. That's an eight-grand piece o' leather. If you jizz on it I'll rub y'face in it."

"Give it a rest," Paul scolded. "You're not even funny. *And* you're in public."

I laughed at both of them. "No screwing on the couch. Scout's honour." I saluted Derek, hiding my anxiety behind a smile. I hadn't thought about being with Cameron intimately again yet. I wondered if it would be different, if he'd be able to love me the same knowing I'd let him down again. After all, he didn't touch me while I was here, didn't hold my hand unless I held his first. The thought had been plaguing my mind, tormenting me, making me doubt his commitment to me.

It made my addict brain louder.

Maybe it's something I should bring up in our next session.

"Hey, Twinkle," Derek said. "Why don't you tell Dyl about you fallin' on your arse yesterday?"

Sitting back, eyes wide, ears eager, I stared at Paul, but his story never came.

"Dick'ead tripped on the end of the escalator in Selfridges," Derek continued while Paul glowered at him. "Went down like a sack o' shit. He…he…" Choking on laughter as he relived the moment, Derek slapped his knee. "He fell down three of the steps and 'e just *lay* there, lettin' 'em carry 'im to the top on 'is fuckin' belly!"

Sucking my lips between my teeth, I fought really hard not to laugh, but failed miserably. Tears sprang from my eyes, Cameron laughed into his shoulder, and Derek couldn't breathe.

"You're all arseholes," Paul spat. "If this was in the restaurant I could sue the lot of you for bullying in the workplace."

Still laughing, I sank back into my chair. Today was a good day. A *positive* day. I had the best friends in the world.

* * *

Recovery: Week Five.

Jason and I spent this week working through my fear of being alone. I'd experienced more loss in the first fourteen years of my life than some people would *ever* have…and it just kept going as I got older. People left. People died. The only common denominator was *me*. But after working with Jason, my thought patterns slowly began to change.

I couldn't have saved my mum. I was a newborn. It wasn't my fault.

I didn't kill my dad. A drunk-driver did that. I wasn't there. I didn't tell him to get in the car that night. Driving to gigs was routine, something he did every week. I couldn't have foreseen the accident. It wasn't my fault.

My grandma had heart failure for years before the heart attack took her from me. I wasn't a doctor. I couldn't treat her. I couldn't make her better. I couldn't have revived her worn-out heart. It wasn't my fault.

And Bubbles...I couldn't save her just like she couldn't have saved *me*. She was an addict. She had a disease, as did I. I wasn't with her that day. I didn't force her to push off. It wasn't my fault.

They weren't my fault.

I'm not poison.

It seemed obvious, really. Jason didn't tell me I wasn't to blame. He never *told* me anything. Somehow, he managed to make me realise things about myself simply by listening. I had no idea how. Maybe he was a fucking magician or something.

So, this week had been tough. Working through these memories, reliving the pain they caused, overcoming them, was testing...but necessary. It had to happen to get me where I was now; at peace. Content. My body didn't ache with the guilt that had weighed down on it all my life.

I felt...*free*.

* * *

Recovery: Week Six.

One week left. I felt ready and terrified to leave here all at the same time. What if I only *thought* I was ready? What if the only reason I hadn't scored was because I couldn't physically do it in here?

No, I told myself. I could do this. I *was* doing this.

My worries about Cameron, about our relationship and if it would survive, continued to niggle at my head, and so I brought them up in therapy. I *faced* them head-on. I wouldn't let them win, break me, push me back to heroin. Not again.

"I didn't want to push you," Cameron said, while Jason watched us interact, in silence, as usual. "I *wanted* to touch you, to hold you, to kiss you…but I felt that I'd pushed you too far already. I felt like you only tried to stay clean for *me*. Before, I mean. After coming off it at my place. I'd pushed you, made you want to please me without even realising.

"And I get it. I do. I get that you need to do this for *you*. I get why you're going to stay with Derek. I don't like it, but I *get* it. So that's why I didn't touch you. I needed you to touch me first. I needed you to *want* to do it, to want *me*…not just *please* me because you think I expect it."

My smile grew wider with every word he spoke. This talking shit really worked. It made me stronger. It made the light brighter, the dark a mere shadow. My time in this place had given me the tools I needed to succeed, the tools heroin had tried to hide from me. That fucker had taken everything away from me, stolen my power, and I was taking it back.

"I'll always want you," I breathed. "I'll always need you." Leaning forward, I pressed my lips to Cameron's, sparks and shivers igniting all over my body. *Fuck*, I'd missed him.

"Ahem!" Jason forced a cough and I pulled away from Cam, feeling once again like the naughty pupil in the head's office.

"I have something I'd like to talk about actually," Cameron said, addressing both me and Jason.

Jason nodded, while I narrowed my eyes in curiosity.

"I'm guessing Dyl's told you about his interest in food, and his job at my restaurant?"

"He has indeed." Jason nodded.

"Well…the new college season starts in a couple of months. I want to offer Dylan an official apprenticeship. Employ him as a junior chef, work towards getting him a qualification." He turned to me, chewing his bottom lip. "I mean, if *you* want that, obviously."

"I do." Take life by the balls, that's what I wanted to do.

Turning back to Jason, Cameron asked, "But is it too much too soon? I know his time here isn't a magic fix and that the recovery process is lifelong, but…is he ready to take on something like that?"

Shrugging, Jason said, "Ask him."

Turning his head, Cameron's stare fixed to mine. His expression was hopeful, his nervous smile breath-taking. "Are you?"

I didn't even need to think about it. I'd changed so much in these last few weeks. I thought differently, saw things in new ways, in *positive* ways. Maybe I'd struggle at times. Maybe I wouldn't. I couldn't predict the future, but I *could* try my hardest to make it a good one. And if I fell, I'd get back up. If I had bad thoughts, I'd share them, take away their power, crush the fuckers before they crushed *me*. "I'm ready. I want it. I want *everything*. I…I deserve everything."

Jason nodded when I looked at him, and he wore a half-smile like I'd just achieved the jackpot. *I deserve it*, I thought again. *I'm worth it*. I wasn't *bad*. I wasn't heroin. I wasn't my mistakes.

I was Dylan Roberts; the bright and loving boy I used to be, the boy who lost his way, the boy who'd finally found the turning he'd been searching for for sixteen years. That boy deserved better, and I was going to give it to him.

Chapter

Thirteen

~Cameron~

SIX WEEKS I'D waited for Dylan. Six long weeks spent missing him, worrying about him, crying over him to my mum, and Paul. Six weeks, and now he was out…and I had to leave him again. I almost asked if I could spend the night with him when we got to Derek's house, but I knew that contradicted the whole point. He needed to live without me, and it stung like a motherfucker.

It's not forever, I reminded myself as I forced my hand to twist the key in my ignition, driving further away from him. I still had a mountain of questions piled up in my head. How long would I have to wait to spend the night with him? Would it be acceptable to ask him over for pizza and a movie? How much affection was too much? How little was too little? How soon was too soon?

These were all things we needed to talk about, most likely with Jason. If I'm honest, the idea of spilling my private thoughts out to a stranger weirded me out initially. Yet, talking in front of Jason became effortless after spending just a few minutes with him. He didn't really say much himself, but somehow he knew how to coax words and feelings from me, Dylan too. He used the right words, offered little prompts that opened the floodgates to our minds, allowing every thought to pour free into the air. It was kind of wonderful actually, being in that room. Liberating.

Our sessions also made me realise how little I knew about addiction, despite all my Google marathons, and how stupid it had been for me to agree to Dylan detoxing himself in my apartment. The actual physical process of taking drugs was only a small part of his problem. Sure, withdrawal was immensely difficult on his mind and body, but I'd been naïve to think the damage ended there, to believe removing the drugs from his system was all it took to get, and *stay* sober.

That's why his relapse terrified me. I worried that this would be our future; a few 'clean' weeks, followed by months of heartache and instability. Rinse and repeat, until death do us part. But, I no longer felt that way. I'd witnessed Dylan healing, physically and emotionally, over the last few weeks.

I saw the change as it happened. It filled me with hope, positivity, and more pride than I'd ever felt in my life.

He could do this.

We could do this.

* * *

One week later…

My positivity didn't last long, and it had nothing to do with Dylan. He was doing good, as far as I knew. He'd kept up his therapy sessions. He'd had the all clear on his repeat HIV test. He'd done everything *right*. I just didn't know how to *do* this, how to be strong for him. I was weaker than I thought.

"How's he doing?" I asked Derek. We were in the prep-kitchen, alone, and it was the first time I'd had the opportunity to probe him without anyone overhearing.

"Good. I think."

"You *think*?"

Derek shrugged, his stare focused on the sugar basket he was creating. "Well, I'm no therapist. I don't exactly 'ave a lot of experience wi' this kinda stuff. He seems okay to me. He's talkin', and that's good, right? He's supposed to talk rather than score?"

"What kind of things does he talk about?"

"Ooh, no. I'm not goin' there. I ain't no go-between."

Damn.

"Here's a radical idea. Why don't you try talkin' to 'im yourself? You've not been by the 'ouse all week."

"I've been busy."

"Liar."

I opened my mouth to reply, to disagree, but then closed it again. "I'm…I don't know, scared I guess. I don't know what I'll do if he's struggling."

"You'll listen to 'im. Isn't that what that Jason fella told you to do?"

"Yes, but…"

"But?"

Pushing out a heavy, frustrated sigh, I leaned back on the wall, crossing my arms over my chest. "I hate this. The uncertainty. I don't know if I can live like that."

"Maybe you wouldn't be so uncertain if you fuckin' *talked* to 'im. Do you not wanna be wi' 'im anymore?"

"Yes! Of course I do." What a ridiculous question. "I can't imagine my life without him."

"I'm guessin' it'll be kinda like it is right now."

Hmm.

"The pair o' you need to man the fuck up and 'ave a fuckin' conversation. Come on, Cam, after everythin' you've been through is talkin' really that scary?"

I looked down at my foot as it drew invisible circles on the white-tiled floor. I felt just the same as the time when I got busted trying a cigarette by my dad outside the school gates when I was fifteen.

It was the first one I'd ever had, and after I coughed up half a lung and spewed all over my shoes, it was my last. Derek had that affect on people. He told things straight. He didn't suffer fools. He refused to mollycoddle. And, especially in the kitchen, he was a bossy sod. But I loved him all the same. "Guess not."

"I'm gonna stay at Paul's tonight, and *you* are gonna stay at mine. Got it?"

"Uh…"

"Grow some balls, Cam, before all you've been through ends up bein' for nothin'."

Well, that's me told. "You ever thought of becoming a therapist," I teased.

"Fuck no. I 'ant got the patience for other folk's problems. I don't think my sort-it-out-or-quit-fuckin'-whinin' approach would go down too well."

It probably wouldn't, but it sure as hell worked for me. Derek was right. The future seemed pretty bleak if I spent it avoiding Dylan, avoiding his, *our*, issues. We only spoke honestly in front of Jason. He'd almost become our comfort blanket which, on reflection, seemed ludicrous…and kind of pathetic.

"And don't forget my rule about the settee," Derek said as he placed another pan of sugar on the stove.

Plucking a clean tea-towel from the trolley behind me, I swatted him across the back with it.

"Boilin' fuckin' sugar 'ere!" he yelled, sidestepping away from me.

"Stop being dramatic. It hasn't even started melting yet." I laughed at him, and he flipped me the middle finger.

"He's a good lad, Cam. Don't let fear balls it all up for you." His tone came out heavy, without a hint of mockery, which was unusual for Derek and it made his words punch me square in the chest.

"I won't."

We *could* do this. I'd thought so before, I just didn't have the courage to actually make it happen. That ended today. No more fear. No more uncertainty. Just strength. Honesty.

Love.

* * *

"Oh," Dylan said, eyes widening when he opened Derek's front door to me. His skin was flushed, his hair damp, like he'd just stepped out of the shower. "Derek said you were coming, but I wasn't expecting you till after service."

"Paul and Derek have it covered. So I went home for a bath and came straight here." Dylan didn't move, so I *couldn't* move. "Can I come in?"

Stepping aside, he freed the doorway and I walked past him without a word. I headed straight to the living room, still impressed by the size and magnificence of this place despite having been here a thousand times. Sitting down on Derek's couch, I couldn't prevent the snort that burst from my nose. The childish part of me wanted to have sex in fifty different ways on this leather, just to piss him off.

"Drink?" Dylan asked as he stood in front of me, his posture awkward, fingers fidgeting.

"What are we doing, Dyl?" I said, sighing. "We're acting like strangers. It's stupid. We're Cam and Dyl. We *know* each other. We *love* each other for Christ's sake."

Blowing out a single, humourless laugh, he nodded. "Yeah." Tilting his head to the side, he looked down at me with a hesitant, yet stunning, smile.

I patted the space next to me on the couch. "Get your arse over here."

He did as I asked, well, as I *told*, and perched on the edge of the cushion with far too much distance between us. I'd had enough of this. Not just the physical separation but the *emotional* detachment. I wanted him back. I needed him. Needed *us*.

Grabbing his shoulder, I pulled him backwards, twisting his body until I had him pinned beneath me. His expression was a little startled, his chest rising and falling faster than usual. I palmed his cheek before running my fingers through his hair, mussing it up before settling on the back of his neck.

"I've missed you," I whispered, brushing my nose against his. His warm breath tickled my face, sending delicious shivers through nerves I didn't even know I had. "You're incredible," I said against his lips. "Strong. Brave. *Beautiful*. There are no words to describe how important to me you are. You know that, right?"

His eyes searched mine, delving right into my soul and taking it, *owning* it, owning every piece of me. "Yes." Smiling his striking, soothing smile, he kissed me softly, tracing the seal of my lips with his tongue. "I'll make you proud, Cam. I swear I will."

Pulling back a little, I stared right into his green eyes, admiring the tiny grey specks peppered around his irises, and ran the pad of my finger down his cheek. "You already have."

I didn't come here for sex, but apparently the memo didn't reach my cock. The sight, feel, scent of Dylan overwhelmed my senses and as my cock swelled it strained uncomfortably against my jeans. I had no choice but to wedge a hand between our bodies and re-adjust it, even though I knew it would ruin the tender moment we were sharing. "Sorry," I said, grinning as I dropped my forehead onto his. "It was bordering on painful."

Stroking through my hair, Dylan said, "Come upstairs with me."

My pulse raced with anticipation. I felt almost nervous as I climbed off Dylan and followed his lead to the bedroom. It wasn't dissimilar to that excited, yet quietly terrified feeling you get right before your first time.

Smiling as we reached his bed, I shook my head at my irrational anxiety. This was Dylan. *My* Dylan. I'd been with him before, yet it felt...*different*, this time. More important.

I lay down on the mattress, on top of the black duvet, and Dylan crawled on next to me, propping himself up on his elbow. "I don't feel like the same person anymore," he began, cupping my neck. "I'm changing. All that fear, regret, all that pain and hatred…it's going away. I don't want to be that guy. I'm tired of being bitter, of feeling worthless. I can't change the last sixteen years, but I can stop myself repeating them."

"Dylan…" I breathed.

He silenced me by placing a finger over my lips. "This is it, Cam. Our future. It starts here. Right now. I'm not dependent on you. I don't feel the need to pretend to be who you want me to be. I'm terrified of losing you, but not because I can't live without you, but because I don't *want* to. This means *we* need to change too. We need to start over. No more fear. No more lies. Honesty. That's the important one. You can't trust me. Not yet."

"Dyl-"

"You *can't* trust me," he repeated. "Not after what I did to you. And that's okay. I have to earn it, and I will. But that's where the honesty comes in for both of us. If you doubt me, tell me. If that needs to be in front of Jason then that's what he's there for. So new start. No fear. No lies. Just honesty. Just *love*. Yeah?"

With a quivering smile, I reached out to touch his face. "Yeah."

Sitting, I pulled Dylan up with me before teasing his T-shirt over his head. I smoothed my palm over his chest, across his narrow shoulders, down his side, needing to feel every inch of his warm flesh. When I reached the bump of his scar, I no longer felt sad. He'd survived that scar. He'd survived so much *more*. What put it there didn't matter anymore. It was simply a part of him, part of the past he'd worked so hard to escape, therefore that scar was beautiful, just like him.

Within minutes we were naked, a ball of tangled limbs and heated skin. Rolling Dylan onto his stomach, I straddled his legs, my heavy cock resting on the dip of his arse. I ran the heel of my hand along his spine before kneading the muscle between his shoulder blades. I rubbed and pressed every inch of his back before stroking down his arms, exploring his entire body. Every groove, every hair, every blemish…I needed to feel it *all*.

Shuffling down the bed, I massaged each leg from ankle to thigh, pinching and kissing every part of him before caressing the two firm globes that made my mouth water. Working the pads of my fingers into the spongy flesh, I felt Dylan tense beneath me.

"It's *me*, Dylan," I whispered, kissing one perfectly round cheek, and then the other. "I love you. You're safe."

His rigid muscles relaxed under my touch as I massaged the small of his back. Reaching down, I gripped my cock, giving it a gentle squeeze in an effort to relieve the throbbing ache, before bending back down and kissing along the back of his thigh. Using my hands, I encouraged his legs to widen, exposing his tight, pink hole. I approached it slowly, keeping him relaxed as I circled it faintly with the tip of my finger. Dylan groaned into his pillow, the sound diving straight into my balls.

Keeping his cheeks spread with my hands, I licked a trail down his delicious crack, and over the underside of his balls, making his legs quiver.

"Fuck," he breathed, fisting the duvet with both hands.

"Do you like that?" I asked, already knowing the answer as I flicked my tongue against his hole before pushing inside a little.

"Yes. God…yes."

He felt, *tasted*, amazing against my mouth and I completely buried my face in him, licking, sucking, teasing him over and over again until his whole body writhed on the mattress.

Without warning, Dylan flipped over, grabbing my face and pulling me into a rough kiss; a kiss saturated with so much passion and longing it made my knees buckle. Flat on my stomach, my legs dangling off the edge of the bed, my mouth became perfectly aligned with Dylan's leaking cock.

Taking it in my hand, I moulded my lips to his tip before pushing them all the way to the root. As I dragged back up, digging the tip of my tongue into the ridge circling his swollen head, he tipped his head back and gasped into the air. "I can't keep going," his voice came out like a hiss through gritted teeth. "I need you, Cam. I need to feel you filling me."

My eyes sprang open, my mouth releasing his cock with a soft pop. I stared up at him, studying his face. What he just asked for was monumental. Dylan was afraid to bottom; we'd discussed it in therapy with Jason, which was kind of embarrassing, but necessary. He associated it with feeling cheap and dirty. He worried it would make him see me differently, like one of those...*johns*, as he called them.

"Dyl-"

He interrupted me. "I trust you, Cameron. I *love* you. I *want* you. I need you to make it different for me. I need you to give me new memories. I need you to make it feel...good. Pure."

"Dylan," I whispered, crawling onto my knees. Curling my fingers around the back of his neck, I kissed him. Slow. Gentle. Sensual. Lowering him onto his back, I kissed away all his fears, his doubts, his bad memories. I kissed him with love. Patience. Hope. *Promise*.

There were nightstands on either side of the bed and, never taking my lips off Dylan's, I blindly fumbled in one of the drawers, praying Derek kept lube and condoms in here. Lube, yes. Several different bottles in fact, but... "There're no condoms in here," I said through a heavy, thwarted sigh.

"My tests were negative," Dylan said before biting nervously on his bottom lip. "I mean, I don't blame you if you don't want-"

"No condom?"

"I'm okay with it if you are."

Holy shit. The mere thought of feeling him close around me, bare, exposed...our bodies joining in a way I'd never felt with *anyone* else before, made my cock weep and my heart swell. "I'm more than okay with it."

Pulling out the first bottle of lube my fingers landed on, I broke away from Dylan, already missing his touch, while I dripped some onto my fingers. I delved between his cheeks, slowly, gently, pushing one finger inside him. Eyes never leaving mine, his mouth dropped open, expelling a shallow, stuttering gasp. Moving on to two fingers, I slid inside once again, then out, then in... He felt tight and hot, the hidden flesh springy and supple under my touch.

As I withdrew my fingers, I scissored them, stretched him, made him moan my name. Straightening my back, I hooked Dylan's legs over my thighs, positioning the tip of my aching cock against the heat of his puckered hole before pumping several generous squirts of lube onto it.

Pitching my hips, I spread the lube along my cock by dragging it up and down between Dylan's cheeks. "You're beautiful," I whispered as I pushed inside. Stilling, I gave him a moment to adjust to me before sliding torturously slowly back out again. "*This* is beautiful." I drove back inside, jolts of pleasure shooting down my spine. "What we have is *beautiful.*"

Chewing his bottom lip, Dylan reached out, running his fingers along the grooves of my chest, his touch slick against the fine beads of sweat misting my skin. "It feels...you feel...amazing," he breathed, his tone almost surprised.

I rocked into him steadily, gripping the top of his thighs. I couldn't keep this up for long. He felt too good. Too tight. Too warm. I was no longer just *me*. I was *his*. We were *one*. We always had been, always would be.

This moment was special. *He* was special. There was nothing cheap or nasty here. Only love. Only *us*.

My speed increased. I couldn't help it. I'd never been so connected with anyone before. Body and mind, we owned one another. "I need you to come, Dyl," I moaned, pressure building deep in my belly. "Need to feel you tighten around me."

Grabbing his wrist, I dragged his hand towards his cock. He took it in his fingers, gripping it tight, and began to stroke.

"God yes," I breathed, watching him pleasure himself the hottest thing I'd ever seen. "That's it. Go faster."

His strokes turned into rough tugs, his back arching off the mattress. Pink heat crept across his neck, his legs trembling as they wound around my waist.

"Oh…holy…" He tugged harder, his knuckles white, and I felt the familiar tingle of an impending orgasm rip through my balls.

"Do it, Dyl," I choked out, driving in and out of him as fast as my hips would allow. "Faster. I'm gonna come."

"*Oh….fuuuuuuck!*" he yelled into the air, his words strangled as jets of creamy cum spurted from his tip, coating his stomach and fingers.

His hole pulsated around my dick, the vibrations pushing me over the edge. I cried his name as I came, my cock jerking inside him, and collapsed onto his chest.

"That was…incredible," he whispered as I kissed breathlessly along his jaw.

"*You're* incredible," I said, running my fingers down his arm. "And our future will be too."

"Yeah," he said, combing through my damp-from-exertion hair. "Yeah it will."

* * *

One month later…

"So, how are we this week?" Jason asked, settling into his leather chair.

Taking Dylan's hand, like I always did now during our sessions, I squeezed it and smiled. "Good," I said. "At least *I* think we're good." I turned to Dylan. "We good?"

Through a heavy chuckle, he nodded. "Yeah. We're good."

"And how are you finding living separately?" Jason asked, gaze trained on Dylan.

"Okay." Dylan nodded. "I get bored a lot, but-"

"You do?" I cut in. "Why don't you call me?"

"Because I don't need to. That's the point. I get bored. When I get bored, I start thinking, *remembering*, and it's okay. I'm okay."

A proud smile tugged on my lips. Christ, I loved this man. Everything about him. His strength. His courage. His fragile heart.

"And why do you think that is?" Jason questioned. "What's changed?"

"*I* have. I crush the bad memories with good ones, just like you told me to. The more I do it, the more good memories I pick out. I remember my dad, my grandma, and…it still hurts, but I'm not afraid of that pain anymore. I'm not letting them down now. I'm trying, you know? I'm achieving things. I like to think they'd be proud of who I'm becoming."

"They are," I said, squeezing his hand a little tighter. "And so am I."

"There's just one thing I can't get past. I don't know why, but…I keep thinking about Bubbles. I keep wondering what happened to her, if she had a funeral, if anyone even noticed she'd gone. Or if she ended up with a crappy state service with no mourners and a plain, generic headstone. I know I didn't *know* her, not really. Didn't even know her real name. But…it kinda haunts me. She didn't deserve to die alone. Nobody does."

Holy shit. I had no idea what to say to that, so I bowed my head, staying silent.

"My story could've ended just like hers," he continued. "Probably would've if I hadn't found Cam again."

"You need to say goodbye," Jason said, clicking the pen in his hand. "You're absolutely right, everybody deserves someone to miss them."

"I…I don't know how. I have no way of knowing where she is. Whether she was buried or cremated."

"It's the sentiment that matters. Go somewhere you feel close to her, talk to her, maybe leave her something."

"No." Dylan shook his head. "I can't go back to the places that remind me of her. Not yet. Maybe not ever." Dylan sighed, picking at a loose thread on the hem of his T-shirt. He was hurting, and I felt so helpless.

"Why not go somewhere you think she would've liked?" I suggested, hoping I didn't sound stupid. "Somewhere you wish you could've met her, instead of…well, instead of where you did."

When silence descended, I definitely felt stupid. Until Jason said, "That's a great idea, Cameron."

"Will you come with me?" Dylan asked, his eyes meeting mine for just a second before he looked back to the loose thread. "You don't have to. I mean I know you didn't know her, and I know her name reminds you of all the bad stuff I've-"

"Of course I will," I interrupted.

Nodding, his tense shoulders relaxed instantly. "She'd never been to the beach. I always found that really sad. All kids should go to the beach. My dad used to take me to Brighton every summer. I think she'd have liked the beach."

"Brighton it is then," I said. "We'll go this weekend."

"I…It feels a little silly." Dylan shrugged. "It's not like she'll ever know."

"You don't know that." I didn't really believe in heaven, but like everyone else, I had no proof either way. "Nobody knows that. You need closure, and this seems like a good way to get it."

After a few seconds with his eyebrows pinched together, deep in thought, he asked, "What would I take? The only thing I know Bubbles liked is heroin, and I hardly think tossing a bag into the sea is a good way to remember her."

"How about some daisies?" Jason suggested. I knew they'd discussed the counting thing in their private sessions because Dylan told me, but it was the first time I'd been a part of the conversation.

Dylan's neck snapped upwards, shock paling his face. "No," he said, his voice curt, adamant. "Daisies…" He took a deep, flustered breath. "They remind me of bad things."

"Do you think that's what your grandmother intended when she gave you that tool?"

"I…I don't…" Dylan's voice cracked, his words getting lost in his throat.

"Daisies are beautiful flowers, and they have lots of meanings to different people. In Victorian times, for instance, the Michaelmas daisy represented farewell, or departure. They also represent afterthought, the wish that things had happened differently. White daisies signify new beginnings. Fresh starts."

"Have you just made that up?" Dylan questioned, his tone sceptical.

"No, Dylan." Jason chuckled. "I researched it after our first discussion."

"You…you *did?*"

"It's my job to *understand* you, and how you think. I think it's time to reclaim counting daisies for the way your grandmother intended. Her aim was to help you turn scary thoughts into beautiful ones, was it not?"

"Yeah. Yeah it was." Dylan's lips twisted into a sad smile, and I knew he was remembering Granny Roberts. "And...they really mean those things?"

"They do. Google it. You'll find plenty more connotations if you don't think they suit what you're trying to achieve here."

"No, they're perfect. I hope, wherever Bubbles is, she's found a new beginning. A *better* beginning."

I squeezed his hand again because it was all I *could* do. I'd said it a thousand times, and I'd say it a thousand more...I'd never been more proud, more in awe, of anyone in my life.

* * *

We arrived in Brighton just after noon the following Saturday. Dylan remained quiet for most of the journey, and spent most of the car ride staring at the bunch of purple asters in his lap. I gave him time to reflect, didn't ask what he was thinking. We'd talk later.

He wanted to head straight to the beach, presumably to get his goodbye over with, attain his closure, as soon as possible. We took off our shoes, leaving them on a large rock, before padding over the sand. It was hot under my bare feet, the summer sun beating down on my face. Perfect, yet rare, beach weather.

"It's busier than I remember," Dylan said, gazing across the sand towards the crowd of noisy families, couples, and dogs fetching balls from the water. "You don't notice as much of the world as a kid, I guess."

Reaching the shoreline, soft waves rippling over my toes, I put my hand on his shoulder. "Do you want me to leave you alone for a while?"

"No," he said, reaching up to press his hand over mine. "Stay."

I watched him as he stared out into the sea. He looked so lost in thought, his eyes haunted by twenty different types of pain.

"Makes you realise how small you are." He jerked his chin towards the water. "How insignificant we are in the grand scheme of things. All that space. All that world…"

"I don't see it."

Turning his head, he looked at me, confusion narrowing his eyes.

"No matter how much space, when I look around all I see is you. *You're* my world."

He blew out a small chuckle through his nose. "Which movie did you nick that from, huh?"

"It was a book actually," I admitted with a coy smile. "Still true though."

Dylan's gaze fell onto the flowers he held and, taking his hand off mine, he stroked the fragrant petals with the tip of his finger. "What do I say?" he asked. "I feel kinda dumb now I'm here."

"Say whatever you would if she were right in front of you. Just…tell her how you feel."

Closing his eyes briefly, he dragged in a deep breath before blowing it steadily back out through pursed lips. He took a step forward, my hand falling off his shoulder, and I stayed where I was – still with him, but giving him enough space to do what he needed to without the feeling of being watched.

"So, uh, hey Bubbles," he began. "It's me – Titch. Never did get to ask you your name. Stupid, right? I'm Dylan, by the way. Can't remember if I told you. Don't think I did. Fuck, this is awkward."

Tipping his head to face the sky, he took some more deep breaths. "I wish we could've known each other at a different time. I wish…I wish we knew each other sober. I wish I'd known the *real* you, before life fucked us both up. I wish I could've helped you. Wish you could've had the chance I've been given.

"I'm doing good, Bubbles. Real good. Wish you were here to see it, see how great life can be if you let it. I've done it. I've gotten off the shit. For good this time. It's a different world. One we never knew about. I hope, wherever you are, your world is good too. I hope you're not hurting anymore.

"I, um, I brought you these flowers. A little lame, I know, but they're supposed to represent new beginnings apparently. It's cheesy as shit, but I've been given a new beginning. I want you to have one, too. They also mean goodbye, which is what this is…"

Tears stung my eyes, pooling around the edges, clouding my vision as Dylan started tossing the flowers one-by-one into the sea.

"Goodbye, Bubbles. I'll never forget you. Fucked up or not, we were friends. You meant something to me. You deserved better. We both did. Maybe we'll see each other again someday. Until then, rest in peace and all that shit. Stay outta trouble, yeah? And, uh, thanks. Thanks for being my friend when I didn't have anyone else. Guess that's it." He threw the last flower. "Bye, Bubbles."

Snorting my tears, I wiped the dampness from my cheeks on the back of my hand before Dylan turned around.

"Okay," he said before blowing out a sigh. "Done."

"How do you feel?"

Gnawing his top lip, he thought for a moment. "Lighter," he said. "Free."

Emotion ballooned in my throat as I lunged forward and crushed him to my chest. Gripping the back of his neck, I buried my head in his shoulder. "I love you, Dylan. So much."

Hands around my waist, he hugged me tighter. "Thank you. Thank you for saving me. Thank you, in advance, for my future. I love you, too, and I'll spend the rest of my life proving it to you."

For several minutes we just…stood. Holding each other, we breathed. We felt. We *loved*.

Afterwards, we walked along the beach, hand-in-hand. We kicked the tide, we talked, we laughed.

343

We were just Cam and Dyl. Together. Like we used to be. Like we were always *meant* to be.

"This way," I said, tugging his hand, guiding him into a souvenir shop. "Got to get some cock-rock for Paul and Derek. You can't go to the beach without getting cock-rock. It's the law."

Shaking his head, Dylan laughed. "It was all about the fake fags when I was a kid."

"Ah, yes!" I said, remembering them well. I used to think I looked so bloody cool blowing on a plastic cigarette filled with cotton wool and some kind of white powder that puffed out like real smoke.

"Feels good, you know?" Dylan said, studying the vast selection of rock in front of us. "Remembering the past. My dad. Doesn't hurt so much anymore. Just…it just makes me smile."

"I know what else will make you smile."

Puzzled, he craned his neck in an effort to see what I was hiding behind my back. Pulling out two 'rock titties', complete with perky pink nipples, I pressed them to my chest. I'd turned into a thirteen year old again, but I didn't care. We'd missed this. The years we were supposed to spend dicking around, being juvenile, growing up together, were stolen from us.

"You wanna lick my titties?"

Dylan laughed; a deep, throaty, *genuine* laugh that echoed through the small shop, making people stare at us.

It didn't matter that we'd lost those years, because we had so many more to come. I planned to treasure them, use them to be his best friend again. I would make him laugh. I would make him feel important. I would hold him when he cried, and care for him when he was sick.

I would love him, forever, with all that I was.

Epilogue

~Dylan~

Six months later…

"SORRY I'M LATE!" I called, shrugging out of my jacket as I bustled into the kitchen. I pecked Cam on the cheek as he stepped away from the pass. "Service ran over. We had some slow eaters."

I was a college student now. *How cool is that?* I couldn't help feeling a twinge of fulfilment whenever I thought about the life I was living. I attended classes twice a week, studying towards an NVQ. On Monday's we worked on the theory side of things, and on Thursdays we got to work in the college restaurant, preparing, cooking, and serving plates of food to paying customers. Then, once a month an assessor from the college would come to

O'Neil's to watch me work. I loved it. Every single second of it. I was *good* at it too. The cooking, that is. I tried balancing plates along my arms like the servers did a few weeks ago. The four shattered plates scattered across the kitchen floor told me I *wasn't* so good at *that*.

"Think Derek needs you downstairs," Cameron said. "But change first." He pointed at my college uniform, which was similar to the one I wore here at O'Neil's. Currently, it was splattered with bright orange stains after an exploding soup incident I experienced earlier. That was one of Cam's big no-nos. He expected the same clean and presentable standards back here as he did front of house.

"Sure."

He was busy, so I left him to it. I had a session with Jason before college this morning which I wanted to fill him in about, like I always did, but I'd have to do it later. I still saw Jason once a week, with Cameron coming with me every fortnight. A couple of months ago, during one of my one-on-one's with Jason, we discussed all the people I'd hurt through my addiction, and how I could make it up to them. This was one of the twelve steps, and it was important for not only my recovery, but for my mind too, which I guess is kinda the same thing.

Truth is I had no way of making it up to all the people I'd hurt. I could repay Cameron, Paul, and Derek, every day by being a good partner, a great friend. I could tell those guys how sorry I was with words and actions. I could stay strong, keep clean, and work damn hard to prove myself. But...I didn't *know* everybody I'd ever hurt because of fucking heroin. I either didn't know them personally, or I couldn't remember half the shit I'd done. I could never right my wrongs to those whose houses I'd broken into. I couldn't return the personal belongings I'd taken and sold.

Talking through this with Jason felt like I was teetering on the edge of a deep, dark well, and I had to fight really fucking hard not to lose my balance and fall inside. He told me to think of those things as crimes against society, rather than the individual people, which helped a lot. I couldn't help the individuals I didn't remember, but I could help people in general.

That's when I started dedicating my Friday evenings to the local youth centre. As a volunteer, I was there to hang out with the kids. We'd kick a football around the yard, we'd listen to music, we'd talk. It was my job just to *be there*. Support them. Some of these kids had been dealt a really shitty hand in life, like I had, and they just needed to know they weren't alone. Some were addicts, most weren't, but they were all a little fucked-up and I knew what that felt like.

I'd taken a real shine to one kid in particular, Simon. At just fourteen years old he was a full time carer for his disabled mother. He missed a lot of school, got in trouble a lot on the days he *did* go, and just last week he told me he was gay. I made no secret of my sexuality from the start, which I liked to think really helped this kid. He'd only told *me* how he felt, said he felt like a big enough of an outcast already because he didn't go to school often enough to make friends. So, I made it my mission to get him more friends here, at the club. No one would judge him here. Every one of these kids came with their own issues.

I started putting together group activities, with the help of the guy who ran the place, that would force them all together; football matches, cooking-nights – which they laughed about at first but they all participated nevertheless. If high school these days was anything like when I was there, it was full of cliques and not a positive atmosphere for someone who felt different to everyone else, someone who didn't belong to any of the groups. You had the popular clan, the boffins and nerds, the misfits…but what if you didn't feel part of *any* of those circles?

That's what this club was about. Embracing different. Accepting flaws. Overcoming problems, or at least escaping them for a while. Underneath all the crap life had thrown at them, they were good kids, and I not only felt obliged to help them out to aid my own recovery, redeem myself, I also really enjoyed it. If just one of these kids could learn from my fuck-ups then it made every mistake I'd ever made worth it.

As far as my own recovery went, I didn't really see my sponsor. I never took to the guy they paired me with. He wasn't a *bad* guy, we simply didn't gel. Jason said that was okay as long as I had *somebody*. I had Beverly. She kept in touch like she promised, and we went to NA together once a month, meeting up for regular lunches in-between. We were at similar stages in our recovery and we connected with each other from the start. I guess you could say she became my *unofficial* sponsor. She was my friend, one of many, and I felt insanely privileged for that every single day.

The internal war continued. Every day was a fight. Every day I had to make the right choice. Every day, if only briefly, I thought about heroin. Every day I had to say *no*. Every day I had to remind myself of everything I'd achieved.

Every. Single. Day.

And it was the most empowering feeling in the world, knowing that I was winning. Without the bad, as Jason once told me, how would we recognise the good? Still, the fear of relapse kept me awake at night. But that was *good*. Being afraid of that fall made me more determined to stay upright.

I just wished my dad was here to see the progress I'd made, Granny Roberts too. I started visiting their graves once a week. Cameron came with me sometimes, and the first time we took cleaning supplies and some gardening tools, washed down their headstones and pulled up the weeds. I told them how I was, all the good things I was doing, even though I didn't think they could actually hear me. I'd talk to my mum as well. Even though I didn't remember her I still felt like I knew her from all the things my dad had told me. I liked to think I'd become the man she thought I would be while she was pregnant. My dad used to tell me all she ever wanted was for her child to be happy and healthy, and I was both of those things now. Maybe, wherever they were, they were celebrating with me. The notion was comforting.

Once Derek learned about exercise being one of my recovery tools, he took it upon himself to make me fit, dragging my arse to the gym with him several times a week. Jason was right. It *was* kinda euphoric. Well, it was after a couple of weeks. The first few times on the treadmill made me feel like my calf muscles were trying to rip themselves free from my body. Overall, I felt healthier. My body was stronger. My scrawny muscles had even started to fill out a little. Mostly, I just enjoyed spending time with Derek. Underneath his tough, no-bullshit exterior lay a gentle, caring teddy bear, who I had no doubt would give up his life to save any one of his friends.

After changing quickly into a clean, crisp uniform, I headed downstairs.

"Tuiles!" Derek barked the second I ploughed through the swinging doors in the prep-kitchen. Cooking wasn't just something I did in my spare time these days. As a commis, it was my job. It was hard, dirty work. I, and my fellow commis, were in charge of unloading deliveries, lugging heavy crap around the kitchen, cleaning down…being general skivvies. *But* I also got to cook now, so that made the tiring, laborious work worth it.

I prepared and plated food all on my own, under Derek's scrutinising gaze of course. My skill set was nowhere near his level, but I was getting better. If I ever eventually became *half* the pastry chef Derek was, I'd be incredibly fucking proud of myself.

"Actually, fuck the tuiles," Derek added, grabbing a knife and waving it in the air for me to take. His cheeks were beaming red, and the tell-tale vein in his forehead that showed when he was stressed, bulged with every word he spoke. He wasn't angry, he just turned into a fanatical monster during service. "I need more strawberries for the mint side salad."

"Yes, chef!" Taking the knife from him, I walked briskly over to my station, grabbing a stack of punnets from the fridge on the way. Prepping fruit for Michelin star-worthy desserts was harder than it looked. It needed to be diced into perfectly identical, tiny cubes. It was intricate, time-consuming work, but again, I loved doing it. I'd gotten faster at chopping, but still only ran at half the speed of the head chefs.

"Oh, *fuck!*" I hissed, dropping the knife and clutching my wrist. Blood dripped furiously from the tip of my finger which I'd just ripped a hefty chunk out of. "*Fuck! Fuck! Fuck!*"

"Oh for fuck's sake!" Derek bellowed, rushing over to me. He picked up my hand, studying the deep gash. "You've gotta be kiddin' me. That's gonna need stitches! You've got really crappy timin'. The floor's packed tonight and Evan's off with the shits!"

The pain made me dizzy and I stumbled back a step. Derek jogged over to the cupboard where we kept the first-aid kits, telling Anna to go and fetch Cameron while he did. Returning to me, he bound my finger tightly in a bandage, the blood soaking straight through it.

"I think I'm gonna be sick," I groaned, tipping my head back.

"Don't you fuckin' dare," Derek said, pulling the bandage even tighter.

"Jesus Christ! Are you trying to kill me?"

"No, I'm tryin' to stop you bleedin' out on the kitchen floor, you ungrateful shit."

My head swam. I felt too hot. Lightheaded. Nauseous. "Fuck, I think I'm dying."

"Quit the fuckin' dramatics. I 'ant got time for it."

"What happened?" Cameron called, slinging a towel over his shoulder as he ran towards me. He took one look at the blood dripping from the bandage and said, "Shit."

"Dickwad can't even cut a fuckin' strawberry, that's what 'appened. I'm gonna be ten minutes late with my plates, chef." Like I said, Derek was...*passionate* in the kitchen.

"Let's get you to A&E," Cameron said before turning to Derek. "I'll send someone else to help you down here."

Arm around my waist, Cameron walked me upstairs, pausing to tell Paul what'd happened, before leading me to his car. I whined all the damn way. I was being a total wimp but the pain was excruciating. Take the worst paper cut of your life and times it by three hundred thousand.

At the hospital, I was taken straight through to a cubicle. I hated these places. The smell of disinfectant reminded me of death. Every time I'd ever been in a hospital someone had died on me. "This isn't a good sign," I said to Cam. "They're not making me wait. Oh, God…I'm gonna lose my whole finger aren't I?"

"You're *not* going to lose your finger," he said, and I could tell he was trying desperately hard not to laugh at me. *Wanker.*

Minutes later, a nurse wearing blue scrubs appeared, drawing the curtain closed behind her. She carried a yellow tray containing whatever supplies she needed to patch me up, and placed it on the end of the bed before snapping on some gloves and pulling up a chair next to me.

"So, you lost a fight with a kitchen knife, eh?" She sounded chirpy. Everyone was so damn chirpy and it irritated the hell out of me.

I'm dying over here!

"Let's take a look." Slowly, she peeled away the bandage and the loss of pressure almost made me pass out. She poked and prodded at my sliced flesh, and I have *no* idea how I managed to refrain from punching her in the face.

"*Ouch!*" I cried out, sucking in a hiss through my clenched teeth.

A small chuckle, which he quickly tried to disguise as a yawn, pushed through Cameron's throat. I was *never* going to live this down. I'd be the joke of the kitchen for years to come.

After squirting my bleeding skin with some orange stuff, the nurse pulled out a needle that, for the briefest of seconds, made my pulse quicken. *Heroin.* It was still there, in my head. It always would be. Only now I had the power to tell it to fuck off.

"This might sting a little."

Oh, shite. As if I wasn't in enough pain already, she wanted to make it worse. Closing my eyes, I blocked out the needle and...I counted daisies. I'd reclaimed them. I used them for the reason my grandma told me to. I turned the pain of the cut, the pinch of the needle, into something beautiful.

One, two, three, four...

"All done," the nurse said. "That should start to feel numb very soon."

Quite quickly, the pain dissolved, and the relief rivalled the best orgasm of my life. "Ugh. Thank God," I groaned, the wound still open but not hurting at all.

Three tiny stitches is all it took. The cut wasn't actually as big as I thought it was, which made me feel like an even bigger wimp. *It fucking hurt though.*

She finished by binding my finger in a clean bandage, which I had to leave on for twenty-four hours. "Rest it for a couple of days. It will swell, but that's normal. An ice pack and some ibuprofen should settle it down. If you need something stronger, I can get the doctor to write you a prescription for some Co-codamol."

"No," I said. "No drugs." I didn't trust myself, most likely never would. The strongest I was willing to go was paracetamol, and I'd only taken those once, for a killer-headache, since leaving Riverside. It was just one of the prices I had to pay for being an addict, because that's what I was. That's what I'd always be. Those same three options still applied...

Using.

Recovering.

Dead.

I chose recovery. I chose Cameron. I chose a future. I chose an education and a career. I chose friends. Family. Stability. Happiness.

The point is *life*.

~Cameron~

I texted Paul before driving home from the hospital, updated him on Dylan, and asked him to ring me after service to let me know how it went. Back in my apartment, I shoved some boxes out of the way to clear a path for Dylan to get to the couch. At present, he still lived with Derek, but we were getting a place of our own. *Together.* We put a deposit down on a two-bedroom town house, closer to the restaurant, last month. So, now, all of our belongings were packed into boxes and suitcases, one of which contained clothes and supplies for our upcoming trip to Edinburgh.

I signed the final paperwork for the new restaurant two weeks ago. It'd all progressed fairly quickly, and smoothly too. This weekend we were travelling up to check out the renovations which began last week, and to interview potential staff. When we got back, the keys for our new home would be ready.

I couldn't wait to live with Dylan again. Start afresh. Build a future. Live the life we mapped out at fourteen years old. I knew it wouldn't be all sunshine and tulips. Loving him was tough sometimes. He still got cravings, 'jonesing', as he called it. Some days all it would take was a hard day at work, a fuck-up at college, and he'd *change*. He'd withdraw. He'd take himself away and sit in perfect silence for a few minutes, or he'd go running. Christ, he ran a lot these days. It made me nervous. I didn't know where he was going, or what state he'd come back in. At first, I followed him. I tracked him down and I held him until he fell apart in my arms. But he *needed* that space, that time alone, and so I had to let him do it.

Love wasn't enough to keep us strong. I had to *trust* him too. And I did. It took some time, but I got there. *We* got there.

"I've got something for you," I said as Dylan lowered himself down onto the couch. "I've had it for a long time, but…well, I didn't know what kind of emotions it would stir up."

"What is it?" he asked, his voice hesitant, a little nervous.

Wandering to the back of the couch, I pulled his dad's guitar case out from behind it. I'd been too scared to show it to him before now. I worried it would fill him with guilt, or regret, bring back the bad memories. But he was stronger now. Healthier, body and mind.

Dylan's gaze roamed over the leather case, his mouth dropping open. "You...you found it?" Reaching out, he stroked along the black leather, tears misting his eyes. "I thought...I thought I'd lost it forever." His voice was quiet, as if speaking to himself rather than me.

"I went looking for it while you were in Riverside. You weren't yourself when you sold it. I know how much it means to you."

"But heroin meant more," he muttered on a sigh.

"Don't do that. You're not that person anymore. You've forgiven yourself, remember?"

He nodded slowly, unlocking the brass clasps before stroking the dark wood inside. "What about the things inside the lid? My songs, the photos..."

Bowing my head, my heart stuttered. "They're gone. I guess the shop owner threw them away."

Dylan nodded again, his sorrowful stare transfixed on the instrument in his hands. I remembered that look on his face. He used to look at the guitar in the exact same way right after his dad died.

"My mum has boxes full of photos from our childhood. She doesn't have one of your mum, but your dad's in there. Granny Roberts too. And us. *Lots* of us." I hoped that would make him feel better. I think it did because he smiled. "I can't replace the things you wrote though."

"I still remember some of them," he said, his voice timid. "The songs I wrote. I…I could play one for you. I mean, if you *want* me to."

"Christ, Dylan…" My words fell out on a deep exhale. "I've wanted to hear you play since we were kids. I'd feel *honoured* listening to you."

Leaning forward, he balanced the guitar on his lap, holding the neck with his injured hand. "Might not sound too great with the finger and everything. But I'll give it a shot."

It would sound stunning regardless. I had no doubt.

He took a moment to familiarise himself with the strings, his gaze flitting between the neck and the body as he strummed a few chords. Then, clearing his throat, he *really* started to play. He mesmerised me. His long, skilled fingers danced along the strings, producing a melody that came second in beauty to only his voice. His body relaxed with each chord he struck, his mind lost in a whole other world.

And then he started singing…

If I could go back, I'd take it all away
Take away the pain of missing you each day
I'd tell you I was sorry, I'd tell you I'll be good

Maybe then I'd get to live the life I always thought I would

The words poured from his mouth, slow and sombre, and each one pierced my heart. In all the years I'd known him I'd never heard him sing, but after today I'd never stop asking to hear him do it again. His voice was rich, a slight crackle coating every lyric. Husky. Soothing. Magical. Utterly fucking captivating.

As expected, a few chords were off, his bandaged finger unable to curl around the neck, preventing him from hitting all the right notes. It didn't matter though. It was still the most beautiful, inspiring thing I'd ever heard. The melody dipped and rose along with his voice, and my chest ached with raw, aching *love* for this brave and beautiful man before me.

Maybe it wasn't meant to be, I guess I'll never know
Perhaps it was my destiny to end up all alone
If you saw me, would you need me, would you keep my fears
at bay
Or would you take one look, turn around and walk away

I know I don't deserve you, I'll only cause you pain
But baby if you're listening I'll try to find a way
My life is filled with errors, more darkness than the night
But every time I think of you I know I'll be alright

If I could go back, I'd take it all away
Take away the pain of missing you each day
I'd tell you I was sorry, I'd tell you I'll be good

Maybe then I'd get to live the life I always thought I would

Pressing his palm against the strings, a silent tear leaked from the corner of his eye, rolling mournfully down his cheek. Dropping to my knees in front of him, I reached up and caught it with my finger. "Thank you," is all I said. "Thank you for coming back to me."

"I wrote that for you," he whispered, his cheek pressed to mine. "Two or three years ago. It's cheesy as shit, I know, but I never forgot about you. I tried. I tried because it hurt. But in here…" Setting aside his guitar, he took my hand and held it to his chest, his heart thumping against my fingers. "In here you never left."

I couldn't speak, could barely breathe. I'd loved Dylan Roberts for as long as I could remember. He'd been my best friend, my everything, since we were kids, and he always would be.

"We're gonna make it, right?" Dylan said, laying his forehead on mine.

"We already have," I spoke against his lips. "I love you, Dyl. Always have, always will."

"We're Cam and Dyl. Just like we were meant to be."

"Yes." Brushing his lips with my own, I cradled the back of his head with both hands. "Cam and Dyl. Forever."

The End.

Acknowledgements

Lisa, thank you for your inspiration. Thank you for sharing your story with me. Thank you for your honesty, your courage, and your strength. I'm glad I got to know you!

As always, thank you to Reese Dante for another stunning cover. I am in awe of you!

Emma, you have to get a mention. It's the law. You're shit. You smell, probably because, as I said, you're shit. But you put up with *my* shit, and you send me funny memes, so I love ya anyways!

TRACY McKAAAAAAY! You're my person, even though you're a pervert. Actually, it's probably *because* you're a pervert. Thank you for brainstorming with me, for supplying my porn, and for being an awesome friend!

Denise, my favourite bellend, thank you for your support and encouragement, and for embracing me as a princess. I love you!

Oor Janie. As I've said a thousand times, thank you for being you! Thank you for loving my guys, for being fantabulous, and for pimping my arse out and making me pretty teasers! And remember, what happens in PM stays in PM ;-)

Theresa Golish, you fantabulous lady you! I can always trust you to pick up those sneaky little bastards known as typos! So thank you for your beady eyes, thank you for our chats, thank you for being my friend, and for being a fellow princess! MWAH!

Sanna Solin. Thank you for everything you do for me; for the pimping, the support, for the advice and tips, and for being a friend. You are very special to me. <3

Now for my beta readers! I have the best in the whole damn world. Emma, Tracy, Keeley, Denise, Theresa, Janie, Danni, Lisa, Melanie and Karen. THANK YOU! Thank you for lending me your keen eyes, for loving my stories, for being there. I love you all to the moon and back and I'm insanely grateful to each and every one of you. I feel lucky to know you guys, and relieved I don't have to send my baby out into the world without having your approval first! (I totally copied and pasted this bit from my last book because I'm lazy, and because it's TRUE!)

Thank you to the whole MM genre, and all the fantabulous people in it. I've never experienced a community like it. I have made some very special, lifelong friends in this genre. The support from readers, fellow authors, and bloggers is incredible and I feel insanely privileged to be a part of it. (Ok, you got me. I copied and pasted this too. But seriously, I think of this genre as my home now. I feel very privileged to be a part of it.)

Bloggers. Yes, I'm a copout because I won't name any specifically, and that's because I just know I will forget to mention someone important. But know that I love and appreciate everything you do for me, and the book world in general. Thank you for signing up to my tours, for reading my words, for promoting me. I would be nowhere without your support. Thank you for everything you do.

Again, it has been a pleasure working with Ena and Amanda from Enticing Journey Book Promotions. Thank you for all the hard work you dedicate to the authors who work with you. You're freakin' awesome!

Finally, my readers. Thanks to you, I get to live my dream, doing something I *love*, every single day. Thank you for reading, for supporting me, for interacting with me. I love each and every one of you.

About the Author

Nicola lives in Rochdale, UK, with her husband, four little shi- children, two cats, and a dog. She is addicted to tattoos and Pepsi Max, hates even numbers and metal spoons, and is altogether a little bit weird. She's also really crap at referring to herself in third person and making herself sound interesting.

Nicola Haken

If you want to keep up with my crazy world, you can do that by following me here:

http://www.facebook.com/nicolahaken

http://www.twitter.com/NicolaHaken

Haken's Heroes Facebook Group:
https://www.facebook.com/groups/11190586181
44158/

https://www.goodreads.com/author/show/70942
94.Nicola_Haken

http://www.pinterest.com/nicolahaken/

Follow my Tumblr page at your own risk!

http://nicolahaken.tumblr.com

Instagram - @nicolahaken

Counting Daisies

Other titles by Nicola Haken

MM Romance

Broken

Being Sawyer Knight (Souls of the Knight #1)

Taming Ryder (Souls of the Knight #2)

The Making of Matt (Souls of the Knight #3)

MF New Adult Romance

Saving Amy

Missing Pieces

Take My Hand

Hold On Tight (Take My Hand #2)

Lean On Me (Take My Hand #3)

Never Let Go (Take My Hand #4)

85431953R00226

Made in the USA
Lexington, KY
31 March 2018